THE
BLACK
DRESS

By Deborah Moggach

You Must Be Sisters
A Quiet Drink
Hot Water Man
Porky
To Have and To Hold
Driving in the Dark
Stolen
The Stand-In
Smile (short stories)
The Ex-Wives
Changing Babies (short stories)
Seesaw
In the Dark
Tulip Fever
Final Demand
The Best Exotic Marigold Hotel (previously
These Foolish Things)
Heartbreak Hotel
Something to Hide
The Carer
The Black Dress

DEBORAH MOGGACH

THE BLACK DRESS

TINDER
PRESS

First published in Great Britain in 2021 by Tinder Press
An imprint of HEADLINE PUBLISHING GROUP

1

Cataloguing in Publication Data is available from the British Library

Hardback ISBN 978 1 4722 6052 9
Trade paperback ISBN 978 1 4722 6053 6

Typeset in Sabon LT Std 10.75/14.5 pt by Jouve (UK), Milton Keynes

Printed and bound in Great Britain by Clays Ltd, Elcograf S.p.A.

HEADLINE PUBLISHING GROUP
An Hachette UK Company
Carmelite House
50 Victoria Embankment
London EC4Y 0DZ

www.tinderpress.co.uk
www.headline.co.uk
www.hachette.co.uk

This one is for Susan Jeffreys and Helena Ramsay,
with love

Prologue

I saw it in the window of a charity shop. A little black dress. Scoop neck, clingy. It spoke of cigarettes and Martinis – a surprisingly vampish garment for a seaside town at the height of summer. It was worn by a mannequin with painted eyebrows and crimson lips, who bore a distinct resemblance to Petula Clark. She leaned at a slant and her head was tilted towards me, as if she were about to burst into song. A feather boa was draped around her neck.

They have a certain smell, don't they, charity shops? All those pasts, all those lives; no amount of laundering can wash that away. After fingering a few cardigans I'm usually out of there, but not that day.

My swim had invigorated me. For half an hour it had washed away my past few months, the horror and betrayal. The sun shone. I felt purified, and about time, too. I'd lived in darkness for far too long. I gazed at the dress, waiting for me behind my own ghostly reflection in the glass. I had no idea why I was drawn to it, not yet. Or whether it would fit.

But it did. Knobbly black wool, snug but not outrageously tight – I was seventy, after all, mutton and lamb – hinting but not revealing, with its scooped neckline and quarter-length sleeves. Standing in the curtained cubicle, I gazed at myself in the mirror. Even in that pitiless light, with my hair damp from swimming, the transformation was startling. I was an alluring woman of a certain age, hardly recognisable even to myself.

It all spins on a sixpence, doesn't it? Chance, decisions. Why that high street, in that town? Why that dress? Why did somebody throw it out just then? Did somebody die, or get too fat, or simply realise that nobody has cocktail parties any more?

I stood at the counter. 'I'll take it.'

PART ONE

One

It was a sort of madness. I realised that at the time. How could a woman like me be capable of such a thing? But I'd been horribly betrayed, and was reeling from the shock. I was in freefall, all the branches cut off, nothing to catch me as I fell. And I was insanely lonely.

That's no excuse either, but maybe you've never been there. Howling loneliness, month after month. I was alone when the lawyer's letter arrived. No Greg beside me to look at those words wiping out our life together. *What's this all about? Leave it to me. It must have come to the wrong address.*

I was alone when the car broke down on the North Circular Road at one in the morning. When a gutter got blocked and water ran down the walls. When a plumber ripped me off, and my laptop crashed.

I was alone when a rosy-cheeked vet arrived – just married, she told me – to put down the dog. I played Joni Mitchell, that song about her lover sniffing his fingers as he watches the waitress's legs, Sidney's head lowered and rested, a dead weight, in my lap.

So that was it. I was sixty-nine, and alone for the first time in my life. My friend Azra said: 'Good sodding riddance. Greg was a tosser, I can say that now. You're not too old to find another man. Go to the park. There's plenty of them there, walking their dogs.'

'I haven't got a dog any more.'

'You've still got his lead, haven't you? Walk about calling "Sidney, Sidney." Somebody's bound to come and help.'

I laughed – a startling sound; I hadn't laughed for weeks. Azra could do that to me. Glorious Azra, sprawled on my sofa in a fug of cigarette smoke. God, I loved her.

Greg didn't fight me for the house. He'd moved onto a higher plane; he made me well aware of that. Our family home had mausoleumed into a repository of junk.

'Who needs all this *stuff*?' he'd said. 'People bust their guts doing jobs they don't like to buy stuff they don't need, just to help corporate criminals ruin the planet.'

He said he was shedding his possessions and going on a silent retreat in Rutland.

'*Rutland?*'

He was already removing himself to an unknown county. We'd never said the word 'Rutland' in our lives. So many unknowns he was going to discover without me. His tone was sorrowful but weirdly exultant.

'I need solitude, to start my spiritual journey.' He'd said this without a glimmer of humour. I knew then that I'd lost him. 'I don't want anything, you can have it all.'

That wasn't quite true. He'd kept the cottage in Dorset. That's where he was going to live. We'd talked about retiring there but decided we'd die of boredom.

Not now. Greg had moved beyond boredom. Gazing at the immensity of the ocean would restore him to himself, a prelapsarian Greg, unmuddied by compromise and familiarity, by a mortgage and a thickening waist, by family rows, by the chronic hopes and disappointments of simply weathering the years. By me.

'It's not you,' he'd said. 'It's nothing you've done. It's just that since my cancer scare I've realised that life is so very short, one must live each day fully, concentrate on what's important—'

'So *I'm* not important?'

'Be honest, Pru. You've felt it too, I can tell. We only have the one life—'

'Oh, shut up.'

'And you must admit that our marriage has run out of steam. It's become stale and predictable. We've lost that joy in each other's company. To be brutally honest we haven't been happy for years. Isn't it time we had the courage to part as friends—'

'*Friends?*'

'And rediscover the aspects of ourselves that have lain dormant all these years, nurture them and let them flourish – you as well as me. Don't we owe it to ourselves—'

'Who is she?'

'What?'

'Who're you fucking? There must be someone waiting in the wings or you wouldn't be spouting this drivel.'

But he swore there wasn't and promptly burst into tears.

Since starting therapy Greg had been more in touch with his feelings. He'd gone to treat his depression and it seemed to have worked. My bookish, gloomy husband had morphed into a cult member, bland and glazed, with a visible lifting of the spirits and a whole new vocabulary of self-awareness. No, self-absorption. Quite honestly, I preferred the old Greg, whose leaden footsteps on the stairs sounded like a man going to his own execution.

So there was no woman waiting in the wings, just his

so-called 'facilitator', who seemed to have facilitated the end of our marriage.

The madness came later. At first I was simply shell-shocked. Everything unravelled so fast, because how can you fight someone who gently, and oh-so-patronisingly, makes it clear that he no longer loves you? Who says it's not your fault, it's his? Who's attempting to relive his youth, or have a late-life crisis, or whatever the heck it was, leaving you to face the future alone?

There was, simply, nothing to say. Of course we'd had our problems but we'd always managed to talk. Now the rubber band had snapped and we'd sprung apart, two ageing strangers. Had it all been a delusion, those decades together? I listened to the cupboards opening and closing, his footsteps on the floorboards above, the rumble of his suitcase wheels. And then with a sorrowful hug he was gone, sprung free, without a single shouting match.

'You're such a wimp, letting him get away with it,' said Azra. 'You should've put up a fight.'

'You can't *fight* somebody back into love with you.'

'Or gone for counselling, or something.'

The truth was, I'd thought Greg and I had been getting on fine in the past few months. His depression had lifted. We still held hands in the cinema. Now we'd both retired we were talking about walking the Coastal Path; we'd discussed selling up and buying a communal house where we could live with equally ancient baby boomers, playing Led Zeppelin and snorting coke. We'd given up flying so we spent whole evenings on the internet working out how to get to Italy by train. *Anything but a cruise*, was one of our running jokes. *What a ghastly thought . . . a fifth circle of Hell . . . why on earth would anyone do it?*

Though, actually, now I remembered, it was *me* who led these discussions. Maybe Greg's mind was already elsewhere, plotting his release, wondering what to shed and what to take. Working out when to tell me. Rehearsing what to say to our middle-aged and far-flung children, who may or may not have seen it coming.

Or maybe it was an impulse decision, prompted by a single moment, an utterly irrelevant moment, like the sight of me slotting a tablet into the dishwasher. *I no longer want to be married to this woman.* Once he realised this, he was swept along helplessly and there was no turning back.

Who knew? It was too late to ask. I was alone in my stagnant house with no other person to stir the air. The slightest noise made me jump. Those first weeks I felt too exposed to go outside, yet indoors the hours stretched endlessly. Friends asked me to supper but that still left the rest of the day to kill. It was November, and darkness fell at four. When I could rouse myself I'd go round switching on the lights but then I thought: why bother, just for me?

I missed him. I missed him *so much*, despite my bitterness and humiliation. I missed him groaning with me when Trump came on the TV. The companionship we shared, in an ever-more dismaying world. The chatting and banalities. I missed the talking, more than anything, even his annoying habit of asking me a question when I had a mouth full of toothpaste. I had so much to say, the words silting up as the days passed. All those thoughts rolling round my head, all those unsaid words – what could I do with them all? Needless to say, I couldn't sleep. I missed his arms around me at night, keeping me safe. His naked body, the smell of his skin. How could he bear to be alone?

For now he was settled in Dorset, living his new life. What did he do all day? Didn't he miss our arguments? The squabbling seagulls were no substitute. I wanted to know about his niece's latest love rat, and his friend Bing's scan results. But these conversations were no longer appropriate. He'd made that clear.

I'd been dumped out of the blue, and overnight become one of those women I'd secretly pitied and kept meaning to invite to supper. Single women with their single cinema ticket and single hotel room and single Serves One Vegan Bake. And a cat, always a cat. That was me, now.

Our house was in Muswell Hill, which made it even worse. Muswell Hill was entirely populated by smug couples leading enviable lives. At dusk I'd walk the streets gazing into my neighbours' windows, each a lamplit tableau of middle-class contentment. Ten-year-olds playing the violin. Candlelit dinner parties. Teenagers romping with labradoodles. The women sang in choirs and did Pilates, and the men played football with the other husbands and they sent their children to private schools even though they read the *Guardian*. They had date nights and said they were each other's best friend – how nauseating was that? Some of them were on their second marriage and even smugger. Some weren't married at all because they didn't believe in a piece of paper, and they were the smuggest of the lot. And every Saturday they all went to the farmers' market where everybody smiled at everybody all the time.

'Ugh! They make me vomit,' said Azra, who lived

above a Turkish takeaway. It was only a bus ride from Muswell Hill but it was another world. 'Anyway, I bet the husbands are banging their PAs.'

Azra lived alone but there was nothing pitiful about *her*. Quite the opposite. She was a fierce, feral creature. Long legs and masses of hair, which she streaked pink and blue, or sometimes dyed jet black. She didn't give a toss about her age. Both men and women had fallen under her spell and been spat out when she'd finished with them. I'd known her for ever and her adventures had thrummed through my marriage like a distant tom-tom in the jungle. How timid my own life seemed, compared to hers! She was my best friend and I loved her with all my heart – even more so now that I was on my own.

For Azra was my inspiration, my role model for this new me. 'Who needs men cluttering up the place?' she said. 'Go, girl. Eat what you like, do what you like. Reclaim your territory. Stay in bed all day if you want to. Go out all night if you want to. Fart in bed, pamper yourself, *don't* pamper yourself, who gives a shit? Come on holiday with me, get drunk, have a laugh. Get rid of his stuff and make the house *your* house. It's fun, and you haven't had much of that with boring old Greg, have you, sweetheart?'

Her contempt for Greg surprised me. Azra wasn't normally the soul of tact but in this case she'd kept her feelings hidden, out of consideration for me. Now it all gushed out.

'He'd become such a pompous old git. Didn't it annoy you, the way he cleared his throat before giving his opinion on anything? And how he let everybody know he'd been a professor at the LSE? He always got it in somehow. And how he'd met Mick Jagger – he got *that* in, too. He was such a starfucker.'

'Was he?'

'God, Pru, didn't you notice? But much, much worse was the way he undermined you.'

'Did he?'

She rolled her eyes. 'All the time. Little squelches. Squelch, squelch, squelch. Contradicting you in front of other people, putting you down, that sort of thing. Being a control freak. No wonder you felt so inadequate.' She gripped my arm. 'But you're not, you're *so* not! You taught for twenty years in the toughest comprehensive in Hackney – catch *Greg* doing that – and you're funny and clever and gorgeous, and you've brought up two fabulous children—'

'He really wasn't that bad.' Ridiculously, I felt a throb of loyalty. 'I think, deep down, he felt inadequate. That's why he was so moody and difficult. It's all the fault of being sent away to boarding school, feeling abandoned. He was so damaged by that. I could've killed his parents. He was depressed for years – you know that – but he was trying to sort himself out. Better late than never. I think it was the cancer that shook him up. He was trying, honestly. He was going to a therapist.'

Azra shrugged. 'I don't know why you're standing up for him when he's been such a shit. I was only trying to help.'

I grabbed her bony shoulders and gave her a hug. It was awkward, on her kitchen stool. She pushed back her hair and took another gulp of wine. Her bangles tinkled as they slid down her arm.

'I'm sorry,' I said.

'No, *I'm* sorry. I shouldn't have let rip. It's just such a relief, to say what I feel.'

People don't, do they, when you're married? They can analyse your lovers to bits when it doesn't really matter, but the moment you get married the curtain is lowered and nothing critical is said until the marriage is over, the curtain is lifted, and they're stumbling over each other to tell you how ghastly your spouse was.

Azra was particularly tense that day, and fell silent after we'd spoken. She obviously felt that even by her standards she'd blurted out too much.

Of course I was buoyed by her criticisms of Greg. But I was also hurt that she hadn't, even in the most guarded way, hinted at some of this before and offered her support. After all, she'd known the two of us for years.

And, quite honestly, he wasn't *that* bad. If he were, she must have thought me an idiot. Azra was a passionate woman and inclined to lash out in all directions, sometimes missing the mark. Maybe her hostility stemmed from Greg's ambivalent attitude towards *her*.

I'd long suspected that he found Azra threatening. He'd kept quiet because she was my friend, but sometimes it would slip out. *Bit of a ballbreaker, isn't she? And the way she wangs on about the patriarchy and racial profiling, all that stuff, nobody can get a word in edgeways. Bloody bad manners.* I had to agree about the manners, but Azra felt things deeply and didn't give a toss if that upset people. I'd been the target of this myself, often enough.

Besides, she'd had a tough upbringing. She'd been born in Sunderland to a single mother, and known real deprivation. In her teens, however, she'd escaped, hitch-hiked south and reinvented herself as Azra, simply because she liked the name. I so admired her courage; in fact, I was a little in awe of her. She was a free spirit, utterly classless, and beholden to nobody. In the circumstances, good manners seemed irrelevant.

I think, too, that Greg was threatened by her bisexuality. I've noticed this, with men. They suspect that their dicks aren't enough to satisfy a woman and that anybody bi must really prefer another female. So where did that leave *them*? Pretty disposable, that's where.

But Azra was beyond all that. *When I fall in love, that's the last thing that concerns me. They're just a person – who gives a fuck?*

I gave a fuck. However, I pretended to agree. In truth I found her airy pronouncement a bit pretentious, but she was my soulmate, something Greg had never been, not really. My soulmate and lifesaver.

He'd been gone four months by then. Outside, the sun was sinking. Azra and I had finished the bottle of wine and were taking turns to swab bread around a tub of guacamole. It was eerily warm for January and Azra's window was open. The smell of kebabs drifted up from Karim's takeaway. On the nearby rooftop, amongst the satellite dishes and extractor fans, sat a crow. It tilted its head and eyed me speculatively, sizing up my thoughts, before bouncing sideways and flying off.

Azra rubbed her thumb along my forearm. 'I shouldn't have said all that. What happens if you two make it up? I'll feel such a twat.'

But he was gone. It had taken a long time for it to sink in, that he was gone for good.

14

Two

I thought I'd get used to being alone. Spring had arrived, with its lambs gambolling and hope abounding, but if anything I felt worse. I'd find myself standing for hours looking into the garden but unable to move. The grass needed mowing but what was the point, with nobody to see it?

Things started to break down. The kitchen grew dimmer as one by one the halogen lightbulbs fused. It was only Greg who could prise the bloody things out. I'd never understood the display panel on the dryer and it started manically beeping and leaving the clothes sodden. I know I should have worked it out but when I found the instruction booklet it seemed to be in Japanese. The car needed oil but I couldn't wrench out the dipstick and found myself standing in the street, weeping, as I gazed into the open yawn of its engine.

I wasn't just helpless; I was gripped by a sort of panicky inertia. Maybe, even then, I was starting to go crazy. I'd resumed work and was tutoring half a dozen pupils, and seemed to cope with that, but the moment they'd gone I sank into torpor and could barely move. I'd find myself stilled in the hallway, hypnotised by the colours on the floor where the sunlight shone through the stained glass. Yet my heart was racing.

My friends were sympathetic and still asked me over for supper, but less often than they'd done in the early days. I seemed to be becoming one of those single women I myself had so cruelly let slip through the net. When I did get an invitation, however, and the countdown began, I found myself becoming pointlessly agitated. Despite my longing for company, I was becoming fearful and agoraphobic. And I hated the preparations: pulling off the baggy trousers I wore all day, putting on make-up, a dress. When Greg was around it had been a companionable thing, sometimes the best part of the evening. *Want a glass of wine before we go?* Now, as I twisted round laboriously to zip myself up, I was already dreading coming home alone, and the number of days before I could ask my hosts back to my house without sounding needy. There were only so many times that one could phone.

Alex and Bethany, Jim and Rachel, Tish and Benji . . . they were my friends, but looking back now, I'm ashamed of the envy I felt. Envy of the easy familiarity between them. I remember watching Tish and Benji, married for ever, playfully butting each other's hips as they stood side by side, dishing up.

Sometimes they said, *It's only us, I'm afraid,* and my heart would sink. Sometimes they said, *You'll love Brian; he's just moved back to London after his divorce,* and my heart would lift. Brian, however, would be bald and overweight, and after asking me, *Do you ski?* would swing round and talk to the woman on his right.

I knew my hosts talked about me afterwards, bonded together by my situation. *Poor Pru. How lucky we've got each other.* It gave them an erotic jolt, and that night they'd make love for the first time in weeks with an ardour that startled them both.

My envy became all-consuming. I can admit it now. Even more than the laughter, I envied the bickering and arguments, because that was so familiar. Whether Greg and I were happy seemed irrelevant by now. I simply envied the normality of what I'd taken for granted. Not trips to Venice, not big things. Just the 'we' so casually scattered through the conversations. Just being a couple.

And now the weather was warmer you couldn't avoid the bastards. I didn't mind the young ones, of course; it was the old ones who upset me. Walking hand in hand in Highgate Woods; queuing at the cinema. I'd see them in Aldi, helping each other at the checkout – you had to be fast, in Aldi – a practised team, like grizzled, synchronised dancers, loading the trolley for their grandchildren's visit.

If I'd had grandchildren, it might have been easier. I'd have someone to love. But my daughter, who lived in Reykjavik, was a workaholic with a same-sex partner, and too busy to be pregnant, and my son, who lived in Pasadena, was a computer nerd and seemed to find it hard to relate to anybody, let alone breed with them.

Besides, I suspected that Max, my son, sided with his dad. He'd always been a loner and no doubt understood Greg's need for solitude. Working in IT suited him fine as he didn't have to talk to anyone at all. Lucy was more communicative, FaceTiming each week, but I didn't want to worry her and pretended that I was coping OK. 'To tell the truth I've seen it coming for years,' I lied. 'It's actually rather a relief and I'm enjoying my new-found independence!'

It didn't help that Azra and I had one of our rows. Azra

had been supportive for months, treating me with unchar-acteristic kindness, but she could flare up unexpectedly. She probably thought I was recovering and could take it. At the doorstep she'd crossed paths with one of my pupils, and when we sat down in the garden with our tea she launched into an attack.

'I can't believe you're helping these kids,' she said, 'someone like you, with your politics. Drilling them with all that stuff to get them into *private school*! Haven't they got enough bloody advantages already, the rich little cre-tins?' She dredged out her teabag and flung it into the flowerbed. 'Don't you feel guilty?'

Of course I did, but I wasn't letting on. 'I need the money,' I said. 'And anyway, aren't they just *people*? I seem to remember *you* saying that.'

'When?'

'About sex.'

'You're having *sex* with them?'

'No! When you said it didn't matter what gender a per-son is. "That's the last thing that concerns me," you said. "They're just a person – who gives a fuck?" You were quite sneery, actually. Quite squelchy.'

'I don't know what you're talking about.'

'Oh, forget it.'

'No, tell me what you mean. You're saying I undermine you?'

'No! I'm sorry, it's just that sometimes you do just what you say Greg did.'

'Greg? What's he got to do with it?'

'Squelching.' I paused. 'Never mind, I probably am a bit pathetic.'

We were sitting on the patio. I gazed at Greg's collection of herbs, each in its terracotta pot. They were already choked with weeds. He'd been a terrific cook, much better than me. Ottolenghi recipes, using ingredients one never used again; our cupboards were full of the obscure little packets and bottles. And he'd loved giving dinner parties. It was one of his best qualities. He liked preparing in advance, the rows of chopped herbs, the more arcane the better, the obligatory heap of pomegranate seeds. He even wrote out placements, standing at the kitchen table, biro in hand. *Who's going to sit next to your stroppy friend Azra?*

She was stroppy, he was right. Suddenly I missed him so much my eyes filled with tears. Why had he left me, just when we were free to go anywhere and do whatever we wanted? We had so many plans. It was so companionable, getting old together. Did he ever regret abandoning our shared life? Did he really want to live like a hermit, gales roaring around him and only a bike for transport?

Today Azra seemed a poor substitute. How difficult women were, compared to men! She sat beside me, rolling a cigarette while she gazed into the middle distance. She'd painted her nails silver, and wore her red velvet leggings and a beautiful stripy jumper she'd found in a charity shop. Somebody must have spent weeks knitting that, and finding its star-shaped buttons. Azra wasn't beautiful, but she was stylish and sexy and utterly confident of the effect she had on other people. It was hard to believe she was seventy.

To change the subject, I told her about the men at the local car wash, who I'd discovered were Syrian. One of

Azra's many jobs was working with Syrian refugees at a community hub in Tottenham. I said how courteous and kind the car-washers were. 'Trouble was, they've retuned my radio to Kiss FM and I can't get it back to Radio 4.'

'Oh, don't be such a pantywaist.'

I burst out laughing. 'Pantywaist?'

'You're a perfectly capable woman, don't pull this help-less shit.'

'What's got into you?'

'Nothing!' She tipped back her head and drained her mug. 'I'm just saying you *can* learn to tune a radio. It's not rocket science.'

In this mood she needed careful handling. I didn't reply and we sat there in silence. It had rained during the night and the daffodils' lovely heads were still bowed from their battering. I remember that day so well, how distracted Azra seemed, tense and quivering, like a racehorse. I thought: sometimes I don't really like you at all.

In mid-April something happened that was to change every-thing. It didn't seem significant at the time. It simply seemed material for a comic anecdote, funnier in the telling than in the experience.

I was invited to the funeral of a man I hardly knew. He was the husband of someone I'd met long ago when I'd briefly joined the local choir. We'd gather on Monday eve-nings to eat home-made flapjacks and tackle Handel's *Messiah*. I liked the people there, I really did: they despised the Tories and did their recycling. But their woolly liber-alism and cars matted with dog hairs didn't fool me. Beneath the self-deprecation thrummed a ruthless ambition for their children and a networking system of nepotism and queue-jumping that would impress the ruler of Uzbekistan. Nowadays they'd be called the Metropolitan Elite, and blamed for Brexit. In those days I simply called them Smug Marrieds, whose offspring all seemed to slide into jobs at the BBC or top legal chambers without any trouble at all.

Having children who were stubbornly unachieving, I didn't stay in the choir long. I could hardly remember Anna, the grieving widow. At that time, in Muswell Hill, the more goody-goody wives had a certain look: navy-blue outfits, velvet Alice bands and patent-leather shoes with little brass buckles. You could barely tell them apart.

Because of this, I nearly didn't go to the funeral; it seemed intrusive to join people I hardly knew, who were mourning a man I couldn't remember. But I needed to get out of the house. A roofer was fixing the leak in the kitchen extension and he was being laboriously flirtatious. I could see his heart wasn't in it – I was far too old – but once he'd started he obviously felt obliged to carry on. I dreaded the creak of the ladder as he descended for yet another cup of tea. I also suspected he was ripping me off.

So I put on some suitably sombre clothes and drove to Golders Green Crematorium. The mourners were already filing in when I arrived. I didn't recognise anyone, but that was scarcely surprising.

I sat down near the back. I could hardly see the coffin, or what looked like a display of photographs. Nor had I thought to pick up the order of service. So it took me a while to realise what had happened. We all rose for 'All Things Bright and Beautiful'. Then we sat down again and a young man in army uniform made his way to the microphone.

'We're here to celebrate the life of Dawn,' he said, his voice shaking. 'My sister was taken from us far too soon. Her struggle against ill health and her bravery in these last challenging months have been a lesson to us all. Even when she lost the use of her legs she kept on smiling, because that was Dawn all over. She was the best sister in the world, and I'm sure there isn't one of us here who hasn't benefited from her kindness and generosity. I'd like to celebrate the Dawn we loved with a short poem.'

Heck. I'd come to the wrong funeral.

It's easily done. They run a tight ship at Golders Green, in and out in thirty minutes, no hanging about. Surreptitiously, I checked my watch. There had been so little traffic that I'd arrived half an hour early.

I shifted in my seat, blushing furiously. I'd been hemmed in by some late arrivals and couldn't sneak away.

So I sat it out. Dawn was obviously a wonderful woman, but then everyone's wonderful when they're dead, aren't they? Despite being fearful of discovery I found myself drawn into Dawn's life story, which seemed one of battling against a series of personal tragedies that would have defeated a lesser spirit. When it was over I made my escape into the drizzle. As I did so, a stranger turned to me and said: 'I don't know half these people, do you?'

Maybe it was then that the seed was sown. At the time I was just filled with suppressed giggles as I hurried away. I remember thinking: I wish Greg were at home, so I could tell him about it and we could have a laugh.

But there was nobody at home. When I arrived back,

having sat through the next funeral, the one I was supposed to attend, the roofer had gone. He'd taken his cash and left an ashtray full of cigarette butts and a turd in the lavatory.

I rang Azra to tell her about it but she was away. She was away a lot that spring. It turned out she was in France, yet again. One of her money-making schemes was trawling *brocantes*, buying old lace and linen bedsheets – apparently they'd become popular again now people had forgotten what a pain they were to iron. She'd bring them back in her van and sell them in antique markets.

A week later she was home. Her door was open and I glimpsed her in her kitchen, leaning against the draining board, reading a magazine and eating cold tortellini out of a saucepan. I was flooded with love.

She turned round. How great she looked! Radiant, in fact, with that wild hair and big, generous mouth. She was one of those sexy women who looked as if they have a secret, like a child sucking a forbidden sweet, up to something that only they find amusing.

I was suddenly suspicious. 'You got a fancy man out there?'

'What?'

'In France. Is that why you keep going?'

Azra laughed so hard she ended up coughing, her thin shoulders shaking. This seemed an overreaction and I was mildly surprised. When she recovered, however, she assured me it wasn't true. I couldn't help feeling relieved. I realised, yet again, how much I needed her. The thought of her disappearing into a love affair filled me with desolation.

I told her about being an imposter at Dawn's funeral and how I'd started to feel weirdly close to this unknown woman. How it seemed somebody had to die before people travelled across the world to express their love – why didn't they do it when the person was still alive?

'And nobody questioned me being there,' I said, 'because at funerals all sorts of people crawl out of the woodwork: people from the past, from bits of the past nobody knows about. We have such different compartments in our lives.'

'My friend Tabitha gatecrashes weddings,' said Azra. 'She lives in Kidderminster, near a big hotel where there's always weddings, so she puts on a nice frock and joins the guests, gets sloshed on Prosecco and snarfs the canapés. That's her weekend sorted. Sod all else to do in Kidderminster.'

Who was Tabitha? It confirmed my point. When Azra died, this unknown Tabitha would pop up at the funeral and nobody would have a clue who she was and where she'd fitted into Azra's life. From Azra's brief career as an actress? From the time she lived with a sculptor in New Mexico? From Greenham Common? From primary school?

I remember gazing at Azra, who was making us coffee. She wore a turquoise shirt, psychedelic leggings, and a pair of earrings I'd given her – little silver acorns that bobbed when she moved. I'd know her for thirty years but there were so many things I hadn't asked her. So many unknowns, yet she was my closest friend. Maybe she felt the same about me.

Actually I doubted this. Azra lacked curiosity. She lived in the moment, unreflectedly. I'd always admired this animal spirit, but today I felt another lurch of loneliness.

Would I ever meet somebody who wanted to look at my photograph albums? Who asked about my schooldays? I don't think she even knew the names of my parents.

I sat slumped on her sofa. The rain battered the window. My visit to the crematorium had shaken me up. Time was running short. Was I really going to die alone?

This naked fear could drain my blood. And the bitterness . . . oh, it was eating me up. I was still smarting from the subsequent funeral, the choir one, the one I was supposed to attend. I'd recognised some of the people there – couples who were still together, after all these years. And they looked perfectly happy! I watched them at the wake, fetching plates of sandwiches for each other, brushing crumbs off each other. How I envied them. What had those women done, to deserve such devotion? *They* hadn't been dumped. *They* had arms around them at night to ward off the terrors.

I was cornered by a woman called Anthea Mills, now fatter and older but still insufferably complacent. She boasted about her grandchildren, all doing marvellously at school, all living nearby, in and out of her house all day. 'We hardly have a moment to ourselves, do we, darling?' She jabbed her husband with her elbow. 'So we're sneaking off to Paris for the weekend, just the two of us. Can't wait!'

'I could have shot her,' I told Azra.

Needless to say, Azra treated this bourgeois crowing with contempt. 'They're probably miserable. Just too cowardly to split up.'

'They didn't look miserable.'

She raised her eyebrows. 'Do you really want to find

somebody? Isn't it a relief to be on your own? I thought you were coping better, now.'

Humiliatingly, my eyes filled with tears. An old woman crying is not a pretty sight. It's best left to the young, and nowadays they have plenty to cry about.

'Oh, lovey.' Azra sat down beside me and put her arm around my shoulders. 'Don't be sad.'

It came out in a rush. 'I can't bear it. I hate everyone being a couple and me being the gooseberry and put in the back seat of the car. Don't they understand how lonely that is? And going to the cinema alone, it makes me feel like those grubby men in Soho, when Soho was Soho—'

'You can always go with me.'

'—and rushing out before the lights come up so nobody's sorry for me. I hate it, hate it, *hate it*. And I hate myself for resenting people being happy.'

'Sweetheart, it's only been seven months—'

'*You* manage it. You love living alone but you're not the same as me.' Shamed by my outburst, I got up and tore off a piece of kitchen roll.

'Get another dog, then.'

I wiped my nose. Down in the street a siren wailed. Azra lived in Tottenham and this was the chorus of her days. Only the week before there had been a stabbing across the road; the police tape still sagged from a lamp-post. She took these things in her stride. I, on the other hand, felt myself becoming more and more timorous. Even the sound of the doorbell made my heart jump. I pictured myself in the years to come, a wrinkled hermit cowering behind the shutters.

'I'm not myself,' I said. 'I'm becoming deranged. I keep

waking up, thinking there's a burglar downstairs. Or on the roof. Or was it a very heavy squirrel?' Even opening letters filled me with dread. I didn't tell her that; it was too humiliating. Azra didn't need a man to protect her from the vast and threatening world.

Instead I said: 'I wonder if he misses me.'

'Forget him! He's an arse. You've got to move on.'

We sat there in silence. I had a suspicion that Azra was losing patience with me. Did she resent the weight of my dependence? Even a friendship like ours had its limits.

She was so brave, that was the trouble. There was a mosque down her road, where the worshippers left their shoes in the porch. A week before, she'd come out of the greengrocers and seen a man pick up the shoes and throw them into a skip. She'd yelled curses at him, chased him down the street and thwacked him with her bag for life, carrots flying everywhere.

Another time she'd slashed the tyres of a brand-new SUV, which was blocking an anti-racist march. And more, much more. She didn't give a fig about getting arrested. How fearful I felt, next to this urban warrior. And though she sometimes embarrassed me, how proud I was of her uncompromising courage.

Azra rolled a cigarette. She was the only person I knew who still smoked. 'It can be better with a woman, you know.'

'Yes, you've told me.'

'We know each other's bodies and we have more laughs.'

'I'm not that way inclined,' I said primly.

She raised her eyebrows. 'How do you know if you've never tried it?'

From anyone else this would have been an invitation, but I knew Azra too well for that.

'Look, you can be all fluid and non-binary and whatever, but I want a man,' I said. 'I want to find the loo seat up. Call me old-fashioned.'

She laughed, and slumped back on the sofa. 'All right, you win.' She pulled a thread of tobacco from her teeth.

She sat there, smoking. I sat next to her, lining up her remote controls. Back home I had an even larger selection. Several of them were a mystery to me and now I would never find out what they were for. Did we once own a Panasonic?

'If you want a bloke you'll have your work cut out,' she said. 'If they were going to leave their wives they'd have done it by now – they'd have done it ten years ago, for a younger model. It's a bit late in the game, at our age. They're starting to get lots of ailments and need to hunker down with the woman they've got, because who else'll nurse them? And they've come to adore their grandchildren because they give them hope when the world's so shit, and they can give them back to their parents when they're being a pain.' She shrugged. 'So you'll have to wait till their wives die and then move fast because a whole lot of women will be crawling – no, galloping – out of the woodwork with their casseroles and condolences—'

'—and their gardening skills, because he'll have let it go to rack and ruin—'

'—being too busy nursing his wife,' said Azra.

'And they'll listen to him banging on about how marvellous his wife was,' I said, 'and agree with him even if they didn't like her – they're not stupid—'

'—and they'll be charmingly helpless: *Could you possibly look at my car, it's making a funny noise*—'

'—but not too needy, because that's a turn-off,' I said.

'And they know he'll be attracted to somebody younger so they pull out all the stops, conversation-wise, so he'll get interested despite himself. You have to work at it when you're old—'

'—and they'll make him laugh—'

'—something he hasn't done for years because his wife was dying and he'd been feeding her mashed potato and holding back her hair when she's been vomiting from the chemo—'

'—if she's *got* any hair,' I said.

'—because he's lived with death for so long, with all its smells and sadness, that he wants somebody bursting with health, so for God's sake keep quiet about your ailments. He's had enough of all that—'

'—and these young women, despite their tight little pussies, don't understand this, and they don't know who Alma Cogan is, and when he's not shagging them it'll make him feel so bloody lonely.'

We collapsed against each other, exhausted.

'Or you could go on the internet,' said Azra. 'But it's full of wonderful, intelligent women and the men are all crap—'

'—or weirdos—'

'—because why would they bother to go online when they can take their pick of gorgeous women like us?'

We sat there, slumped together, bemused by the mystery of it all.

*

During those months I became more and more reliant on Azra. It shamed me, how when I was married I'd forgotten about her for weeks on end. Not that she'd minded, I'm sure. She probably didn't even notice. But when I was teaching I was busy, and in the holidays Greg and I would disappear to Dorset. Being an academic, he did much of his research online and could work anywhere.

Besides, we had children and Azra didn't. From the day they're born, children shift the centre of gravity, and it stays that way for ever. In this respect, Azra was an outsider. Sometimes I pitied her; sometimes I envied her life of freedom in her tiny flat in North London's premier crime hotspot, flooded with sunshine and vibrating from the passing buses. Even if she had the money she wouldn't have moved. She'd been there for ever and knew all the shopkeepers – the Turks, Afghans, Bengalis – and the names of their children.

In Muswell Hill, on the other hand, everyone went to Waitrose. And, unlike Azra, they'd benefited from the property boom. Our generation had been the lucky ones, buying at the right time, sitting on our backsides and watching our houses turn us into millionaires. *So unfair,* we'd say, with sorrowful exuberance. My friends had been cannily investing, too, whilst downplaying their purchases: 'Oh, it's just a tiny buy-to-let,' or, 'It's for the children, to get a toehold on the ladder,' or, 'Of course we couldn't have afforded it, but I got this surprise legacy from my uncle, and of course we've had to take out a huge mortgage.'

I, too, was sitting on a fortune. And I was living in a house that was far too big for me. It had been too big even when Greg was around. He'd said, 'I don't want anything, you can have it all,' but I suspected he'd soon regret this reckless passive-aggression and come to his senses. His sparse, infrequent emails gave no sign of this, but then I was in a state of limbo, too, and unable to make any decisions. There were three spare rooms upstairs, including his abandoned study. I knew I should take in lodgers but the thought of strangers in the house was even worse than being on my own. The creaking footsteps on the stairs, the shuffling around each other in the kitchen, the hesitant tap on the bathroom door. Azra said I should take in a Syrian family – they'd be cleaner and more polite than an English one – but I'd prevaricated.

'Why don't *you* come and live with me?' I said. 'You say you're skint – well, you could rent out your flat and make some real money. You're always saying you want a garden. And it could be fun.'

She shook her head. 'I'm good,' she said. It was a phrase I particularly disliked. I knew she valued her independence but I still felt rebuffed. *Squelched.*

I had to conceal my all-consuming need. Stiffen my sinews and learn from her. I was phoning her far more often than was healthy. Desperation is all very well in the young but, like a short skirt, it's not a good look for a seventy-year-old.

In May I lost two of my pupils when their families moved out of London. I knew Azra disapproved of my tutoring but I'd been particularly fond of those boys. They'd made me laugh, and I missed their company. So I asked her if she needed help with any of her various jobs.

'I wouldn't want any money. I just want to be useful.'

My voice cracked with self-pity. 'It would get me out of the house and stop me brooding.'

Azra had a young friend called Shania, who ran a florist's shop in Dalston. I also knew Shania because I'd taught her at school. I liked her a great deal; she'd been a serious, single-minded girl who'd set her sights on floristry, even at that early age, and now ran her own business, supplying the local gastro-pubs and hipster hangouts. She also did the usual weddings, funerals and home deliveries. Azra, with her van, helped her out when she was busy.

Azra said we could do it together. It would be fun, and I could sit in the van and watch out for the bastard traffic wardens.

I was feeling strangely weightless that day. I'd hardly slept, and then was plunged into a dream where I fell off a cliff while my mother stood at the top, her mouth gaping in a silent scream. I only remembered this when I stepped into the back room of the florist's. Shania stood there, poking carnations into a floral 'DAD' that took up half the table.

I'd also woken to upsetting news about my daughter. Greg had sent one of his terse, formal emails, this time about renewing the house insurance, and had added a PS, saying our daughter had split up with her long-term partner, Freyja. This had thrown me into confusion. Why hadn't Lucy told me? Why her dad rather than me? Did she think I'd be too upset? Was she unhappy, or was it her decision to leave her girlfriend? Was she planning on quitting Reykjavik and coming back to England? I'd tried to phone but only got her voicemail. She worked at a TV studio and switched her mobile off when they were recording.

All in all, everything felt disconnected that morning, a

jolt away from reality. My nightmare was still a taste in my mouth. I looked at the floral 'DAD', lying on Shania's work-table. It was a hot day and the fan was whirring; DAD's white petals shivered as if they were aware their life was to be extinguished. I remembered that time, a month earlier, when I'd been the imposter at a stranger's funeral. How I'd felt awkward, but oddly invigorated.

Azra was chatting to Shania as she collected bouquets to load into the van. They were propped against the wall, sheathed in Cellophane and bound with raffia. Sachets of plant food were sellotaped to them like little colostomy bags. Slotted between the stalks were cards bearing messages of love, congratulations and condolence, written in Shania's beautiful copperplate handwriting. At school she'd been top of her class at art.

'Pru broke up with her husband last year,' said Azra.

Shania turned to me, her face softened with concern. 'Oh, no. You all right?'

'And she's looking for a new bloke,' said Azra. 'I've told her she's got to move fast if she wants to get a good one, know what I mean? They get snapped up pretty sharpish, all those hungry women just waiting to pounce. Of course, they'll have a lot of baggage – at our age we all do – but I think it's weirder if they *don't*. And widowers are a better bet than divorcés because they won't be bitter, just bereaved. But she's got to watch out, because who wants to be a rebound fuck? She should let another woman do that job, then nab him for the long haul. Which Pru seems to want, but God knows why.'

They both laughed. This conversation annoyed me. Azra was talking as if I wasn't there. And did I really want

Shania to know about my private life? Wasn't that *my* business?

Later that morning we did the deliveries. Sitting in the van, I read the cards. 'Thank you, Mummy, for making me a little brother to play with,' said one. 'To the best wife in the world,' said another. So many kisses; so much love. I watched Azra, lithe as a panther, bounding up front steps and ringing doorbells. She wore a singlet and jeans, a butcher's apron tied round her waist and her hair bundled up with a rag. Needless to say, she was greeted with delight – who doesn't like getting flowers?

In the van, however, we hardly spoke. She seemed pre-occupied. I presumed she was just concentrating on driving. Traffic was heavy and it was hard to find anywhere to park. Sometimes, when Azra leaped out, I slid into her seat and had to drive around the block or double-park to a chorus of honking horns.

I hardly noticed. I was thinking about Lucy, how much I loved her and how I longed for her to come home. All my old emotions flooded back. I could be a mother again. Lucy was admittedly a grown-up woman, and a truculent one at that, but she was still my daughter and it would be a relief to be needed. Feeling obliged to others, even my dearest friends, was such a strain. Lucy might bully me but she was family, and I'd forgotten what family was like.

Just then my mobile rang. It was Lucy. Never one for chit-chat, she came straight out with her news. She'd split up with her girlfriend because she'd fallen for someone else – a woman who worked with her in the props department at the studios.

'Why did you tell your dad first?' I blurted out.

'Christ, Mum, is that all you can say?'

'I'm sorry. I just thought it might mean you were coming home.'

'This is my home; Iceland's my home. All my friends are here. And I only told Dad first because he phoned me from a narrow boat.'

'A narrow boat?'

'To tell me about his holiday. He was on the Kennet and Avon Canal.'

'Your *dad* in a *narrow boat*? He doesn't know anything about narrow boats.'

'He was having a great time. I've never heard him so happy.' Lucy paused. 'Aren't you going to ask about *me*? If *I'm* happy?'

I apologised and asked her, but I wasn't concentrating. A *narrow boat*? I was parked on a double-yellow line behind a Londis lorry. A man unloaded a crate full of boxes and wheeled them into the shop. In the rear-view mirror I saw Azra walking towards me. She was on her mobile, and in no hurry. In fact she stopped, still talking animatedly, so she could carry on her conversation. I felt irritated; she'd hardly said a word to me all morning.

Finally she clambered into the cab and I slid into the passenger seat.

'Greg's been on a narrow boat holiday,' I said.

'What?'

'He's got a woman.'

'Why do you think that?'

'Because the only thing I know about narrow boats is there's got to be two of you. It's always couples. You see them, one at the front and one at the back.'

She reversed, the gears crashing, and pulled out into the street. I knew she was fed up with me talking about Greg, but I soldiered on.

'The one at the back steers it and the one at the front jumps out and does the locks and stuff. Greg's never been interested in narrow boats. He's got no *friends* who're interested in narrow boats. I just know.'

'Aren't you a tiny bit jumping to conclusions?'

'It's always couples, middle-aged couples with their little folding chairs for when they stop in the evening to drink Prosecco on the towpath. They look happy. *He* sounded happy. They're all *Daily Mail* readers, of course.'

'Doesn't sound like Greg.'

'Exactly. That's why I know there's a woman involved. Men do all sorts of unlikely things if they're having sex. Like your pal whatshisname voting Brexit. We all knew he must be shagging that ghastly woman.'

Azra stopped with a jolt at some traffic lights – she was a terrible driver – and swung round to glare at me.

'Listen, pet, you've got to stop obsessing. Maybe Greg *has* found somebody. He's probably quite a catch. After all, *you* fell in love with him once. And he's not too bad for his age – plenty of hair, nice flat tummy, and pretty intelligent if you can bear him banging on about the Monetary Fund, or whatever it is he's writing about. And a nice cottage in Dorset.' She shrugged. 'I mean, what's not to like, if you're desperate?'

'You've changed your tune.'

She wrenched the stick into first gear and turned left. The car behind hooted. 'I said he was a tosser because I'm loyal to you and can't bear you being hurt. Of course he was bloody annoying, but then so are most people. That's why I don't live with any of them. Nor would they want to live with me.'

'Can't you just ring him up and find out?'

'What?'

'In a subtle way.'

'Pru, he doesn't even *like* me!'

'Of course he does.'

He didn't. Not only did Greg find her threatening, he thought her pretentious. 'That silly name "Azra" – she's Linda, for God's sake! And all that self-invented bohemian I'm-such-a-free-spirit-compared-to-you-lot stuff, and that phoney voice. Never trust a person who's lost their regional accent. And she hates men.'

Greg had been jealous, of course. The way I laughed with Azra on the phone, the endless talking. 'Nattering', he called it. *What on earth do you find to natter about for so long?* He wouldn't call it nattering if she were a man.

Azra was right. I knew I should let Greg go. My mother was in my thoughts that morning, my dream still curdling my brain. She'd suffered years of dementia before she died. Was something loosening in my own brain? It is often triggered by trauma, or some sort of shock, and I was still feeling the effects of what had happened. More so, as the months went by.

I thought I'd feel better by now. 'Get over it and move on,' said Azra. Linda. Azra. Whatever she called herself. She was my friend, my ally in the wilderness. She seemed to cope all right, but I couldn't.

Because I wanted a man. I was so hungry I could scream. The warmth of a man in my bed, scaring away the demons.

His arms around me, the smell of him. The weight of him between my legs.

Who could I cling to if there was a third world war? Or a pandemic, killing millions? Was I to die alone, abuzz with bluebottles?

The next day I saw my dog, Sidney. He was tied up outside Waitrose.

'Sidney!'

My heart leaped and I stumbled towards him, my bags bumping against my legs. My darling dog, he'd been waiting for me all this time. *Months*. Almost a *year*. That's how faithful dogs are. How had he survived? Who had been looking after him? There were several other dogs tied up but only one Border collie. Only one Sidney.

'It's me!' I shouted, tears springing to my eyes.

He remained sitting there, panting in the heat, his tongue hanging out.

Of course it wasn't my dog. Slimmer, younger. I veered away, my eyes stinging, and made my way to the car.

Mad or what? I sat in the car, quite undone. Of course he was dead, my faithful friend. Nobody had loved me quite like he did. His head had rested on my lap and Joni Mitchell had sung him out of this world.

Doors slammed, cars came and went. I sat there, overcome with grief. For my dog, for my marriage. For Greg's tenderness, the way he warmed up the car on frosty mornings before I drove to school, the way he cleaned my specs. He was a terrific dancer – he could *jive*, for God's sake. Most English men danced like publishers. We'd had a good life together and I thought he loved me.

Consumed by self-pity, I sat there sobbing; once I started I couldn't stop.

I had to shake myself out of this. There were worse things than living in a five-bedroomed house in Muswell Hill with bookshelves and shutters and an open fire, with an apple tree in the garden and nice middle-class neighbours I'd known for ever. What right had I to sob in my car when the world was burning and migrants were drowning and hedgehogs were becoming extinct? Every day when I read the *Guardian* I felt another plughole opening and the hope draining away, thousands of bath-tubs and gallons of tears. And here I was, fretting about my marriage.

So the next week I asked Azra if I could help with her Syrians. Every Saturday she drove to supermarkets where she loaded up her van with leftover food, which she distributed to families around her neighbourhood, and then helped out in the community hub in the furthest reaches of Tottenham.

Azra had already collected the food. I buckled up for another Wild West ride through the mean streets of North London.

'Fatima likes peanut butter,' Azra said. 'So I nicked her a jar when I was signing for the other stuff. She has a son with cystic fibrosis and her husband beats her up.' We swung round a corner. Behind us, the bin bags shifted and slumped. 'We always have too much bread. Trouble is, they can only take the sliced loaves because most of them don't have chopping boards.'

How I loved Azra that day! All was forgiven, for although she could be snippy with people like me, with the vulnerable she was at her best: warm and solicitous, asking about their children and helping them rummage in the bags for the choicest items, like punnets of strawberries.

When we'd finished the deliveries we drove to the community hub. It was in a former carpet shop on a particularly desolate stretch of road. Lorries thundered past in clouds of exhaust fumes. Its interior was decorated with murals of sunflowers and skipping kids. There was a café, where Azra stored the food we hadn't given away. Men played backgammon and mothers bent over exercise books with their children.

Azra seemed to know them all and went round shaking hands and chatting. I lingered by the door, distracted by the thought that I might never have sex again. I looked at a little girl who was sucking the leg of her teddy bear. When I was her age, seventy years was unimaginable. You'd be dead by then. When I was a schoolgirl, our teacher was forty and that meant practically dead, too. No doubt, all those years I was teaching, my schoolchildren thought the same about me. The thought of sex would not only be disgusting but inconceivable. If, that is, it ever crossed their minds, which I doubted.

Azra was on her mobile again. She stood hunched against the wall by the toilets, her back to the rest of us. Her shoulders shook with laughter and my warmth towards her evaporated. She wore her green leather jacket and the long lacy skirt she'd bought at the Oxfam shop. It was one of her less successful purchases, with its foolish cobwebby hem. Why did she agree to this trip and spend the whole time on the phone?

I felt too shy to introduce myself and gazed out of the window. Opposite, above a mini-cab office, there was a poster for some clothing company – a model wearing ripped jeans. What an insane world, I thought. Ragged children, on the other side of the planet, toiled in factories to make jeans that were purposely torn into rags for well-off Western kids to buy as a fashion statement. I wanted to share this no-doubt clichéd observation and suddenly felt bleak.

Loneliness, I realised, was making me increasingly strange. As I rattled round in my empty house, I was dwindling into something not quite human. The social constraints were lifted. I farted in bed, just as Azra had suggested, and didn't wash enough. The hairs had grown on my legs. I wasn't talking to myself, not yet, but I'd realised the civilising effect of another human being, simply by their presence in the house. And they would restore my sense of time, surely they would. In recent months I'd have a drink, make supper, eat it, wash up, get ready for bed, then look at my watch and realise it was only half-past eight.

Maybe a lodger would give me back my evenings, simply by being there. Even if we didn't have much in common.

Azra finished her phone call and came over. She was perspiring in that jacket. It was an inappropriate outfit for a food run, even for her, and I wondered if she was meeting someone later.

I asked: 'Is there anyone here who needs a room? Any of these people? Is there a list or something? I don't know how to go about it.'

'We can't do that now,' she said. 'I've got to go. Thing

is, I'm going in the opposite direction, but I can drop you off at the tube.'

And she hustled me out.

Azra's acting career had been short-lived. A brief appearance in *Casualty*, avant-garde stuff in pub theatres, that sort of thing. I remember how Greg and I would trek out to godforsaken venues in Zone 3 and sit on benches watching Eastern European productions in a state of buttock-numbing bafflement. She never made the big time. The trouble was, Azra was not beautiful enough for leading roles – too tall and angular, with her big features and tombstone teeth. More to the point, she wasn't a company player, one of the gang. Actors survive on charm as well as talent and she gained a reputation for being difficult, especially with directors, and especially if they were men.

So her career petered out and she went on to other things. But she was born with a talent for fabrication and reinvention; her very accent, that middle-class drawl, had been created somewhere between Sunderland and London. Greg once said, 'There's something phoney about her, don't you find? Something not quite real.' But then Greg had never trusted her.

But I did. I trusted her with my life.

I never did get a Syrian lodger. I'd hoped to do the food run again the following Saturday, and planned to investigate further then. The community hub seemed to be run by an amiable beardie who'd been nailing up notices when I was there. He might be the person to ask.

But Azra said she was going away for the weekend –

another flying visit to France, apparently – and somebody else was taking her place. So I thought I'd put it off for another week.

Besides, I was having second thoughts about the whole enterprise. I realised I'd been doing it largely to impress Azra. To be honest, I'd been hurt by her shuddering recoil at my suggestion she moved in with me. She could have been more graceful about it. Now I could turn the tables and surprise her. There'd be a touch of the *touché* about co-habiting with a Syrian asylum-seeker.

During the last few days, however, I'd been getting cold feet. What happened if my lodger and I didn't get on? I could hardly chuck them out after all they'd been through. Yet another expulsion, after so many.

So I didn't go to the hub. But I needed to go in that direction because I had something to drop off at Azra's flat. Her birthday was on the Sunday, and though she dismissed birthdays as irrelevant, I'd always given her a present. I'd bought her a book about rewilding and a tasteful Gwen John card, both of which would fit through her letterbox.

And I fancied a jaunt. The street outside her flat was filled with shops selling cheap vegetables and spices. So I decided to go shopping and deliver the package. At least it would get me out of the house.

I took the bus there. It was full of children clambering over their parents, who snapped at them but who were unconditionally loved. That morning I was filled with even more self-pity than usual. I thought: I come first with nobody. I'd thought I came first with Azra, but she obviously had somebody else. The signs were unmistakable: the absences, the phone calls. I thought she was my companion in the wilderness, my ally and inspiration. With her as my guide, slashing away the undergrowth and clearing a path, we could face the future together.

The bus stopped at some roadworks. That year, 2018, it seemed that the whole of London was being dug up and turned over like a giant compost heap. Later I remembered every detail of that day. I had a strong feeling of foreboding. I presumed I was just nervous about the simple act of shopping in a different area. Taking any decision nowadays filled me with dread; a mundane Saturday, with people thronging the streets, made my heart pound. So I decided to delay going to the shops. I'd drop off the package first.

I got off the bus and walked towards Azra's flat, above Karim's takeaway. There were a lot of Turkish restaurants in her street. Her favourite was called Yassar Halim.

It was there that I saw her, in Yassar Halim. She was sitting at a table by the window, half-obscured by a rubber plant, and talking to a man.

It was Greg.

Three

I knew. I just knew. You can tell, can't you, when two people are sleeping together? You can tell by the body language, the way they mirror each other's gestures. They do it unconsciously, of course. I knew it straight away.

The two of them were leaning towards each other across the table, both resting their chins on their hands. They were talking intently, lost in their own world. Greg was wearing an unfamiliar blue shirt.

They hadn't seen me. I swung round and stumbled away. I told myself: Azra's reading him the riot act. She's telling him I'm miserable and he's been stupid to leave me, that we'd had a great marriage and he's thrown it all away. That it was a late-life crisis and he should pull himself together and come home. That she was a loyal friend and worried about me.

I told myself: she lied about going to France because she'd arranged this meeting and hid it from me in case it failed. She is my friend; she is on my side. She loves me.

I seemed to have got on the wrong bus and it took a long time to get home. I poured myself a vodka and sat down at the kitchen table. For the first time in thirty years I longed for a cigarette, but my hands were shaking too much to light one anyway. In the garden a squirrel scrabbled in the flowerbed, trying to find something it had buried, earth flying everywhere.

They hated each other! *She's such a fraud, so pretentious!* Greg had said. *He's such a tosser,* she'd said. Doggedly, over the months, they'd created a smokescreen. Or maybe they *did* find each other annoying; after all, friction is often the basis for sexual attraction: look at Elizabeth Bennet and Darcy. Greg and I'd had a generally amiable relationship, not a passionate one, not since the early days. Even then it was companionable rather than tempestuous. We'd *liked* each other; we were friends, woolly liberal friends. We had so much in common.

When had it begun, him and Azra? Months ago? *Years* ago? Lie after lie after lie. No wonder she'd been testy with me recently; she was feeling as guilty as hell.

I scraped back my chair, rushed to the lavatory and threw up.

'How was France?'
　'Fine.'
　'Where did you go?'
　'A little town in Brittany.'
　'What's it called?'
　'St Suplice-Deux-Eglises.'
　'Why?'
　'Why what?'
　'Why did you go there?'
　'It has a big *marché aux puces* on Sundays.'
　'What's a *marché aux puces*?'
　'A flea market.'

'Successful?'

'What?'

'Your trip. Successful?'

'So-so.'

'What did you buy?'

'This and that.'

'What?'

'Some bedspreads. A little chest. Why?'

'Why what?'

'Why are you so interested?'

'I saw you with Greg.'

'What?'

'I saw you with Greg. On Saturday.'

She didn't miss a beat. 'Oh, that.'

'Yes, that.'

'I didn't want you to know.'

'So you lied.'

'Yes.'

'Pretending you were away.'

'Yes.'

'Why didn't you want me to know?'

'Because I needed to talk to him. To bring him to his senses. I didn't want you to know because it might have raised your hopes, but it didn't work. He's never coming back.'

'Because he's got you.'

'What?'

'All those times you were going to France you were going to Dorset, weren't you?'

Finally, a silence down the phone.

'How long has it been going on?'
Another silence. I could hear Azra breathing.
'Five years,' she said.

Do you know? She was too cowardly to come and face me. My bold, fearless friend. Ex-friend. The woman who slashed tyres and chased Islamophobes down the street. She sent me an email – how pitiful is that?

'I'm so sorry,' said my friend Linda – my ex-friend Linda – this totally unknowable person.

Actually it's a relief. I've felt so guilty because I love you too, it made me sick to my stomach to lie to you. I know you'll think it's a betrayal but what Gregory and I have is bigger than all of us.

She'd laid it out neatly in paragraphs. No spelling mistakes either, and she was borderline dyslexic. Care had been taken.

What I've realised is that life is short and if we are lucky enough to find love we must follow our hearts. I truly apologise for my behaviour, but for a while I was in a state of denial. In fact I was hoping it was just a fling and would soon blow over. You know me! Nobody would be the wiser and Gregory and I would have got it out of our systems. But as time passed we realised we'd both met the love of our lives.

We kept meaning to tell you, but kept putting it off. Unforgivable, I know, but there you are. It's terrible to cause pain and, as they say, ignorance is bliss. But when you saw us, that's exactly what we'd decided to do. Gregory came up from Dorset to discuss it with me. We were then going to phone you up and come round to the house to tell you.

You would have known soon enough. I've got a tenant for my flat and I'm moving out, in a couple of weeks, and going to live with him in Mortimer's Creek. It may not work – who knows? – but to be honest I've never been happier, and I'm just sorry it has been on the back of your pain. I've always loved your part of Dorset and it will be a new life for both of us.

I was astounded. She'd practically asked me to wish her luck. I'd always known Azra was thick-skinned but the brutality of this was jaw-dropping.

And no question of asking my permission to live in what had been *my* cottage, with *my* husband. She was obviously deranged by sex.

I couldn't shake off the images. Azra's long, dry, olive-skinned legs wrapped around Greg's pallid, spongey midriff. She had the most beautiful legs. When she came down to Dorset we'd sit on the beach, side by side. She'd give me a squirt of her tea-tree moisturiser. Rubbing it in, I'd gaze with envy at her neat, chiselled knees and slender feet. Next to hers, my legs looked unappetisingly pale and mottled with bruises which, as I grew older, stubbornly remained, blooming under the skin.

I imagined her big, hungry lips clamped around Greg's cock.

Where had they done it? In her flat, no doubt, but had they sneaked into my bedroom when I was away? She said it had begun five years ago. I was still working full time, then, and out of the house all day. Greg was at the LSE, supposedly, or researching at the British Library, supposedly, but his hours were flexible and he had plenty of time to sneak off. Then he'd retired and had all the time in the world. And after that, when he dumped me to 'find himself' . . . the bastard. The *bastard* . . . That sorrowing look. *We haven't been happy for years, isn't it time to part as friends? . . . I need solitude, to start my spiritual journey.* His gaunt, bony face, his Adam's apple moving up and down. There had always been something of the ascetic about Greg. Not the face of an adulterer.

Of course I was furious. And horribly, horribly hurt. I kept searching through the past for clues. Greg going to a conference in Scarborough and not responding to my calls; Azra, coincidentally, going on a Fiction Writing course in Devon. Funny, when she never read any fiction – in fact, never read any books at all. Greg's narrow-boat holiday – of course she was with him. Those endless phone calls. Then there was her sudden and surprising enthusiasm for beauty treatments – not her thing at all. She even took me to a spa where we were massaged, bikini-waxed and rubbed with hot pebbles. We had a laugh and drank Sauvignon, very *Birds of a Feather*. It was soon after Greg left and I thought Azra was simply giving me a girly treat – paying for it, too. In fact, of course, she was buffing herself up to pleasure my husband.

Countless other incidents came to mind. Greg on the phone in another room, *Oh it's just that needy student*; Greg taking up running, *Ah, the endorphin rush, nothing like it!* Greg at the cottage, leaning over Azra and inspecting the boring parsnip soup she was stirring; she was a hopeless cook: *That looks interesting, how do you make it?* Greg sitting on the beach, watching Azra in her lime-green swimsuit striding into the sea, buffeted back by the waves, laughing, then plunging into the water. Greg watching her, shading his eyes with his hand.

Greg's therapist, lifting his depression and enabling him to get in touch with his feelings. Ha! Ten guesses who was responsible for this magical transformation?

How could I have been so stupid?

'Why didn't you tell me?'

'I'm sorry.'

'Is that all you can say?'

Silence.

'Don't you realise how I feel?'

'I'm sorry, Pru.'

'She's my best friend. Well, not now, of course.'

'No.'

'And she's going to *move in*? To our cottage? Without even asking me?'

'We were going to. That's why I came up to London.'

'Do the children know?'

'They're not really children.'

'You know what I mean.'

'I'm going to ring them tonight, now it's all out.'

'Why couldn't you have been honest? With me? With

them? You're totally pathetic, a totally pathetic, lying, pathetic, fucking total creep. I can't believe you could be so, so . . .'

'Look, we can't talk if you're going to be like this. Why don't you calm down—'

'*Calm down?*'

'—and we'll talk about it later. I'll ring you tomorrow.'

Greg didn't ring, or reply to my emails. That's the sort of coward he was. Azra, too. They had that in common.

It was early June, and beautiful weather. You could practically hear the plants growing, rustling and jostling and mocking me in my misery. I stabbed at dandelions and yanked them out, the little adulterers, flinging them into a pile on the lawn.

Do you know what I mourned, even more than my marriage? I mourned the loss of Azra, the way we'd laughed and bitched together. Most of all, the vision of independence she'd given me. She'd been my beacon as I strode into the future, and now it had gone. Her fearless, solitary life was a lie. All those years she'd been cheating on me, and now she'd not just destroyed our friendship but the possibility that I could carry on alone. It was all a sham.

Now she'd disappeared from my life. All I knew was that in two weeks she'd be moving into the cottage with my husband. At night I lay awake, picturing them in excruciating detail. Azra sitting on Greg's lap, in the sagging armchair next to the fire, the two of them nursing mugs of tea. Morning, and sunlight streamed through the bedroom window; Azra stood there, naked, breathing great gulps of sea air. Greg stepped up behind her. He buried his face in her hair; he ran his tongue down her spine. He'd done that to me, long, long ago, in the early days.

Most painful to contemplate, actually, was the mundane stuff. Washing up, shopping at the local Spar. Walking round with their phones in the air, trying to get a signal. Greg and I had agreed we couldn't retire to Mortimer's Creek. It was wonderful for a holiday but after a month we'd go stir-crazy.

Not them, obviously.

Lucy was furious, on my behalf. 'The lying sod,' she spat down the phone. 'I'm never going to speak to him again!' Our daughter had always had a difficult relationship with her father. I suspect he'd wanted an intellectual, girly daughter and she was neither of these things. She was forthright and sporty – pretty aggressive, at times. I adored her, of course, and so did the crew at the TV studios, where she was one of the gang. She was strong and gutsy; in her spare time she was always up some glacier.

Max was less engaged. 'You OK, Ma?' That was it, really. He was trying to be sympathetic but didn't know where to start. He was brilliant at IT; the world of emotions, however, was an uncharted sea and best avoided. A bit on the spectrum, bless him. I didn't know the phrase when he was young, but when Greg and I heard it applied to our son it had come as something of a relief.

I loved Max dearly, of course, and had always tried to protect him from my problems. So I asked him about work.

He relaxed and started explaining something I didn't understand. As he did so, my heart started pounding.

For I decided to do something so bold that it made my legs turn to jelly.

Four

You might ask, what was my motive in driving down to Dorset? What good would it do? I had no idea. I was simply boiling with fury at Greg's silence. If he wouldn't speak to me, I'd give him the shock of his life when he saw me on his doorstep. Didn't I deserve this small gratification?

I wanted to see the whites of his eyes. I wanted to hear him jabber some sort of explanation. I wanted to make him suffer at my misery and feel a lurch of remorse. I wanted to shout at him and make him cry. I wanted him to realise what he'd done and what he'd lost.

God knows.

I just wanted to see him.

Time was short. Azra would be arriving in a few days. I drove fast, overtaking lorries, cars hooting. I slewed around roundabouts, gears crashing, and hit the A303. It was mid-morning; thunderclouds piled up ahead. A motorbike roared past; on the back of the man's jacket was printed '*If You Can Read This the Bitch Has Fallen Off*'. I'd done this journey countless times; as I sat there gripping the wheel the car seemed to be driving *me*, from some trace memory.

Of course, Greg might not be there. I had no idea of his movements. He could be in London with Azra; he could be anywhere.

If the cottage was empty, I had a key and could let myself in. Then what? Chop up his clothes? Set fire to the place? Do that thing with rotting prawns stuffed into the curtain-rail?

My emotions fluctuated wildly from the murderous to the mundane. Maybe I'd just make a cup of coffee and bid goodbye to it all. Have a day at the seaside, and finally put my marriage to rest.

I had no plan. I just somehow knew he would be there. And he was.

The cottage was isolated. Our nearest neighbour was a monosyllabic farmer with vicious dogs. His son was currently in prison for child sex offences. There was nobody around and I drove past to a chorus of howls as the dogs flung themselves against the barbed wire.

I parked further down the lane, out of sight of the cottage. I wanted to surprise Greg; if he saw me he might run away, the pantywaist.

Pantywaist. Tears sprang to my eyes; I suddenly missed Azra, even her contempt. For a while I sat in the car; now I'd arrived I had a sudden attack of nerves. In fact, I nearly turned round and drove home.

It was midday. The clouds had cleared. I sat there, waiting for my heartbeat to return to normal. The lane went downhill to Mortimer's Cove, which was tiny and basically sheer cliffs and rocks. Our cottage was halfway down, surrounded by trees and rough pasture.

Greg was at home. His bike was leaning against the porch. I hid behind a hawthorn bush and had a look.

He'd painted the front door blue. A new creeper had been

planted against the house; even from this distance I could see its bamboo stake, with the label still attached. On either side of the path the lawn had been mowed; I could smell the grass. We'd never done much to the garden, but over the past year Greg had evidently been busy, a busy bee, readying the place for his lady love. There was a new raised bed to one side, the gardening fork still stuck in it, and a regimented row of pots under the sitting-room window. Good luck with that; it faced north and never got any sun.

The place was immaculate. Greg was a neat man. He ironed tea towels. I wondered how he would cope with Azra's slovenly ways.

Of course I knew the answer. He wouldn't give a toss.

We'd had the cottage for thirty years. That first summer . . . oh the joy. The children were young then and spilled out of the car, released from the long journey. Skipper, our dog at the time, raced around the garden and relieved himself against the water butt. I remembered moments of such intense happiness they still caught at my throat. Silly things. The time some sheep got in, the four of us waving our arms and yelling, Skipper herding them out through a gap in the fence, their foolish bottoms bobbing with dung, like baubles on a Christmas tree, as they jostled in the exit. The two of us painting the living room, singing 'Mockingbird' in harmony, the children's shouts drifting in from the garden. At night, the moths flying through the window and fixing themselves like brooches to the wall. Our own Aladdin's Cave.

The cottage wasn't picturesque – a plain, stucco farmworker's dwelling – but we loved it. When the tide was out we'd run down the lane, have a swim and lie on the tiny pebbly beach. There was hardly anyone around, even in high summer. Above us reared the cliffs, chattering with birds: crows and seagulls, hidden in their nests, gossiping and squabbling. 'Just like suburban housewives,' said Greg, squinting upwards. 'Do shut up, Mavis, she'll say the same about you.'

I stood in the lane, unable to move. This was no longer my place. The past was gone. Those joyous, sunburnt children were middle-aged, jerky blurs on Skype, mouthing out of sync, miles across the world, with their own troubled lives. I hardly knew them any more.

'What are you doing here?'

I swung round. Greg was standing behind me. His hair was damp and his T-shirt dark with sweat.

'What are you doing?' His voice was squeaky with alarm. 'Has something happened to Azra?'

'Of course not!' I snapped. 'She would've phoned you. Anyway, I don't speak to her any more.'

There was a silence. Greg stood there, panting like a puppy. His hair seemed thinner. His beaky face was sheeny with perspiration. Already, he had altered. So much time had passed that he'd turned into a sinewy stranger out for a run, his head filled with his own dreams, almost a year's worth of them. It seemed inconceivable that for most of our adult lives we'd slept in the same bed.

Of course I should have gone home. Now he knew that Azra was OK, Greg just looked distracted. I thought: how can I be mad with a man I hardly know?

He mopped his brow with his green spotted handkerchief. This, at least, was familiar. 'I need a shower,' he said. 'Do you want to come in or something?'

It was not the most enthusiastic invitation, but I nodded and followed him into the house.

I shouldn't have gone in. Of course I shouldn't. Nothing I had to say could alter anything. Besides, I was in such a state that I'd forgotten why I'd come, even if I'd known in the first place.

Nor had I prepared myself for the shock of stepping into the living room. Everything was the same – the two armchairs, the rag rug, the wood-burner with its cracked glass. The desiccated spider plant on the windowsill – God knows where we'd got it; we'd both found it dreary, but it had proved to be more durable than our marriage.

Everything the same, yet not the same at all.

Greg gestured to the armchair. 'Why don't you make yourself—'

At home. He stopped. There was an awkward silence, then he went upstairs.

I heard the familiar creak of the floorboards and the bathroom door closing, then the sound of the bolt. We'd never used the bolt when we had a shower, or even closed the door.

I remembered those last, terrible days in Muswell Hill, when he'd moved into the spare room. How the two of us had lain low, alert to the sound of the other moving around the house, the rattle of cutlery as we each made our solitary breakfast. How I'd disappear and he'd creep out, then vice versa, like figures in a Swiss clock. Once, when we happened to be in the same room, Greg had put his arm around my shoulder, out of habit, and jerked back as if he'd been stung.

By the time Greg came downstairs I'd recovered. He

stood in the doorway, so tall that his head was tilted sideways. This gave him a quizzical look. I had a flash from the past – Greg standing there smiling, wearing his Habitat apron. *Supper in half an hour, OK?* Ducking under the door-frame to give me a glass of wine.

Today he wore a new grey tracksuit. He'd never liked tracksuits. Perhaps Azra had bought it for him. But then I couldn't picture her doing that, either. I knew nothing any more.

I shouldn't be here, torturing myself.

'I'm going to have some lunch,' he said. 'Do you want some?'

I followed him into the kitchen. He opened the fridge and squatted there, gazing at its contents.

'There's a bit of risotto from last night, but not enough,' he said. 'We could have some hummus and toast. Want some of that?'

His voice was chilly, but that was hardly surprising. I sat down at the table. The silence weighed between us as he moved around, slotting bread into the toaster, filling tumblers with water – new red tumblers, I noticed, rather nice. He put the tub of hummus on the table. No question of spooning it into a bowl, or adding anything to it. I could see a pot of basil and a dish of tomatoes on the windowsill but he wasn't going to bother with that sort of thing. Fair enough. Anyway, I wasn't hungry.

The toast popped up. We both jumped. He put a slice on my plate, sat down opposite, and pushed the tub of hummus towards me. I could feel his eyes on me as I picked away at the plastic lid, trying to open the seal. He didn't help me. Finally I levered it off and spread some on my toast.

I slid the hummus over to him. He spread some on his own toast, then looked up at me.

'So how can I help you?'

'What?'

'Why are you here? Is there something you need to collect?' He cleared his throat. 'Before things, you know, change?'

'No.'

'I'm well aware that you're entitled to take what you want, but I'm also aware that you're living in a much more valuable property—'

'That's not why I'm here!' I snapped.

He put down his toast. 'So what is it?'

I paused. 'Nothing. I just wanted to get out of London. It's such a lovely day. I wanted to go for a walk.'

'A walk?'

'For one last time.'

See? *I* was a coward too. Just as bad as him and Azra. Of course I should have said, 'I'm here because you've not responded to my emails, you snivelling little shit. I want to have it out with you. Don't you owe me that?'

'Fair enough.' Greg looked mildly surprised. Probably relieved. God knows what was going on in his head. We were simply two strangers, having a cheerless and meagre little meal.

He looked at my plate. 'Don't you want to finish that?'

I shook my head.

He leaned over the table, grabbed my toast and crunched it down. Love had obviously given him an appetite. In a few days it would be Azra sitting opposite him. I bet she'd get salad and a glass of wine. I'd seen a bottle of Chablis in the fridge. Christ, I longed for a drink.

I should have left then. I could feel the fury building up. Blind, reckless fury. I watched Greg posting the last piece of toast into his mouth. This man I'd loved, who'd danced with me around this kitchen to our Beach Boys CD. Who, by his demeanour, seemed to be having a perfectly normal day, despite its unwelcome interruption.

Greg tore off a piece of kitchen roll and patted his lips in the prissy, actorish way that had always irritated me.

'Want some apple?' he asked.

He reached for the bowl, cut one in half and passed the half to me. Once, this had been a companionable act; he'd quarter the apple and cut out the core, before giving me two pieces. Once, our life had been like that. Small shared considerations, too small to even register.

And then he said something that took me by surprise. 'Shall I come with you?'

Behind the cottage a track led up through gorse bushes to the coastal path. You had to walk in single file, your legs brushing the prickles. I followed Greg's grey tracksuit. We'd done this walk a thousand times. It led along the cliff, the grass springy and littered with sheep droppings. Each year we'd pointed out the harebells dancing to their secret tune. After a mile the path descended in a series of steps, to the next cove. We'd branch right, turn inland and return through Scragg Wood.

Greg was walking so slowly that I nearly bumped into his back. This puzzled me. He was super-fit and usually strode along so briskly that I had to scamper to keep up. I just presumed he was tired from his run.

When we reached the cliff top the path widened out and we could walk side by side. I opened my mouth to ask, 'Are you OK?' but that was inappropriate so I shut up.

For a while we trudged along in silence. Above us the swifts screeched past like Spitfires. It was eerily still; not a breath of wind. The sun beat down. We hadn't seen a soul. It was as if the world had emptied, just leaving the sea glittering beneath us and vapour trails crisscrossing the sky. It seemed a shame to spoil it.

Greg was walking along like a professor – head down, hands behind his back, a thoughtful look on his face. He *was* a professor.

'Don't you owe me an explanation?' I said.

'What?' He raised his head.

'An apology. An explanation. Simple courtesy, you know.'

'What exactly do you want me to say?'

'It would have been nice if you'd replied to my emails.' My voice shook. 'To have treated me like a human being.'

'I told you I was sorry.'

'*Sorry?* Isn't that just a tiny bit inadequate?'

He stopped. 'What else can I say?'

'All that "finding myself" bollocks. You've been fucking my friend, my *best* friend. You could at least have found somebody I didn't know. Have you any idea how painful that is? All these years and you didn't even have the decency to come clean—'

'Calm down, love.'

'*Love?*'

'There's no point in raking it up now.'

He put his hand on my shoulder. I shook it off.

'You haven't got a clue how I've been feeling, have you?'

He sighed, and pushed his hand through his hair. 'What do you want to know?'

'Everything. When it began . . .'

'All right, all right.' He raised his hands in surrender. 'If you really want to know. Do you? Really?'

I shouldn't have nodded. Because his face changed. It softened with the memory. 'That trombone recital,' he said.

'What?'

'That's when it began.'

'What trombone recital?'

'Your ex-pupil, what's his name? At the Methodist Chapel in Finsbury Park.'

'Ah, yes.'

'For some reason Azra came along.'

Now I remembered. The recital only lasted an hour, and afterwards the three of us had planned to go to a movie at the Holloway Odeon, something with Cate Blanchett in it, some thriller. But I wasn't feeling well, so I bailed out and went home.

'Do you know? Azra and I had hardly ever been alone together, ever,' Greg said. 'All those years. Isn't that funny? I used to find her a bit scratchy, to be honest, in fact quite aggressive sometimes; very loyal to you.'

'Oh, yes?' I laughed.

'Always banging on about women's rights, quite anti-men really. And then all that lesbian stuff – well, it was quite off-putting. I had the feeling she just tolerated me for your sake, that she didn't really like me at all.' He paused. 'But that night, everything changed.'

He was actually smiling . . . a dreamy smile.

'You see, as we were sitting there in the dark, in the cinema, something happened. She felt it too. It was most extraordinary – like a bolt of lightning through our bodies. I've never felt anything like it. I mean, we didn't touch or anything, we were just flooded with this . . . sort of *bolt*. I don't think we were conscious of the film at all, I can't remember anything about it.' He paused. 'Afterwards I saw her to the bus stop, and when the bus pulled away I literally felt my heart exploding, and know what? I burst into tears. In the middle of the Holloway Road. So embarrassing.' His eyes grew moist. 'I was lost. I was lost, but I was found. Do you know what I mean?'

'No.'

'Of course we fought it—'

'You can stop now.'

'—but it was bigger than both of us, it was totally consuming. And as the weeks went by it grew stronger and stronger, and deeper, and oh . . .' He broke off. 'I can't really describe it . . . Body and soul, I was possessed. I never thought I could feel like this, that *anybody* could feel like this . . .' His voice quickened. 'I *ached* for her, day and night, it was a physical pain, it tore me apart . . .'

I stared at his face, flushed with love. He'd completely forgotten I was there.

'I'd come alive for the first time in my life.' His voice throbbed. 'The hunger for each other, it was all-consuming. The snatched moments of joy, the lovemaking – oh, the lovemaking, I can't start to describe it—'

'Don't then.'
'It was like nothing I'd ever known before.'
'Stop it!'
'The passion, the total, shattering passion—'
'Shut up! *Shut up!*'
But, would you believe it? He didn't.

PART TWO

One

It was two weeks later that I saw the dress.

Maybe two weeks; I've lost my bearings. As I said, I was in freefall. It was a superhuman effort to function at all. In the morning I put on my clothes, usually the same clothes as the day before; I seemed to manage to get through my tutorials, though the words blurred on the page. Occasionally I washed. I ate, now and then.

Did I tell you this? What *did* I tell you?

It was killing me, being stuck in the house. I had to get out of London. I had a sudden need to swim in the sea. Needless to say, Mortimer's Creek was out of the question. In fact, the whole of Dorset was poisoned. So I turned east and drove to Kent, the nearest beach I knew.

It was another beautiful day. *The passion, the total, shattering passion.* The words rolled around my head as I drove along the motorway. How could a man say that to a woman he'd loved, the mother of his children? What sort of human being could destroy someone so brutally? Of course I'd asked for it, but that was no excuse. I drove fast, overtaking a row of lorries. *I ached for her, day and night . . . The lovemaking, oh, the lovemaking.*

Later that day I was wandering down Deal High Street. I knew the town; when I was a child I'd come here on holiday with my parents. I was thinking about their fractious relationship when I stopped outside a charity shop.

In the window, something caught my eye. It was a little black dress. A classic little black dress – ostensibly demure, yet deeply seductive. A dress that someone's mistress would wear, back in the 1950s, when people smoked and went to cocktail parties and called mistresses mistresses.

It was a surprising garment for a seaside town at the height of summer, whose shops were full of matelot leisurewear and pastel shorts. It spoke of Martinis and adultery. Of sex, and death.

Of funerals.

I don't know anyone here. The words came back to me. Golders Green Crem, and the crowd of strangers, filing out of the funeral of somebody I'd never known.

It spins on a sixpence, doesn't it? There I was, stepping out into the dazzling, dizzying sunshine, the dress in its bag, the bag in my hand. I found I was smiling insanely at passers-by, even dogs. Especially dogs.

You'll have to wait till their wives die and then move fast. Azra, licking a cigarette paper with her neat cat's tongue. *Widowers are a better bet than divorcés because they won't be bitter, just bereaved.*

I drove home, my head spinning. It was heatstroke; I shouldn't have sunbathed. Tomorrow I would have forgotten the whole mad idea.

And the next day I did forget it, for the entire morning. It was only when I was leaving the house that I noticed the carrier bag lying in the hall and it all came back to me.

My first thought was: why would I wear a black woolly dress in high summer?

Then I remembered, and burst out laughing. I looked at my reflection in the mirror – sunburnt nose, unbrushed hair. I'd been searching for my specs and there they were, sitting on my head. Mad, you see. Mad old bat.

Mad to even consider, for one nanosecond, such a plan.

Two

I used to be pretty wild. I haven't told you this. Even Greg didn't know the half of it. When we met I'd put all that behind me and become a hard-working student at teacher training college. Then I'd had children, which changes everything. I could scarcely remember the person I'd been and the risks I'd taken.

I wasn't the only one. Look at them in Waitrose, those Muswell Hill matrons, those doting grandmothers with their choirs and sourdough. They, too, might have younger selves they could scarcely recognise without blushing. Sex with two different men at the same party, one in the loo and one under the coats. A knee-tremble in a Soho alley with a West Indian drummer who was high on heroin. Threesomes in the Swiss Cottage Holiday Inn. That sort of malarkey. Even now I can be brought up short, remembering a man I haven't thought about in fifty years, who's probably a grandfather now. A great-grandfather. Who's long forgotten me, too. Who might well be dead.

Azra had carried on with her adventures. I'd knuckled down and remained faithful to Greg. There had been the odd temptation along the way but I'd snuffed it out due to cowardice and loyalty. Due to love, in fact – even the frayed and darned love of a long marriage.

And look where that had got me.

It all remained a fantasy until I opened the local paper, one day in July. In fact I'd forgotten all about it.

But as I turned the pages my eye was caught by a death notice. 'Susan Edwardes, beloved wife of Evan, mother of Gina and Lisa . . .' A photo of a doughy, plain face. Susan had died aged sixty-eight. Her funeral was to be held in two days' time at Golders Green Crematorium.

My heartbeat quickened. Why not just go along for a lark? A dare? A diversion from the aching loneliness of summer? That's how I thought of it at the time. It's hard to remember, after everything that happened, but that was my motive. Maybe I was fooling myself; if I made light of it I wouldn't get scared.

In fact my hands were shaking as I twisted round, trying to zip myself into the dress. I needed another pair of hands. How I longed for a man! Already, ludicrously, I was making up scenarios for me and Evan Edwardes, the grieving widower.

It was a sunny day. The crem was only a couple of miles away so I decided to walk, carrying my smart shoes in a bag. Over the dress I wore Greg's black raincoat, which he'd left behind at the house. Paul Smith, rather stylish. Even if I had a suitable hat I couldn't quite bring myself to wear one. I was fully prepared to flunk it, you see, at the crematorium door.

But I walked straight in.

The West Chapel was packed. She had obviously been popular, this Susan Edwardes. And quite the matriarch. From where I sat I could see the front two rows, reserved for family, filling up with her children and grandchildren. Older people, too, no doubt her husband amongst them. The adults wore black and many of them already clutched tissues to their noses.

I sat next to an elderly lady who peered through her specs at the order of service. As the organ struck up, however, she took out her phone and started texting. This startled me and set me thinking. These people here – how well did they know this dead woman? How well do we know each other?

I thought of Greg, and how little he knew about my past. In forty years we'd hardly spoken about my childhood. Nor had I asked about his. All those years together and I'd never told him about being bullied at school by Stephanie Jenkins, or breaking my arm when tobogganing. About the fox my dad found trapped in the living room the day President Kennedy was shot; how did it get in? Spooky or what? Fur everywhere. I'd never told him about my mother's miscarriage, a boy, and how my dad buried the tragic little parcel under the lilac bush at the end of the garden. Small things, big things. So much unsaid. What *had* we talked about?

I sat there in a stupor, gazing at the dandruff dusting the shoulders of the man in front. He was so big that he blocked the view; I had no idea who was speaking at the lectern. Not that I would have known them anyway. The old woman next to me had put away her phone and was now rummaging for a hanky. She couldn't find one and I passed her a Kleenex. She took it and blew her nose honkingly, like a man.

We stood up to sing 'Abide With Me'. Just for a moment, I felt swept up in the general warmth. I was a gatecrasher, I shouldn't be there, but as the singing swelled I found that tears sprang to my own eyes. For it was only then that I realised the truth: That I'd simply sought comfort. And that I'd found it here, surrounded by the bereaved. We were all grieving for someone we'd lost.

No wonder I'd bought the little black dress. 'I'm in mourning for my life,' says Chekhov's Masha. And no wonder I was drawn to funerals. There was nothing weird about it. I just wanted to be amongst people who were stricken with sorrow. To all be in it together.

A weight lifted off me. I sat dreamily through the rest of the service. Words drifted past. Susan's long career as a nurse ... how devoted she'd been to her five grandchildren ...

I didn't pay attention. The sun had come out. It flooded through the window, bathing me with forgiveness. How stupid I'd been! When this was over I would slip away and go home. Nobody would be the wiser, and this bizarre episode would be consigned to oblivion.

Except that it wasn't. Susan slid into the flames and we, the living, stepped into the sunshine. It was there that I found myself in a queue, waiting to shake hands with a man I took to be her widower, Evan.

It was too late to escape. My hand was clasped in his firm grip.

'I'm so sorry for your loss,' I muttered.

'Thank you.'

He was tall and surprisingly attractive. Fine features, full head of hair. Not what I was expecting, whatever that might have been.

I tried to move on, but he still held my hand.

'And you are?'

'Prudence,' I said. 'I was at nursing college with your wife.'

'So you're a Nottingham lass, too?'

'Yes,' I lied, 'though we hadn't seen each other for ages.'

'Well, it was very good of you to come today.' He smiled down at me. 'I hope we'll see you at the house.'

I gave him a vague smile and moved off. As I did so, a woman said: 'Anyone want a lift?'

Just then the strangest thing happened. A jolt shot through me. It was pure adrenalin. I thought: why the hell not? Suddenly I felt more alive than I had for years – recklessly, thrillingly alive – the scent of danger in my nostrils.

'Yes, please,' I said.

Luckily enough, the other occupants of the car were sullen teenagers. They spent the journey arguing with their mother about how long they'd have to stay at the wake. Somebody called Josh was having a party to celebrate the end of term and they wanted their mother to drive them to Enfield. I kept quiet, working on my story. By the time we arrived at the house I almost believed in it myself.

Evan, I later learned, was a vet. His surgery was on Hendon Broadway and the family home – detached, half-timbered, shadowed by conifers – stood in a cul-de-sac behind the main road. The forecourt was jammed with cars and the front door was open. I heard the hum of voices and almost flunked it, but I was here now and there was no turning back.

The living room was already full of people, with more arriving. A young boy, wearing a suit too large for him, stood by the door holding a tray of glasses.

'I'm Arthur,' he said. 'Would you like a Prosecco? There's sandwiches over there. Are you a friend of Granny's? I'm sorry, but there's lots of people here I don't know.'

His forehead was bumpy with spots. I couldn't bear to lie to a grandchild, especially one suffering from acne, so I thanked him and moved into the room.

The teenagers from the car had made a beeline for a sofa. They sprawled there, texting, legs spread, taking up all the space. A middle-aged woman wearing a fascinator glared at them but they didn't move. She perched on the arm of the sofa, caught my eye and beckoned me over with a scarlet fingernail.

'Weren't you at her sixtieth?' she said. 'I never forget a face.'

'No,' I said. 'I'm from long ago.'

'My God, she was pissed, wasn't she? Remember her dancing with Donald? They'd call it twerking now. Quite blatant, but that's Susan for you.' She pulled me close. 'She even tried it on with my Harold but he sent her packing, bless his cotton socks. And she was supposed to be my friend.' She shook her head; the black feathers quivered. 'To be honest, I never liked her. All that gushy-gushy girly charm didn't fool me. Did she have a bash at yours?'

'My what?'

'Your husband.' She indicated Evan, across the room. 'Poor old Evan. No wonder he preferred dogs.'

That's when I learned that Evan was a vet. 'I had a Border collie,' I said. 'He's been dead for nearly a year and I miss him every day.'

The woman drained her glass. 'God knows how he put up with her. Especially after what happened in Hastings.' She wandered off.

Through the crowd, Evan caught my eye. He gave me a smile and made his way over to me.

'So you two were nurses together,' he said.

'Er, just at college.'

'Prudence . . . Prudence . . .' He thought for a moment. 'I'm sure the name's familiar. Did you share that flat in Nethercott Road?'

'Er, no.'

'But you worked together at the Gen?'

'What?'

'The General Hospital. In Nottingham.'

I shook my head. 'Really, I didn't know her well. We just trained together and went our separate ways.'

He nodded. 'She was a popular lass, bless her. Always had a lot of friends.'

'She certainly did.' I felt the sweat trickling down my armpits.

'And a first-class nurse. We were so proud when she got that award.'

I had to extricate myself. 'Actually I never took up the nursing,' I said. 'I moved to London and became a teacher, and got married and had children. But we split up recently, my husband and I, and that's when I saw the notice in the paper, and remembered your wife and how fond I'd been of her.' This mixture of lies and truth scrambled my brain, but I persevered. 'So I came today to pay my respects and tell you how sorry I was.'

Evan's eyes filled with tears. He pulled me to him and held me close. This was so unexpected that the blood rushed to my face.

'Thank you,' he said. He let me go and wiped his eyes.

I was shocked at my reaction. Nobody had touched me for so long that it took me a moment to regain my breath.

Just then somebody tapped Evan's shoulder. As he moved away he turned to me, raised his eyebrows and shrugged. There was something intimate about this, something conspiratorial.

I took an Uber home and sat in the garden. It was early evening and shadows slanted across the lawn. In the forsythia a blackbird poured out its song. Despite my headache from the wine I felt a surge of satisfaction. I'd done it! Azra would have been proud of me. I'd gatecrashed a stranger's funeral and been hugged by her husband. *You have to move fast,* Azra had said. That dress had emboldened me. Clothes can do that, of course; they can transform you into somebody else. Without this there'd be no fashion industry.

But what I hadn't expected was Evan. For, by an extraordinary stroke of luck, the grieving widower had turned out to be remarkably attractive. Tall, tanned, crinkly smile. Not entirely unfuckable.

I was desperate for a man. You know that, of course. But since that meeting with Greg it had grown even more unattainable. For Greg had unravelled the last shred of my already-ravaged self-esteem and filled me with bitterness and bile. It's not a good look in anyone, especially when they're my age.

But now I felt the old machinery rumble into action, like a boiler clicking into life and warming up the house. It was the thrill of romance, a sensation I hadn't felt since I was young.

I know what you'll say. Wouldn't it be cruel, you'll say, to target a man who was grieving? A man weakened and disorientated by loss? Wasn't that like a lion picking out the most vulnerable antelope in the herd?

You bet. Ever heard about the survival of the fittest?

More to the point: how was I going to keep up the pretence that I'd trained as a nurse with Susan? I didn't know anything about nursing. Or, indeed, about Susan.

And even more to the point: how was I going to meet Evan again anyway? We were total strangers. We'd spoken for maybe three minutes. He'd hugged me but then there had been a lot of hugging going on – it was a wake, for Christ's sake. How on earth would I find an excuse to see him again? Pretend I worked for British Gas and arrive to read his meter?

Stupid idea.

You see, I'd already had a better one.

I'd left my raincoat at his house.

Three

The next morning I sat down and Googled 'veterinary surgeries Hendon'. Propped on my desk was a framed photograph of Max and Lucy when they were young. They hung upside down on a climbing frame, like bats, but I didn't let their darling faces stop me.

I found the surgery, phoned it and finally got through to Mr Edwardes. After a moment's hesitation – had he forgotten me? – he recovered and suggested I came round one evening after work.

'I haven't seen your raincoat but I'm sure it's around here somewhere.'

He sounded perfectly cordial. I said I'd drop by on Friday.

My father used to say, 'Don't expect too much and you'll never be disappointed.' This seemed a somewhat downbeat philosophy to pass on to a child, but like many depressives he got a grim satisfaction from his own negativity – indeed, joked about it. I once told him how, when I'd been swimming in a lake, a tern had flown above me, dipping and diving into the water, to which he'd replied, 'The only tern I know is a turn for the worse.'

Now, however, his words steadied my nerves. I had no expectations. I was simply going to collect a raincoat. I didn't bother to smarten myself up, and drove to Hendon with a metaphorical shrug of the shoulders.

There were only twelve dwellings in the cul-de-sac but for a moment I couldn't recognise which one belonged to Evan. I finally found the right house, but it seemed oddly exposed.

'I've had the conifers cut down.' Evan ushered me in. 'The leylandii. Susan always hated them and I wanted to let the sunlight into the bedroom as she was there all day, but of course it's too late now. The end came faster than we expected. Would you like a Bloody Mary?'

I nodded. 'Yes, please. For some reason I only remember I like them when I'm sitting in a plane. Why is that?'

Evan barked with laughter and disappeared into the kitchen. I heard the rattle of glasses.

I looked around the living room. It was beige and unremarkable: heavy curtains tied with tassels; cream carpet; silver-framed family photos. There were plenty of bouquets left over from the wake, some still in Cellophane, some starting to wilt. The raincoat was folded neatly on a chair.

I gazed through the window at the row of stumps where the conifers had been. What on earth was I doing there?

Evan returned, carrying the Bloody Marys on a tray.

'No celery, I'm afraid,' he said.

'I've always considered celery a pointless vegetable,' I replied.

He burst out laughing again – that startling bark. 'You're a tonic,' he said. 'Can't tell you how long it is since I've had a laugh.'

He was wearing jeans and a red T-shirt; he looked

showered and shaved and more athletic than I remembered. Light on his feet; limbered up. As he passed me the tumbler, I imagined him in his vet's gown, caressing a dog's head as it subsided on his knee. One way or another, he must have experienced a lot of deaths.

We sat down, him in the armchair, me on the sofa. 'I found your raincoat,' he said, pointing to it.

'Actually it's my ex-husband's.' Had I told him I was single? I couldn't remember. 'He forgot to take it when he left.'

I waited a moment for this to sink in. Maybe it did.

'Well, it's good of you to come all this way,' Evan said.

'It's no trouble.'

'And to the funeral. I was very touched by how many people turned up. And how kind they've been. I've had an endless stream of visitors. There's enough food in the fridge for an army.'

Azra's husky laugh. *A whole lot of women will be crawling – no, galloping – out of the woodwork with their casseroles and condolences.*

'She was obviously very much loved,' I said. 'I wish we'd stayed in touch.'

'I heard all sorts of stories about her college days.' He grinned. 'I bet you two got up to some shenanigans.'

'We certainly did.'

'Some of it unprintable, I imagine.'

I raised my eyebrows suggestively.

'Susan had such a zest for life, didn't she?' he said.

'Gosh, yes.'

'And yet she was such a deeply caring person.'

I nodded. 'She was.'

'Did you go on that legendary camping trip?'

'Er, which one?'

'Was there more than one? I meant the one to Tenby. When the Hells Angels . . . you know . . . It must have been pretty alarming.'

'Ah, yes.'

'They wouldn't have forgotten *that* in a hurry, knowing Susie. Catch them trying *that* again.'

I had to stop this. So I blurted out: 'Actually my husband died, too.'

Evan stared at me. 'Oh, I'm so sorry.' He leaned across and put his hand on my knee.

'I said we'd split up because if I say he died I start to cry and people get embarrassed.'

'I quite understand,' Evan said.

'And it saves going into the details all over again.'

His hand rested on my knee. 'When did it happen, if I may ask?'

'Two months ago.'

'Good Lord.'

'Cancer. Like your wife.'

Evan's face softened. He took away his hand and rubbed the back of his neck.

'How terrible,' he said. 'How long was he . . .?'

'A couple of years. Prostate. Then it spread to his bones.'

His eyes moistened. 'How are you coping, if I may ask?'

'I just take it day by day,' I said. 'I miss him horribly, of course. It's so lonely, rattling around in an empty house. Especially in the evenings.'

Evan nodded. 'It's just starting to sink in. When the

family was here it was so comforting. Susan was sur-rounded by love during the last weeks. They sent her home from the hospital, you see, because there was noth-ing more they could do and she wanted to be with us all at the end.' We'd finished the drinks; he gazed at our blood-smeared tumblers. 'But they couldn't stay here for ever, and now they've gone and it's . . . well, it's just hit me. That she's not coming back. That it's just me.' He looked up, his face drained. 'Thank God for work. I think I'd crack up, otherwise.'

'It's the only way to stay sane, isn't it? Work.'

Evan nodded. 'Though it's odd coming home and hav-ing to use my key. She always left the door on the latch, you see, because she'd be here in the house. Or in the garden.'

He got up and walked to the back window. I got up and followed him. Side by side we looked at the flowerbeds, choked with weeds.

'Her beloved garden,' he said. 'And look at it now. I know nothing about plants. That was her department.' He shrugged. 'And even the lawnmower's died on me.'

We watched a cat slink through the grass. It paused, glared at us, and slunk on.

I said: 'I've got a lawnmower.'

I arrived home and collapsed into an armchair. It took a while for my heartbeat to return to normal. The whole thing had gone far better than my wildest dreams. *You've got to move fast.* I'd done that all right. Evan and I had had a long emotional talk. When I left, he'd hugged me on his doorstep. On Sunday I'd load the lawnmower into the car and drive back to his house. It was working out surprisingly well.

And the man was a catch, no doubt about it. At my very first attempt I'd struck lucky. Tall and attractive, in touch with his feelings, large close family. Successful, too; I'd noticed the brand-new BMW parked on his forecourt, next to the row of stumps. And he loved animals, for God's sake! He cured their ailments and, if that didn't work, sent them peacefully to their deaths. What was not to like?

And I did like him – truly I did. He was open and honest; we'd made each other laugh. As we'd stood at the window, side by side, I'd felt a lurch of desire.

So why had I entangled myself with lies? The Susan lies were bad enough, but necessary. They were my entry into Evan's life, and I'd made sure that my connection with her was so distant that there was no danger of further complications. That subject was now exhausted, thank God.

But that story about Greg . . . how stupid I'd been, blurting it out. I knew why I'd done it. I'd needed to extricate myself from the conversation about Susan. But it was deeper than that. I'd wanted Evan's sympathy; I'd wanted us to be thrust into intimacy, bound together by a shared sorrow. We were in it together, the two of us; only I could understand how he was feeling.

And it had worked, hadn't it? Suddenly we'd become close, we could both feel it. I'd left those casserole women way behind.

But I had to watch my step. With those impulsive words I'd planted a minefield. The best way forward would be to avoid the subject of my husband altogether. If it came up

I'd simply say the whole thing was too raw to talk about, and that no doubt Evan felt the same about his wife. It would be a relief not to dwell on our mutual bereavement. If the relationship flourished, of course, there might be complications in the future. For instance, what would happen if he talked to my children? Indeed, talked to my friends?

Maybe I'd swallow my pride and confess I'd made the whole thing up. I'd tell him that my husband had run away with my best friend and I'd been so devastated, so utterly humiliated, that I couldn't bring myself to tell the truth.

Fuck it. I'd face all this when the time came. If, indeed, it *did* come. It was perfectly possible that Evan had felt no flicker of interest in me and was just being polite. I might have imagined the whole thing. After all, when it came to matters of the heart I was pretty rusty. It was only ten days ago that Evan had lost his wife; he was in no state for a new love affair. The man might just want his lawn mowed.

I spent Saturday in a state of turmoil. My emotions spun around wildly; I felt like a teenager. I tried to calm my nerves by hanging up the washing in the garden, usually a therapeutic activity. Baking was another soother of the soul but I had nobody to bake for, and I certainly couldn't present Evan with one of my legendary orange polenta cakes. That would be a step too far.

There were three cars parked on Evan's forecourt. What was up? I parked down the road, hauled the grass-encrusted lawnmower from the boot and dragged it along the pavement.

As I eased it between the cars a small girl ran out of the front door. She was wearing a mauve angel dress, complete with tiara. Behind her, a woman appeared.

'Lyra! Come back inside.'

The little girl saw me and stopped. She turned to her mother. 'There's a gardener lady here.'

The woman frowned at me. 'Don't scratch our car, will you?' She pointed to the lawnmower. 'You can take it round the side.' She took the little girl's hand and went back indoors.

I managed to ease the lawnmower between the stumps and pushed it around the side of the house. When I turned the corner, I stopped dead.

Several grown-ups sat on the patio, drinking coffee. They turned to gaze at me. I recognised some of them from the wake. Various children swarmed around; the boy Arthur, no longer a waiter, was listlessly kicking a football around the garden.

Evan came out of the house, carrying a jug of fruit juice.

'Prudence!' he called out. 'How nice to see you! Leave that and come over and join us. I've been descended upon. It's such a pleasant surprise. Come and meet the family. Find her a chair, somebody.'

'No, really,' I stuttered. 'Why don't I leave the lawn-mower here and collect it later?'

'No, no, no, come and have a coffee. Or would you like some pomegranate juice? My daughter Gina made it with her NutriBullet. Apparently it juices everything, including the kitchen sink.'

Gina, it turned out, was the woman I'd just met. 'I am

a twat.' She turned to the others. 'I thought she was the gardener.'

Evan barked with laughter. 'No, no, she's an old friend of your mum's. Don't you recognise her? She came to the funeral.'

Somebody brought me a chair and Evan made the introductions.

'This is my daughter Gina, her husband, Terry, their little girl, Lyra and that's their son, Arthur. This is Lisa, my other daughter, and her partner, Hendrik, and those are their children Lola and Sam, and that's little Anna-Belinda.'

My head spun. Somebody passed me a glass of juice.

'Anna-Belinda's going to show us her dance steps later,' said Evan. 'Aren't you, love?'

Today Evan wore a powder-blue jumper. He looked like a golfing pro – white teeth, tanned skin, as wholesome as Perry Como. In the bosom of his family he seemed a different person. He was a stranger and I shouldn't be here. How did I ever find him attractive?

'Why don't I just mow the lawn now?' I said. 'If you can show me where to plug it in. Then I can go home.'

'Don't be silly,' said Gina. 'It'll make a horrible noise.'

'Gina!' said her husband.

'We won't be able to hear ourselves speak.'

Her husband pushed back his chair. 'Look, *I'll* do it. It's a small lawn; it won't take a moment.'

Gina glared at him. 'Why do you think it'll make *less* noise if *you* do it?' She sighed. 'Men, honestly. You're such willy-wavers.'

'Ssh!' Her husband glanced at the children.

'You do the same with the dishwasher.'

'What?'

'Rearranging the plates with a little sigh—'

'Because *you* put them in wrong.'

'Exactly! It's all about power, isn't it?'

Lisa's coffee cup rattled as she put it in its saucer. 'Look, Mum's just died, can we calm down?' Her voice trembled. 'We're here for Dad. Let's think about him, shall we?'

'Thank you, love,' said Evan. 'But, honestly, it's fine. We're all a bit raw. It's understandable.' He glanced at me. 'Prudence knows what we're talking about. She's been going through this, too.'

I froze. Luckily, just then, it started to rain. Everyone got up and started to move indoors. Gina pulled her cardigan off the back of a chair. I said to her: 'I'll be off. I can collect the lawnmower later.'

Evan overheard this. As the children jostled into the living room he caught my eye and mouthed, *Don't go.*

This sudden complicity made my heart leap. *Aren't I intruding?* I mouthed back. He grinned and shook his head. *Stay for lunch.*

My desire for him welled up again, but just then he was claimed by his granddaughter. We were indoors now. He dropped to his knees and they inspected something she'd found on the carpet. I gazed at his bald patch, tanned as polished caramel. How did a vet become so sunburnt? Did he tend to cattle? Were there any cattle in Hendon? I knew nothing about this man. This beige suburban room was not to my taste, but just then I found my immersion in his family life an unexpected adventure. A risky one, but wasn't that the point of adventures?

I wandered into the kitchen. Evan's grown-up daughters were squatting at the open fridge door.

'Bloody hell, we needn't have brought any food,' said Gina. 'It's quiche fucking central in here.'

'They haven't wasted any time, have they?' Lisa peered at the labels. 'Who's Audrey?'

'She lives at number six.'

'And Mum not cold in her grave.'

'She was cremated.'

'Still, they're probably just being kind.'

'Huh. Like the getting-into-Dad's-trousers kind of kind.'

They turned and saw me.

'Can I help?' I asked.

Gina climbed to her feet with difficulty. It was only then that I realised she was drunk. Maybe she'd spiked her own pomegranate juice.

'We'll have to eat in the dining room.' She gave me two plastic bowls covered in cling film. 'You can take these in.'

The dining room was empty. It was dominated by one of those formal, polished tables you don't dare put anything on in case it makes a ring. I stood there, holding the bowls.

Gina came in, carrying a tray full of cutlery. She tipped it up; the knives, forks and spoons clattered onto the table.

'That'll do,' she said. 'They can help themselves.' She pointed to the bowls. 'Bung them down anywhere.'

She pushed back her hair. Her face was flushed, and sheeny with sweat. She was so thin that I suspected an eating disorder. Her T-shirt read: 'I've Been to Disneyworld Orlando'. There was something about her middle-aged intransigence that reminded me of my own daughter.

'So you knew Mum at school,' Gina said.

'No,' I said. 'At college.'

'So you knew what she was like.'

'Not really.'

'What I mean is, don't listen to anything Lisa says.'

'What would she say?'

'Just don't listen.'

'But she hasn't said anything.'

'Especially if she mentions the red pashmina.' Gina ripped the cling film off a bowl. 'Mum always said I could have it. It was an understood thing.'

We gazed at an uninspiring pasta salad. Not that they're ever inspiring. She ripped the cling film off the second bowl to reveal another one.

'The manipulative cow,' she muttered.

'Who?'

'Mum, of course! I bet she was like that at primary school. Was she? Did she set you against your best friend, that sort of thing?'

'I didn't know her at primary school.'

'It was unforgivable, the way she played us off against each other, her own daughters! Like a puppeteer. A malign, witchy puppeteer. It so damaged our relationship – poor Lisa, I'm quite sorry for her, really. And then there was that thing with Dad.'

'What thing?'

'You know! In Builth Wells. I'm amazed he didn't end up in intensive care.' She snorted. 'Ha! And her a nurse. That would've been funny.'

'What happened?'

'She was an alcoholic, of course, but you would've known that . . .'

'Not really.'

'The way he looked after her when she got ill, he was utterly devoted. Poor old Dad, he forgave her everything, the poisonous bitch. But I didn't. To be perfectly honest, when she died I didn't shed a tear.'

At this point the door opened and the others came in, laughing at some joke and bringing a blast of normality.

During lunch I watched Evan, but he didn't meet my eye. That brief moment of intimacy was gone. He cut up Anna-Belinda's food – he was obviously a doting grandfather – and discussed cricket with his sons-in-law.

My head was still busy with Gina's revelations. Who was this Susan? I couldn't make sense of her. The funeral eulogies still drifted through my head . . . *devoted mother, loving wife, popular member of the community* . . . the bland phrases with which we're all familiar, and with which we'll all be posted on our journey into the unknown. Do they ever really capture the person? For Gina's outburst had bulldozed through it all with the truth. Well, *her* truth. Each of us has our own truth, and this Susan was turning out to be a somewhat contradictory creature, like the rest of us.

Not that it was any of my concern. I'd never met the woman and she was none of my business. Nor, thank goodness, did anyone seem more than briefly interested in our past so-called friendship. However, my own, fictional memory of Susan was thickening up into something so solid I was starting to believe in it myself. High jinks and apple-pie beds in the nurses' hostel; giggles in our jim-jams. I'd never been to Nottingham but I was there now, watching me and Susan sashaying down its imaginary streets to a chorus of wolf-whistles. In my real life, back in the 1970s, I'd been a bit of a hippie chick, but this Prudence was a sporty lass who played netball with her fellow student nurses in the spacious grounds of the General Hospital, wherever that was. Susan and I lost our virginity in the very same week. She subsequently stole my boyfriend, a junior doctor, and I never spoke to her again.

'Are you all right?' asked Evan.

'I'm fine.'

'You've been very quiet, but then with my family it's hard to get a word in edgeways.'

Lunch was over and I was preparing to leave. He apologised for landing me with them all but said their visit had been a spur-of-the-moment thing.

'I hope Gina didn't bend your ear,' he said. 'She can be quite forthright.'

We were alone on the doorstep. I said it had all been lovely and thanked him. He gave me a peck on the cheek and disappeared back indoors.

I didn't hear from Evan for two weeks. Then he sent a text, asking for my address. He said he'd mowed his lawn and would deliver the lawnmower to my house. Five minutes later my phone pinged again. Or would I like to collect the lawnmower and he could cook me a Sunday supper? If so, there was time to dash to Waitrose and if they had any clams left he could rustle up a *spaghetti alle vongole*, his speciality.

The invitation raised my spirits. It had been a wretched fortnight. Outside, Britain was enjoying an August heatwave but I spent most of the time in bed. When I did get up, my leaden legs could hardly take me downstairs. *I'm in mourning for my life.* My situation could suddenly hit me, winding me as if I'd been slugged with a sandbag. The anti-depressants were no longer working, but I didn't have the energy to get dressed and go to the doctor.

I've told you enough about this, haven't I? But during that period it was particularly bad. Traumatised people start to smell and I was in no state for a *dinner à deux*. In fact I'd hardly thought of Evan at all. But his text shook me to my senses and I managed to bathe myself and actually wash my hair. As I dried it I noticed the grey roots were only too visible. 'You're gorgeous,' Azra had said, but she was a liar, wasn't she?

I drove to Hendon and Evan welcomed me in. He wore an apron patterned with pansies that no doubt had belonged to the dead wife.

'Come in, come in, how nice to see you.' He steered me into the living room, his hand resting on the small of my back. It felt firm and authoritative. I knew then that we would go to bed together.

And he made us Dry Martinis, another promising sign. I felt a surge of hope. And of fear. Under my summer dress I was suddenly conscious of my ageing body. How would it cope with an unknown man? More to the point, how would *he* cope with *it*?

Soon, however, the alcohol started to work its magic. My head swam and I felt my inhibitions loosening. To keep off the subject of Susan I found myself jabbering away about my own family.

'Max is a dear person, very sweet – he lives in Pasadena – but he's always found it hard to make friends, let alone find a girlfriend. He stares at a screen all week and then goes on marathon bike rides into the desert. Lycra, gussets, the full Monty, he's frightfully fit. And very gentle – he wouldn't hurt a fly.' I drained my Martini. 'When they were small, Lucy used to beat him up. She's pretty fit as well, canoeing through rapids and whatnot, but she's a lot more intense. She's already broken up twice with her new girlfriend.'

As I rattled on Evan gazed at me speculatively, cocktail stick poised. Was he picturing my children, or was he wondering what it would be like to have sex with me? He popped the cherry into his mouth. I wondered if he was as nervous as I was.

'I wish I could see more of them,' I said. 'Like you do. You're so lucky.'

'We've always been a close family,' Evan said. 'But it was thanks to Susan, bless her. She was always there for them, one hundred per cent. They adored her. She was such a wonderful person, so generous and loving. She had the sweetest nature, always putting others first.'

I stifled my disbelief. Was this the poisonous drunk who twerked with Douglas, whatever that was, whoever he was? The arch-manipulator who was bitterly loathed by her own daughter – a daughter who didn't shed a tear when she died?

'I'm going to tackle those clams,' said Evan, getting to

his feet. 'Would you like to watch, or would that ruin the mystery?'

I laughed. Good Lord, I actually liked this man.

So I stood in the kitchen in a haze of garlic smoke as he cooked the *spaghetti alle vongole*, stirring in the clams with a flourish. I almost heard them cry. Watching their shells opening I thought: poor little sods, victims of mass murder – but I kept quiet. It would hardly be tactful, would it? Though to a clam, of course, its own death would be as momentous as Susan's.

'Would you like to open that very decent bottle of wine you've brought?' asked Evan.

I uncorked the bottle and, under his instructions, fetched a bowl of salad from the fridge and tossed it with some dressing. It was pleasantly companionable, almost marital; I hadn't done this for so long. He'd laid the small table in the kitchen, which was preferable to the sterile formality of the dining room. He lit a candle and dimmed the lights.

The supper was delicious. As we ate he asked me about my husband but I steered the conversation in another direction. We talked about holidays in Italy (both for), cruises (him for, me against), opera (him for, me ignorant), bullfights (both against), Bruce Springsteen (both for).

We'd finished the bottle of wine. I felt agreeably tipsy. He said he was afraid there was no dessert but would I like some coffee? I shook my head. There was a silence.

He leaned across the table and looked me in the eye. 'You don't have a dog, do you?'

'No,' I replied, startled. 'Why?'

'No animal you need to get home for?'

'Only a cat.'

He folded his napkin. 'So there's nothing to stop us spending the night together?'

He led me into the bedroom. We were both unsteady on our feet and collapsed onto the bed – oh Lord, the bed in which Susan had died. The cupboard door was open; I glimpsed a pack of adult nappies. Evan pushed the door shut with his foot.

He held my face in his hands and kissed me. His mouth tasted of wine and garlic. Despite the awkwardness, it was swooningly lovely to be desired.

To be alive.

'I've been wanting to do this all evening,' he murmured into my hair. He pushed the dress off my shoulder, turned me over and expertly unclipped my bra with one hand.

'I haven't done this for a while,' I whispered.

'Me neither.'

He extracted my bra with the expertise of a surgeon pulling out a varicose vein and flung it on the floor. I wriggled my dress down till I was naked to the waist. He turned me over to face him, and gasped.

I have large breasts. There has been a certain slippage over the years, but as I lay on my back I saw his eyes widen with wonderment. His breath quickened. He cupped each breast in his hand, as if he were a boy and he'd never felt such a thing before. He stroked my skin with his finger. Then he bent down and closed his mouth over a nipple. I felt a jolt of electricity. I felt worshipped.

To my horror Evan suddenly burst into tears. He pulled away and buried his face in the pillow, one hand still cradling my breast. He said something but his voice was muffled.

'What is it?' I whispered.

'I'm sorry.' He rolled over onto his back. 'I'm so sorry.'

For a moment he didn't speak. I heard the murmur of traffic down in the main road.

He said: 'She had a mastectomy, you see. A double mastectomy . . .'

He stopped, unable to continue, and took great, hoarse gulps of air. I didn't know what to do. He sat hunched on the edge of the bed, his back to me. I put my arms around him. He was rigid with grief.

'I can't do this, I'm afraid,' he said.

'No.'

'I thought I could, but . . .'

'It doesn't matter. I'm just so sorry.'

He raised his head. 'She was the love of my life.'

We sat there for a while. I noticed a folded-up wheel-chair, shrouded with a blanket, parked under the window. Out in the darkness a fox barked.

I said: 'Would you like me to stay the night? We could just hold each other?'

'I don't think so.' He shook his head. 'I thought I could do this. In fact I was looking forward to it. I even put on my own underwear.'

'What?'

'I've been wearing hers, you see. Her panties. I can tell you this because I don't think we'll ever see each other again, will we?' He spoke to the cupboard door. 'I just wanted to feel close to her. You probably think I'm deranged.' He shrugged. 'I probably am.'

I stroked his back but he didn't turn round. 'I'll go, then,' I said.

He didn't move. 'I wish it had been me,' he said.

The next morning I got a text.

Please keep it between ourselves. You're the only person who might understand. I wish you well for the future and hope you find happiness again, you deserve it. L-mower in your front porch. E x

Four

The little black dress, now dry-cleaned, hung in my wardrobe. When I rummaged for clothes, its polythene shroud shivered and clung to the hairs on the back of my hand. I couldn't touch the thing for weeks.

The summer wore on. As time passed, that evening in Hendon grew increasingly unreal; I could hardly believe it had happened. It was easier to think about Susan than her bereaved husband. By now she had assumed a life of her own – poor, mutilated Susan (why hadn't she had reconstructive surgery?). Susan the flirt, and possibly the adulteress. Susan the bitch-mother. Susan the good-time girl. Susan the caring nurse. Susan, who sent the Hells Angels packing and who did something terrible in Builth Wells. Speculating on her multiple personalities kept my mind off Evan. Oh, Evan. Needless to say I was spooked by my own behaviour, and deeply ashamed.

But I was also strangely energised. Like an addict, I knew I would do it again. It was only a matter of time.

I saw few people that August. It was the holidays and my pupils had gone. Azra had called them privileged little cretins but I'd loved them for the way they'd struggled under the weight of their parents' expectations. I'd loved them for their kindness. For their doggedness and vulnerability. For simply being young. But now they'd disappeared to their vacation homes in Cornwall and Umbria. They'd returned to their families in Tehran. They were sailing round the Greek Islands or visiting school-friends in Cape Cod. They were having fun.

So were my own friends. Most had retired, thrown off the shackles and were having a high old time. They barely had time to unpack before they were off again. 'Your lot, they spend their whole time on frigging airplanes,' said my daughter. 'Don't they give a toss about the planet?' They gallivanted around the world, riding elephants in Nepal, perching on top of Machu Picchu, toasting each other with Bellinis in Venice and posting their grinning selfies on Facebook.

Cull them! Put snipers in World Heritage hotspots! Shoot the women and leave the men for me! They'd been married for years, they'd had a good run for their money. Wasn't it my turn?

My envy was eating away at me like a cancerous growth. But I kept it hidden, I'm sure I did. I wasn't behaving oddly. There was no denying, however, that the invitations had dried up. Not everybody was away that summer. When I was out and about, people waved at me from across the street. But the phone stayed silent. I'd become one of those solitary women who slip through the net.

My birthday came and went. Lucy sent an e-card and Max forgot about it altogether. It was my first birthday without Greg. He'd been a perfectly good present-giver – books, earrings, that sort of thing. Dinner in Soho. But a few years earlier he'd done something unexpected. He'd taken me to Waterloo station, pointed to the departure board and said, 'Choose any destination and I'll take you there for lunch.' I'd chosen Leatherhead, for no discernible reason.

I remember being charmed by Greg's larkiness. It was so uncharacteristic. I'd thought it stemmed from his therapy, which he'd just begun. For I'd noticed a difference in him: he seemed freer and more relaxed. Happier.

Later, however, I made a calculation and realised why. He'd just started sleeping with Azra. Already she was in his bloodstream, influencing him; that jaunt had her fingerprints all over it.

And she was still in my own heart, even though I'd never see her again. Even though I hated her. Perverse, wasn't it? But when did love have anything to do with any sort of sense? She was there in the people I glimpsed in the street. A swinging skirt reminded me of the way she strode so fearlessly, those long legs and silver trainers. Her plastic combs were embedded in other women's hair. A pair of thick eyebrows or a generous mouth reminded me of her *jolie-laide* allure. Greg must have felt this when he'd first fallen in love. That her spirit was everywhere – in the silver birches across the road, in a cup of coffee – because he was always, always thinking about her.

And I was too; we had that in common. *What's she doing now? Does she ever think about me?*

If I saw her again, what would I do?

September arrived, blustery and wild, the nights drawing in. It was the anniversary of Greg's departure and I was utterly alone. I had no students for the next academic year; I seemed to have ignored the agency's emails. The boiler broke down. Only Greg understood its incomprehensible electronic panel. I was gripped with inertia and couldn't bring myself to find a plumber; some days I stayed in my dressing gown until it was time to go back to bed.

I still clung to one routine, however. Every Thursday I left the house, went to the corner shop and bought the local paper.

I know what you're thinking. That this respectable Muswell Hill wife and mother – a retired schoolteacher, for God's sake – had morphed into a mentally unbalanced, sex-starved predator, on the hunt for her next victim.

You're right. That's just what I was. I knew my compulsion was growing out of control but there was nobody around to stop me. The mere presence of somebody else in the house would have jolted me to my senses. I'd never lived alone and had no idea what it would do to my head.

And sometimes I emerged, blinking in the sunlight, and thought: I'm not doing any harm, am I? In fact, I might be doing a good deed. I might make someone happy! Besides, it might never happen. After all, it was the longest of long shots. What were the chances that I'd strike lucky again – that I would fancy someone and they would fancy me?

But it had happened once, and on the first try too. Despite the disastrous ending, Evan had given me confidence. Against all the odds, we'd felt a real *frisson* of attraction. He hadn't considered me too old, either. That had boosted my fragile self-esteem.

So, week after week, I bought the *Muswell Courier*. I followed a strict routine. I'd make a cup of coffee, get a biscuit, sit down by the window, put on my specs, and – just to increase the suspense – read the entire paper before I looked at the 'Family Announcements' page. Sometimes I fooled myself into thinking it was just a game. A lark. A somewhat creepy little experiment to get me out of the house and relieve my loneliness.

But I knew, deep down, it was something more unsettling. Azra dwelled there, deeply buried, but she still had power over me. Searching the Deaths notices kept me close to her. How we would have laughed together! Because it was just the sort of thing that *she* would do. As I sat in my yellow armchair she was there in the room, feet propped on the table, knocking back the wine. *I never thought you had it in you*, she'd say, impressed.

More than impressed. *Admiring.* It was only later that I could admit this.

It wasn't until mid-October that I found a promising funeral. 'Yvonne ('Vronny') Crawley, beloved wife of Trevor', had died, aged sixty-five. Funeral at St Luke's Church, East Finchley.

This time I wasn't going to be caught out. I'd gone on Facebook and done some homework. Why hadn't I thought of this before?

Vronny, it turned out, had been an enthusiastic user of social media and had chronicled her family life in detail. Many of her postings depicted holidays in her and Trevor's trusty camper van. Photos showed picturesque views of the Scottish Highlands, a favourite destination, despite the clouds of insects. 'Trev says I'm a midge-magnet!' Trev was a Glaswegian, apparently, and recently retired from his job at British Gas. They had plans to retire to their apartment in Spain.

I sat there, a Peeping Tom, and gazed at photos of Trevor. He looked fun. Wizened, grinning, something of the jockey about him. I suspected early malnutrition. Stripped to his shorts, sinewy and sunburnt, he stood beside a barbecue holding up a sausage. Dapper in a dove-grey suit, he danced with his daughter Tina at her wedding. There seemed to be three children and one grandchild, Chip. 'The doting granddad' showed Trevor kicking a football around with little Chip. Several photos showed rough-and-tumble sessions with their Yorkshire terrier – 'that little rascal' – in their garden in Finchley.

All in all, they seemed a boisterous bunch. However, an elegiac air hung over these family snaps. Soon, their high spirits would be snuffed out. Only I, a stranger, knew what was coming, for a few months later Vronny's postings stopped, for ever.

Of course I felt uncomfortable. But then I thought: it's Facebook! Anyone can look at Facebook, that's the point of it. So what's wrong?

Nothing. Nothing at all. I was just curious, just doing a bit of research. So why was my heart pounding? Why did I jump, when the doorbell rang, and snap my laptop shut?

I'd lost weight, these past months; the little black dress sagged around the middle. In fact, I hadn't eaten a proper meal for some time. Just bags of peanuts, tubs of three-bean salad, that sort of thing. Washed down with vodka and tonic. Or, when I forgot to go to the shops, just the vodka.

My face looked gaunt. I hadn't looked at myself in the mirror for a while and was shocked at my appearance. Make-up would remedy that. And I'd better do something about my hair.

I drove to the church in time to see the hearse arriving. A floral 'MUM' was propped against the coffin. I remembered that day at Shania's shop. It had happened in another life, a life with Azra in it. Greg had disappeared but in those days I'd still had my best friend. She'd told Shania my troubles but I'd simply thought her indiscreet. What treachery lay ahead! She'd bounded up front doorsteps, muttering into her mobile. No doubt muttering to my husband.

They'd even been on holiday together. It beggared belief. I pictured Azra, supposedly in France, standing in the bows of a narrow boat, chugging along the Kennet and Avon Canal. When a lock approached, she leaped onto dry land. She wrenched the wheel with her thin, muscular arms. Water gushed through the fissures of the lock gates and Greg, standing at the helm, rose up in their barge like a god. Their eyes met; he gave her a thumbs up. This Greg was totally unknown to me. He was the captain of their ship, the captain of Azra's heart, and at night they lay in each other's arms in their cramped little cabin that smelled of toilet chemicals, but they didn't mind; they loved each other.

'You can't park here.' A face loomed at my window. 'Oh, sorry, dear. You OK?'

I wiped my eyes, crashed the gears and drove into the car park.

In the church, sunlight streamed through the stained-glass windows. It was a great barn of a place and only half full. This time, for some reason, I didn't feel awkward. I just felt upset – for me, for everyone. We were all suffering in our own way, some more than others. I might be low down the list but I still felt companioned.

> Lead us, Heavenly Father, lead us
> O'er the world's tempestuous sea;
> Guard us, guide us, keep us, feed us,
> For we have no help but Thee . . .

As the thin, wavery voices rose, so did my tears. Who were these people? It didn't matter. My stupid scheme evaporated and I was overcome with sorrow.

'Excuse me,' I whispered, clutching a Kleenex to my nose. I squeezed my way along the pew and hurried to the door.

Outside I leaned against a gravestone, shuddering and wheezing. Why did this always happen in public? Nearby an undertaker loitered under a tree. He saw me, dropped his cigarette and ground it out with his foot. I really should have confined these meltdowns to the privacy of my own home, but they caught me unawares. For some reason they happened a lot in car parks.

'Don't be upset, love. She's gone to a better place.'

I swung round. A young woman had come out of the church and stood behind me. She held a baby in her arms.

'It's a blessing, don't you think, after all she'd been through?' She looked down at the baby. 'Barney was yelling his little lungs off in there, but now he's stopped. Typical, isn't it?'

'I'm sure they wouldn't have minded,' I said. 'Weddings,

funerals, there's always a baby crying, isn't there?' I thought: like there's always one bluebottle buzzing around a room. Never more than one. Why is that?

The woman shrugged. 'Maybe they know more than we do. That's why they're sobbing their little hearts out.' She hoisted the infant over her shoulder like a sack of vegetables. 'I'm going back in. Want to come?'

I shook my head. 'I think I'll go home.'

'You're not coming to the cricket club?'

'I don't think I should.'

'Don't be daft. We're giving Vronny one hell of a send-off. There's a hog roast, and Trev's booked a rumba band. They've come all the way from Huddersfield.'

She walked off. Over her shoulder the baby's face bobbed up and down. It gazed into my soul, as babies so unnervingly do. Then they were gone, the path littered with yesterday's damp confetti.

Emboldened by this, I drove to the cricket club. I'd liked that young woman. She'd accepted my presence without question. Better than that, she'd issued me a personal invitation. I almost felt like a bona fide guest. And I was suddenly ravenously hungry.

Vronny was being buried, so the family hadn't yet arrived. The clubhouse, however, was already filling up with guests. On the lawn outside, a tattooed youth was turning a carcass on a spit. Indoors, glass cases lined the walls, displaying cricket bats and trophies. As so often with funerals, the atmosphere was surprisingly cheerful. More so than weddings; I'd noticed this in the past. No doubt we were all relieved to still be alive.

There was a raised stage at the end of the room; members of the rumba band, wearing matching waistcoats, were fiddling with an amplifier. I eased myself through the crowd, searching for something to eat. Tea was laid out on a table, but the men were already hitting the bar.

Nobody noticed me or questioned my presence. I munched a cucumber sandwich and drank a glass of juice. See? I hadn't lost my nerve. In fact I felt quite relaxed. I liked the look of these people. They were determined to have a good time and soon they'd be too pissed to notice if I slipped up. Besides, I'd cobbled together a back story. I gathered that Vronny had been a dinner lady, so I could simply say I'd taught at the same school, hardly a lie at all, considering my years of teaching.

So far, however, nobody had spoken to me. I inspected a plaque on the wall. In gold lettering it listed the various captains of the team. The window was open and I could smell roasting flesh.

Somebody tapped my shoulder.

'You've got a nerve, turning up here.'

I swung round. A reddened face loomed close.

'What?'

'I said, you've got a nerve, coming here!'

'I'm so sorry,' I stuttered. 'I didn't mean . . .'

'You've got him to yourself now.' The man glared at me. 'Isn't that enough for you? And don't tell me he invited you. Even Trev wouldn't do something that sodding stupid.' He leaned closer; his spit spattered my skin. 'So why don't you sod off home? Haven't you done enough fucking damage? They'll be arriving any moment. You really think they want to see you here?'

A woman hurried over. 'That's not her, you pillock!'

'Course it is,' he said. 'I'd recognise her anywhere.'

She pulled him aside. 'You only saw her the once, didn't you?' she hissed. 'On the Kilburn High Road. This isn't her! Put on your specs, you moron! This lady's twice her age.' She turned to me. 'No offence, darling.'

So I never met the adulterous Trev or tasted his pulled pork. I drove home in a state of suppressed hysterics. How I longed to tell Azra! Even Greg, not the world's most attentive listener, would have laughed. In fact, of course, I couldn't have told anyone, because then they'd have learned what I was up to. Even putting it into words made me feel a little more bonkers.

It's funny, about compartments. Trev, no doubt, kept his affair in its own little box. Maybe it had been going on for years, sealed off in its own perma-climate, insulated from the drudgery of normal life and never leaking out. But there, always there. While blamelessly frolicking with his grandson, Trev was plotting his next visit to his young mistress – so dispiritingly younger than me. I pictured him on holiday in the Scottish Highlands. While Vronny scratched her midge bites, Trev strode through the heather on his bowed jockey's legs. *Just going for a dump*, he'd say, but, once out of sight, furtively searching for a phone signal. How potent these secret lives could be!

Adulterers, transvestites, serial killers – they all needed to compartmentalise. Me, too. I kept my funeral forays in their own little box. It was safer that way.

*

You might think that I'd be put off the whole idea by now. In fact, it was quite the opposite. My two attempts had ended in failure, but I didn't consider them disasters. I'd managed to pull myself together, get dressed up, get out of the house and attend the funerals of total strangers. In my state of mind, that was a huge achievement. I'd done it! I'd kept my wits about me when I thought I'd lost them completely. I'd entered into the hot, beating hearts of other people's lives and remained undiscovered. The chances had always been slim, I'd known that from the start. All I needed was perseverance.

And it was now November, the dreariest month of the year. Another winter alone and I would kill myself.

So every Thursday I still bought the local paper.

I nearly said, '. . . and then I found my next victim.' Whoops.

His name was Andy Meadows.

Andy and Prisha were the veterans of several marriages – five between them, in fact. They themselves hadn't tied the knot – *we just never got round to it* – but had enjoyed twenty happy years together, never a cross word, but then who reports a cross word on Facebook? They ran their own business selling miniature Schnauzers and ethically sourced garden furniture. Photos showed adorable puppies heaped on teak benches. They'd had *lotsa laffs* together. In fact their life had seemed to be one long party, in the company of their extended family and multitudinous grandchildren. In this respect they reminded me of Vronny and Trevor, but that was hardly surprising. According to Facebook, Instagram and the rest, life was indeed one long party. And one long holiday. Florida. Bermuda. The Swiss Alps. God knew when Andy and Prisha got any work done. And who looked after their puppies?

The old envy rose up in me. No wonder teenagers, addicted to social media, had mental problems. Would my life with Greg have looked as rapturous? Compared to these, our family photographs seemed posed and false, but only because I knew the circumstances in which they were taken. Snapshots of a picnic with the children, for instance, at Burnham Beeches. We all looked happy, Instagram-happy. We were having *lotsa laffs*. In truth, Greg and I were having one of our muttered, low-level rows. It was a well-worn theme. He'd been complaining about the pot-holes in the local lanes, how they could wreck the car tyres, and I'd said why didn't he ever notice anything nice? Like the bluebells? He'd chanted, 'Hello trees, hello sky.' This Fotherington-Tomas squelch had sent me into a sulk. He'd said he was joking. I'd said his negativity was like a toxic cloud, poisoning everything.

Then we'd had our picnic. Greg had made a Spanish tortilla, which Lucy refused to eat because it had olives in it. He'd been snippy. She'd cried. I'd come to her defence. Max, who'd been reading his *Beano* throughout, knocked over his mug of Ribena and it splashed on Greg's trousers. Greg was furious. I said it was just a little splash and would come out in the wash. Greg said they were ruined. Max burst into tears. Greg said he shouldn't have been reading the *Beano*, he'd been reading the bloody *Beano* for the last bloody hour, he hadn't climbed a single tree or joined in anything, what was the point of coming all this way if he was only going to read his blithering comic?

Come on, we're going home. No, we can't, I said, the tyres are wrecked – a feeble joke that fell flat, as Greg accused me of thinking he was boring, but who'd have to take the bloody car to the bloody garage? And Max got up and sat with his back to us and went on reading his *Beano* even though I knew he'd finished it.

And beneath it all thrummed Greg's disappointment with his son, for we were both aware that there was something not quite right with Max, but when I'd tried to bring this up Greg had got angry and said he didn't know what I was talking about, the boy was just a bit eccentric.

And beneath *this* thrummed one of our sexual stand-offs. This one had lasted nearly three weeks, something of a record for us. It stemmed from Greg's birthday. I'd taken him out to dinner. Underneath my dress I'd worn some new underwear – matching lacy bra, knickers and suspender belt. When we came home, however, Greg had stayed downstairs watching *Newsnight*. Upstairs I'd peeled off my black stockings, removed my underwear and gone to bed in a state of seething resentment. Since then, I'd rebuffed his few attempts at sexual congress and now *he* was hurt and he didn't know why because I hadn't told him, it sounded too peevish. It *was* peevish. And because I despised myself I was even rattier with him. You get the picture.

I remember that day so well, but I can't recall what finally unblocked this marital *impasse*. Maybe it just dissolved away. And much of our marriage was perfectly contented. Never thrilling, never that.

Prisha, however, confided to her many Facebook followers that, 'We're still crazy about each other, after all these years. My heart does a little somersault when Andy comes into the room.' Maybe her photographs actually told the truth.

But Prisha was dead. It was reported on her Facebook page. She'd died in a car crash in Lincolnshire, on the way to collect a grandfather clock. If photos did lie, I'd never learn the truth, because nobody except Gina, Evan's drunken daughter back in Hendon, had spoken ill of the dead. More to the point, a death triggers multiple reactions, spawned by the multiple personalities of the person who has passed away. I thought of Trev from Finchley, posed outside his camper van with his arm around his wife. How long had he been double-crossing *her*, sleeping with a woman half her age? Half *my* age? For a moment, on the dead Vronny's behalf, I actually felt jealous of Trev's mistress, so briefly glimpsed in the Kilburn High Road.

There were many, many postings on Facebook of Andy and Prisha. I became so intimate with their lives that I forgot why I was doing this. Prisha was a large – very large – woman who frequently wore a fuchsia-pink trouser suit that did her no favours. She had the steely look of a born businesswoman. Her partner, Andy, was a stocky, fleshy man who enjoyed his drink; in the majority of the photos he was holding a pint. He was a Spurs supporter and, not surprisingly, a dog lover. In fact, with his groomed and shapely white beard he resembled one of his own Schnauzers. I liked the look of his dogs – a breed unfamiliar to me – and I liked the look of him. Third time lucky, I thought. If anyone questioned me, I'd say I'd met Andy and Prisha when I bought one of their puppies.

I know what you're thinking. That I was a psychopath. A

sociopath. Whatever. That I was *seriously* deranged if I carried on like this. Did I really think I could hit on a man at his own wife's funeral and get away with it? That we would both, as it were, hit it off? The whole thing was getting beyond a joke. And now I should stop, before anyone got hurt.

I nearly missed the funeral. This was happening more and more often nowadays. Time seemed to be slipping its leash. I'd write a shopping list, put on my coat, and find it was six o'clock and I was still sitting in the kitchen. I'd come downstairs in the morning, having forgotten when I'd gone to bed, and find the lights still blazing.

That particular day, in late November, I was already dressed and ready. I sat on my bed, the blower heater humming. It was freezing outside and the boiler was still broken. Underneath the black dress I wore a vest I'd found at the back of my cupboard. I hadn't worn it for years, not since Azra and I had gone ice-skating.

It was an unlikely thing for us to do – as unlikely as that spa outing – but I'd suggested it as a treat to cheer Azra up. She had sunk into a depression. I'd never seen her in that state before, my strong, resilient friend. In fact I'd never seen her cry.

In all the years I'd known her she'd hardly mentioned her father. 'He buggered off when I was a baby,' was all she'd said. I thought she'd dismissed him from her life. A violent stepfather had come and gone, but she seldom talked about her childhood and, as I said, she'd left home for good when she was a teenager and strode into the future, armour-plated.

But she wasn't. Nobody is. I realised how little I knew her when she told me, one day, that she was going to track her father down. She was in her mid-sixties by then; it had taken her a long time to come to this decision. I gently suggested he might be dead but she shrugged this off. So then I offered to go to Cyprus with her but she wanted to do it alone.

So she did. She flew to Cyprus. And after a week of following up various leads she discovered that her father had indeed died.

The effect on her was pretty catastrophic. I was surprised. In the past, when I'd mentioned her father she'd airily said, 'He's nothing to me, he might as well be dead.' But now he was actually dead she was distraught.

I was musing about this as I sat on the bed. Azra had said, *the possibilities have gone.* Whatever her father was like, however he'd behaved, whether she'd ever see him again, whether or not he ever thought about her, whether or not he was a shit, the very fact that he was in the world – it was all snuffed out. She was overcome with loss. I remember thinking how strange it was, to be so affected by the death of someone she'd hardly known. I myself had simply felt relief when my much-loved but demented mother died. I thought how grief waits in ambush in the most unlikely places, waiting to pounce at the most unlikely times. I realised, in fact, the importance of a funeral. The closure, the laying-to-rest.

I tried to help Azra, but she withdrew from me. For some months we hardly saw each other. When we did, she seemed closed off and irritable. I blamed it on the father business. But recently I'd realised the true reason;

it was around that time that she started sleeping with my husband.

So I was late for Prisha's funeral. And then I got lost, driving there, and found myself in an industrial estate filled with shipping containers. And I suddenly felt shooting pains in my chest. Ha! I was having a heart attack! That would teach me.

I burst out laughing. For a moment I lost my concentration. Pulling out into the Edgware Road, I nearly collided with a lorry. Horn blaring, it swerved into the centre of the street and nearly crashed into an oncoming bus.

I slewed left and came to a halt in a Dunelm car park. An Indian family were carrying armfuls of pillows out to their SUV. They turned to gaze at my car, which was parked at an angle, blocking the access road.

Oh, to crawl into bed under a Dunelm duvet! To sink into a Dunelm pillow and fall asleep dreaming Dunelm dreams! When I woke, Greg, too, would be stirring. He'd turn, put his arm around me and snuffle in my hair like a dog sniffing for truffles. His leg was hooked around mine. The mammalian warmth of the bed kept us safe. It smelled of sex. Through the wall we heard the tinkle of 'Postman Pat' as the children played in their room. The goldfish was in its bowl; the dog was in his basket; the cat was a slumbering lightweight on our feet. Nothing could harm us.

A car honked. I jerked to my senses and drove off. What was it, about car parks?

After driving through suburban streets I finally found the church. It was an unlovely modern building in Neasden.

The sign outside displayed a golden bolt shooting out of a cloud. It read: 'Be Still and Know That I Am God'. I think it might have been Methodist. Music came from within but there was nobody around except a couple of undertakers loitering beside the hearse. They took no notice of me.

Suddenly I felt a surge of gratitude, simply for being alive. My chest pains had gone. I hadn't been flattened by a lorry. The unknown Prisha had died in a car crash but I'd had a stay of execution. I felt twenty again, on the prowl in my chic, seductive dress. I could turn round and go home; I could jump in my car and go to the cinema in the middle of the afternoon. I could eat french fries! How stupid I'd been to sink into a miasma of misery when my heart still pumped blood around the miracle of my veins.

And who cared whether my plan worked? I didn't. The whole thing was ridiculous. In fact I'd momentarily forgotten the name of Prisha's husband, the luxuriantly bearded whoever, the object of my desire. Andy.

I went in. It was more a function room than a chapel, the walls bare except for a crucifix. The place was packed but there was a space in the back row. The singing had stopped; the moment I came through the door everyone sat down, as if they were so astonished at my plan that they'd subsided in surprise.

A man started speaking into the microphone. It was Andy; I was so familiar with his photograph that I felt I'd known him for years. Even at this distance, however, I could see that he'd trimmed his beard into a natty little goatee. Had he already put the past behind him? Was this a sign that he was ready to move on?

'Prudence!' An elbow nudged me. 'What are you doing here?'

I froze. It was Pam Kidderpore, who lived in my street. She was sitting next to me.

Shit.

'How do you know Prisha?' she whispered into my ear.

'I bought one of her puppies.'

'I thought you had a Border collie.'

'I didn't like it and sent it back.'

'But they're so cute.'

'It peed everywhere.'

My heart sank. Pam lived opposite me, a few doors down. Not only did Pam know me, she was an inveterate curtain-twitcher and the founder of our Neighbourhood Watch. Nothing escaped her notice – who was visiting who and how long they stayed. Who parked in the disabled space or didn't pick up their dog poo. Teenagers hated her because she snitched on them to their parents. Rumour had it that she took in people's Amazon parcels and had a special method of opening them, inspecting the contents and closing them up again.

'How do *you* know Prisha?' I whispered, changing the subject.

'Oh, we did Weight Watchers together, years ago,' said Pam. 'Our group was super-successful. One year, between us, we lost the combined weight of a Ford Transit truck.' She leaned closer, her breath tickling my cheek. 'To be perfectly honest, I found Prisha a bit of a bossy-boots. It was only fatties' solidarity that brought us together. And I didn't trust those certificates.'

'What certificates?'

'For the teak. Sustainable forests, my foot! Those poor orang-utans.' She glared at me as if I were responsible. 'Is it worth their destruction just to have a garden bench?'

'Sssh!' A woman in a huge hat swung round and glared at us.

Pam leaned closer; her breath smelled sour. 'I like that dress, Pru,' she said. 'How do you stay so slim?'

I remembered now that Greg and I had a nickname for her: Pritt-Stick Pam. That was because she glued herself to people, needy and wheedling. And then she'd bitch about them behind their backs.

I hardly heard the speeches. I had to get away. A nosy parker was the last thing I needed. But when the funeral was over and I hurried outside I saw that my car was blocked in by another vehicle. The wake was in a community hall next door and I found myself propelled in there by the press of people. Pam kept close by my side.

'You're the only person I know here.' She butted me with her hip. 'Lucky we met, eh? None of the other Weight Watchers seemed to have turned up, the old so-and-so's.' Gripping my arm, she pushed our way to the tea table. 'That Victoria sponge shouldn't go to waste.'

People glared as she grabbed two paper plates. With the skill of a professional she loaded them up and steered me into a corner. I wondered whose car was blocking me in and if I could make an emergency announcement.

Pam lowered her voice. 'I know you've been going through a hard time. I have to admit that I was slightly miffed to learn about it from the neighbours. But I'm not the sort to bear a grudge so let bygones be bygones. I'm just so glad we've met today so we can clear the air.' She

121

took a bite of cake. 'The important thing is, I'm here for you now, sweetheart, now you're on your own. Cup of coffee, trip to the garden centre, you name it. I was thinking of going to Brent Cross this Saturday for some Christmas shopping, want to come?'

This encounter filled me with panic. How could I escape my persistent new friend? If I could imagine a life worse than living alone it was a life with Pam in it. From her windows she had a clear view of my house. Now bygones were bygones she was poised, ready to pounce, when I emerged. Would I like a glass of wine? A trip to the cinema? Home-made Anzac biscuits were left on my front step. I tried to keep the shutters closed but then Pam would ring up to ask if I was all right. She asked me to supper, 'just us girls and my signature lasagne', and I could hardly pretend I was busy when she knew I was at home.

So I went. After all, I was hardly in a position to sneer. I was as lonely as Pam; this was to be my life, from now on. Those three possible men had faded back into the general population as if they'd never existed. Azra and Greg had gone. After their initial sympathy, most of my friends had stopped phoning. I didn't blame them; I was hardly the best company. Nowadays, it seemed, Pam was as good as I was going to get. She wasn't even one of those single women who had slipped through the net; Greg and I had hardly known her, and had never set foot in her house. We'd laughed at her, you see – poor fat Pritt-Stick Pam in her beige cardigan and beige shoes, still a virgin, still living with her mother and all those cats, nothing to do in her life except sit behind her net curtains, poised for an Ocado van to park in the disabled bay.

How smug we were! Looking back, I can see that we were the very people I've been condemning. Smug and patronising. Smug and married. Ha! Silly me.

Pam's house was immaculate. In the hallway she asked me to remove my shoes. 'I hope you don't mind,' she said. 'Since Mum died I've been trying to put the place to rights, bless her. But it's lonely, isn't it, rattling about on your own? I expect you miss the companionship.'

I was going to reply about lodgers, how I'd thought about getting one, but she was busy uncorking a bottle of wine.

'So what were the kennels like?' she asked.

'What?'

'Their kennels. Andy and Prisha's. You must have gone there when you chose your puppy.'

'Oh, I didn't go there.'

'What?'

'It came by post.'

'The puppy?'

'What?'

'In a parcel?'

'No – sorry. I mean it was delivered.' I paused. 'You know, in a delivery van.'

She poured out the wine. 'That makes sense. I'd heard they were a scandal, those kennels. Faeces everywhere. Have a Pringle.' She passed me a bowl. 'I reported them to the RSPCA – anonymously, of course – but nothing happened. I think they must have been paid off.'

'Who?'

'The RSPCA.'

'Surely you can't pay them off.'

'You'd be surprised. Same thing with the council. I reported number five for contaminating their recycling, and not a dicky bird. Same thing happened with the noise from number twelve. I tested it on my meter—'

'You've got a meter?'

'—and sent *that* off but answer came there none. I'm thinking of taking them to court.'

'The council?'

'But then half of *them* have got their snouts in the trough.' She munched a Pringle. 'And did you know that Elaine next door is a sex worker?'

'*What?*'

'Men coming and going at all hours.'

'But she's at least sixty. And isn't she married to that nice man who works for Amnesty International?'

'He's her pimp. It's all a front. You can't hear what I can hear; the walls are that thin.'

'Goodness. This street has always struck me as rather respectable.'

'Oh, Prudence, get real.' She sighed. 'You're a lovely person. I've always liked you. I hope you don't mind me speaking my mind but that's just the way I am.' She drained her glass of wine. 'I'm so glad we've become friends, after all these years. Isn't it odd how you can see somebody every day and just say hello and never know a thing about them? We're funny that way, aren't we, us British? Stiff upper lip and all that.' She got to her feet. 'But I'm a Yorkshire lass and, to be honest, it's not my style.'

She led me into the dining room.

'Better late than never, anyway,' she said. 'Now we've broken the ice, and we're both on our tod, it's so nice to know we're there for each other, don't you agree? And you must tell me where you got that skirt . . .'

The next day I felt trapped in my own home. If I stepped into the street I knew that Pam was waiting. But I needed to go to the shops. The only solution was to escape through the back alley.

This was easier said than done. There was a door at the bottom of the garden but I hadn't used it since Greg left, fourteen months earlier. It was now engulfed with brambles. The rusty bolt was trapped by ivy, which had climbed up the door and stuck to the hinges. Even in winter there was a Sleeping Beauty air to this door – indeed to the whole neglected garden, which I'd hardly set foot in for months. The lawnmower was rusting in the shed. It had last been used by Evan, poor bereaved Evan, who hopefully had stopped wearing his wife's knickers and found a new love. Men recovered so much faster than women, especially if they were of a cheerful disposition and had a flourishing vets' practice. Those quiches were a promising sign that he wouldn't be alone for long.

I wrenched open the door and stepped into the alley. It was bordered on both sides by the back walls of neighbouring gardens. When the children were small we used to collect blackberries there; it was our secret place.

Today, however, I was shocked by the rubbish. Old paint cans, buckets stuck with cement, bursting plastic bags, an office chair, the obligatory traffic cone. Despite the chill, there was a putrid smell in the air. I'd thought that ours was a respectable street, with its dinner parties and violin lessons. But maybe Pam was right; it had a dark, feral side, not glimpsed from the public front it showed to the world, with those self-righteous rows of recycling boxes. Out the back it was an illicit, fly-tipping free-for-all. Our dirty little secret.

We all have our secrets. For I was halfway down the alley when I saw my dentist, Mr Feinstein, who lived five doors down.

He was opening his garden gate to let out a young woman. She was buttoning up her coat but stopped to kiss him goodbye. For a moment they didn't notice me.

I knew, just as I'd known with Azra and Greg. This time it was a lot more obvious. At that moment they both swung round and saw me.

The young woman hurried away. Mr Feinstein gave me one of his dazzling smiles.

'It's a scandal, isn't it?'

'What?'

'All this.' He gestured at the rubbish.

'Oh. Yes.'

'You haven't seen my cat, have you?' he asked.

'No.'

'My friend popped round to help me have a look. She's very old and suffering from rheumatoid arthritis.'

'Your friend?'

'No!' He laughed his easy laugh. 'My cat!' He didn't even look shifty; he was going to brazen this out. 'Anyway, if you see her, do give me a ring.'

He touched my shoulder, raised his eyebrows, and left.

His gate was wrought iron so I could see into his garden.

I watched him saunter oh-so-casually into his conservatory, then hastily disappear into his house.

His wife was in hospital, having just given birth to twins. Many of us neighbours had put cards through his door, and left cakes and flowers on his step, to celebrate the happy event.

Five

That encounter was to change my life. Of course, I didn't know this at the time. All I knew was that in January, when I was due for a check-up, I needed to find another dentist.

This wasn't just triggered by my fury at what I'd seen, and the awkwardness of meeting Mr Feinstein again. I'd never liked him. He had film-star looks and I've always been suspicious of handsome men, especially smooth talkers. And, my God, the chap never stopped talking. Of course he had a captive audience, pinioned in the chair, mouth open and unable to answer back. But he came from South Africa and some of his monologues were borderline racist. I'd never challenged him because once I was released I just wanted to get the hell out of there. For God's sake, the man had a drill.

I asked around. My old friends Chaz and Sasha suggested Mr Patel in Potters Bar. 'We've had him for years. It's a bit of a faff to get there but, orthodontically speaking, he's the dog's bollocks. And he makes sure it never hurts, not even a root canal. And he's got lovely breath.'

It was February before I could get an appointment. I went by train because my car wouldn't start. One by one, as I said, things were breaking down. Nowadays my DAB radio was filled with static, its voices bubbling from somewhere underwater. A brief power-cut had set digital lights pulsing all over the house. The Velux window was leaking. My printer was jammed. And that's not mentioning the dust. Nobody had set foot in my house for months and it gave me a shock, one day, to notice it with a stranger's eye.

On the train I watched a small boy eat a chocolate coin. He had the usual trouble peeling the edges off with his fingernails; the carriage was warm and the chocolate was already melting. His mother tried to help but he snatched it away. At Christmas I'd always put a bag of chocolate coins in my children's stockings. 'It'll rot their teeth,' Greg had said. Later they'd graduated to pillowcases, which Greg said was over-indulgent. 'It's turned into an orgy of greed and consumerism,' he'd said. At times I could hit him. 'You're just like my father,' I'd said. 'Suffocating the joy out of everything.' Why were women so much more fun?

This had been my second Christmas without Greg, and the first without Azra. She'd always joined us, sometimes in the company of other waifs and strays. That's what Greg called them, *waifs and strays*. Now, on this cruellest day of the year, I'd joined their ranks.

I'd presumed I'd be on my own, hiding from Pam. My daughter was spending it with her new partner's family in Reykjavik and Max had gone camping in Arizona with someone I suspected, and hoped, might be a boyfriend. I'd always thought my son might be gay. I longed for him to be gay. I longed for him to be happy, and thus slightly less strange.

However, the week before Christmas I got a phone call from my cousin in Catford, inviting me over. Dorothy was a lay preacher and we had nothing in common, but she had a large number of children and grandchildren, some of whom I'd never met, and I thought I could blend into the crowd.

And, to my surprise, it had been wonderful. Just for a moment the fog lifted and I found myself in a place of true goodness and warmth. I'd forgotten this existed. Before the meal Dorothy said grace, and when she added, '. . . and this year, Prudence is in our thoughts and prayers,' I felt my eyes filling with tears. There are people like this in the world, I thought. I must remember this.

I arrived early at the surgery. The waiting room was empty except for a receptionist who was busy at her computer. Nothing was momentous about my surroundings – it was a dentist's, for heaven's sake. After signing in I sat down and looked at the reading matter. Amongst the magazines I spotted a local paper, the *Hertfordshire Mercury*.

Something stirred in me. I thought I'd got over my addiction. Meeting Pam had spooked me. What I'd been doing had been mad. Not only mad, but dangerous. Sooner or later, somebody would find me out.

Briefly, in Catford, I'd glimpsed something resembling normality. Curled up in Dorothy's armchair, surrounded by children and laughter, I'd been shamed by what I'd done. Throughout Christmas Day her family had cared for me so tenderly, as if I were ill. I pictured their reaction if I'd told them about the little black dress. They would have been horrified. It didn't bear thinking about.

Besides, my escapades had hardly been a success. The only result so far had been an accusation of adultery and the acquisition of a cloying and fathomlessly boring new friend whom I spent all day trying to avoid. Plus the humiliation of a sweet man who was going through hell.

Funny, then, that I was leafing through the paper, searching for 'Family Announcements'. I just couldn't stop myself. This time, I thought, there'd be no danger of discovery. I was in Hertfordshire, eight miles from home. Nobody I knew would go to a funeral here. Surely I'd be safe?

There was a whole page of 'Deaths'; Potters Bar seemed to have a lethal effect on its inhabitants. Besides, it was the height of the flu season, and there were a lot of geriatrics about; on my walk from the station I'd spotted six mobility scooters. Most of the dead were men, of course, males being the frailer sex. I gazed at their photos, mostly elderly, mostly smiling. *Much loved husband, father and grandfather.* I thought: at least they'd been spared that morning's news: the Isis bombing of a children's hospital in Kabul.

'Morbid, aren't you?'

I looked up. A man was sitting beside me. I hadn't noticed him come in.

He pointed to the dead people's photos. 'Who puts this stuff in the paper?'

'These announcements?'

'I've never known anyone who's done it, have you?'

'No.'

'Maybe nobody liked these guys, and it's to get people to turn up.'

I laughed. 'It's one way of doing it.'

'At least they don't have to go to the dentist any more.'

I stared at him. 'That's a tiny bit tasteless.'

He grinned. 'So sue me.'

There was an Australian twang to his voice and he wore a baseball hat. I hoped he wasn't a Trump supporter. He looked cocky enough.

'Shall we go to one and see?' he asked.

'Go where?'

'One of these funerals. See if we're the only people there.'

'That would be truly weird.'

'It would be a hoot.'

'Like hoots, do you?'

'You bet. Don't you?'

Do you know, I felt a jolt of familiarity. He was around my age, his face creased with laughter lines. Something froggy about his face, like Frank Sinatra. Not unattractive. Not unattractive at all.

He said: 'When I was a nipper, I thought the best thing about growing up was not having to go to the dentist.'

'Me, too.'

'We do, though, don't we? Because we're mature adults.'

'*So* mature.'

'Thank God for that.'

We looked at each other. Then he stood up and grabbed my hand.

'Come on.'

'What?'

'Let's go.'

'To a funeral?'

He shook his head. 'Let's just get the hell out of here.'

My heart turned over. 'What, now?'

'We're adults! We can do anything we damn want.'

I took my coat and stood up.

'Mrs Weston?'

I swung round. It was the receptionist, calling from her desk.

'Mr Patel will see you now.' She turned to my new companion. 'And Mr Fox? Mrs Fernandez will see you, Room Two.'

The man, Mr Fox, looked at me and shrugged. 'Too bad.'

He was taken down a corridor. I watched him leave. He was shorter than I'd realised – probably my height. Jeans that looked ironed. *Ironed*. Not my type at all.

Yet why did I feel my insides melting? Is this what happened between Greg and Azra, in the Holloway Odeon?

Forget it, I thought. He's married. They all are.

I walked upstairs to where Mr Patel waited for me.

My appointment lasted an hour. All thoughts were wiped from my mind as I lay prone in the chair, Mr Patel leaning over me with his lovely breath. Proddings and probings, sudden agonising pain, the rattle of instruments, murmured instructions to the dental assistant who moved around noiselessly, ministering to us like a vestal virgin. She was stupendously beautiful; I've noticed this, with dental assistants. Mr Patel gazed sorrowfully into my mouth like a plumber tut-tutting over a previous plumber's work. It seemed I had periodontal disease due to shrinking gums, not unusual for someone my age, and what he was too polite to call a botched filling. Plus a significant build-up of plaque. He said he could clean my teeth himself and I insisted on injections to numb the pain. I was a terrible coward.

The sun was sinking when I emerged from the surgery. Across the street a Range Rover was parked on a double-yellow line, its engine running. I glared at it disapprovingly, until I saw who was sitting in the driver's seat.

He opened the door and leaned out. 'You got a car?'

I shook my head.

'So? Want a lift?'

'Can't speak,' I mumbled. 'Mouth numb.'

My lips felt like bolsters. I was drooling, and my mouth was dragged down one side like a stroke victim.

'Can't hear a word,' he said. 'Hop in.'

'You could take me to the station,' I muttered, behind my hand.

'What?'

'To the station.'

'Where are you going?'

'Muswell Hill.'

'What?'

'*Muswell Hill!*'

'No worries, I'll drive you there.'

'No!' I put my hand on his thigh. 'No, stop! It's miles.'

But we were off. He drove fast, his vast, silent car sliding like butter through the traffic. He reached down and passed me a box of tissues.

'For the dribble, sweetheart.'

I was touched by his concern and mopped my chin.

'You don't look so bad,' he said. 'Honest, I wouldn't have noticed if you hadn't told me.'

He said his name was Calvin. He'd trained as a paramedic in Australia, flying helicopters into the outback, but had lived in England for the past thirty-five years. 'For my sins, I went for the big bucks,' he said. For he now ran a fleet of helicopters, based in Elstree Aerodrome, and ferried celebrities and captains of industry hither and thither.

'How exciting,' I mumbled stupidly. 'Bit of a daredevil, are you?'

'Maybe, back in the day. My heart's not in it any more.'

'Why not?'

'Since Angie's gone, the stuffing's been knocked out of me, to be honest. It's my team who're doing most of the flying now.'

'Who's Angie?'

'My wife. She passed away three months ago.'

My heart leaped. 'Oh, I'm so sorry.'

'She was a great gal.'

Well, well.

We were speeding along the A1, the sky streaked crimson. Lit by the sun's last rays, passing factories looked as molten as the Promised Land. Bare trees flashed past, soon to be engulfed by the night. I felt a surge of exhilaration. Suddenly I was sixteen again, dreamily in love with a boy who wrote me a poem.

The tall trees, through understanding grieving,
their long black branches weaving,
a dream across the lonely sky.
This dream is the web of God, and I, the fly.

Ungrammatical, but lovely. Goodness, I hadn't thought about him for over fifty years. Maybe he was dead.

I glanced furtively at Calvin. Why was I drawn towards this man? Beefy. Thickish thighs. A tanned, leathery face with eyes that had spent a lifetime squinting into the sun. Sandy hair sprouted from his freckled slabs of hands holding the wheel. His leather jacket was mushroom-beige, with too many zips. As I said, he wasn't my type, and I suspected he was not to be trusted. But here I was, sixteen again and just as foolish; just as senselessly weak with desire.

We talked non-stop. I'd been silent for so many months that Calvin released a stopper and the words poured out. I can't remember everything we said but we darted from one thing to another, veering off this way and that, like a dog sniffing a new scent and bounding into the bushes. Robert De Niro one moment, mothers-in-law the next. I remember a lively disagreement about tinned versus fresh custard. The whole thing got a bit silly.

'What's the most depressing word you know?' he asked.

'Chutney.'

'Because you hoped you'd been given a pot of marmalade?'

'Exactly. Who needs chutney? So what's yours?'

'Bus Replacement Service.'

'That's three words.'

'Fair enough. What's *your* three words?'

'More Stalls Upstairs.'

He groaned in agreement. 'Selling chutney.'

'Scented candles.'

'Bric-a-brac.'

'*Bric-a-brac!*'

'I once overheard a stall-holder telling a customer, "It's more valuable without its saucer." '

I burst out laughing. I hadn't felt so larky since Azra. How I'd missed our conversations.

Finally, however, it had to end. It was dark when Calvin pulled into Talbot Avenue and stopped outside my house. I asked him in, and turned on the lights.

'Streuth, you been burgled?'

I looked around. 'I've been busy,' I said. 'Would you like a cup of tea? A drink?'

'It's frigging freezing in here.'

'The boiler's not working.'

'Want me to have a look?'

I told him it was upstairs in the bathroom. And off he went, bounding up the stairs two at a time. A chatty man. A *helpful* man. Good Lord, he was whistling.

I felt a mild, tingling sensation as my lips came back to life; I touched them with my finger. And as I stood in the hallway I heard the faint, familiar *hurrumpf* as the boiler, too, awakened from its long slumber. The radiators started ticking as they warmed up.

Calvin came downstairs.

'Gosh, that was quick,' I said.

'Easy for me, doll. Got the same model at home.'

'Thanks so much, anyway.'

'No problem. But you need a plumber to flush out the system.'

'Huh, try finding a plumber round here.'

'I've got a great guy, I'll send him round.'

I told him my number and he tapped it into his mobile. It felt curiously intimate, tap tap tap, like a pulse in my blood.

He pocketed his mobile and looked at his watch. 'Better go. Got to feed Angie's horse.'

He laid his hand on my shoulder, and was gone.

*

To be honest, I was relieved he left. We seemed to have been plunged into familiarity at breakneck speed. I needed to catch up and have a think. Maybe, for Calvin, this wasn't unusual behaviour. He was simply an impulsive man, bursting with energy, and easily bored. In the waiting room I'd briefly amused him and he'd fancied carrying on the conversation. Maybe he was lonely. His wife had died; he'd largely given up work. He might have been one of those talkative men who simply need an audience. After all, he hadn't been flirting, just nattering. He probably did this with everyone. Maybe he'd simply been making phone calls in his car and had forgotten all about me until he saw me coming out of the surgery.

Besides, he was bound to have a girlfriend. She'd be half my age, too. A man like Calvin wouldn't be alone for long. He wasn't drop-dead handsome, he had questionable taste in clothes and he said 'no worries', but there was something magnetic about him. It was his confidence, his brashness. And something intimate, as if we were sharing secrets we'd told nobody else in the world. I can't quite describe it. I guess it was charm.

He charmed me, anyway. Besides, he was fun. And I hadn't had fun for a long time.

Maybe I was just desperate, and anyone would do.

Besides, all this was theoretical. In all probability I'd never see him again.

Six

I didn't hear anything for a week. Hope drained away as the days passed and the phone stayed silent. How could I have been so stupid? Of course nothing was going to happen.

And then a plumber arrived. He was a good-looking guy called Lamonte. He said he'd worked for Calvin for years and they'd become mates.

'He and Angie had great parties,' he said. 'Wall-to-wall booze and coke, skinny-dipping, know what I mean? She was a model, gorgeous, legs up to here, but then she got into that Extinction Rebellion malarky and that put the lid on it.'

Sinkingly, my suspicions were confirmed. This Potters Bar Sodom and Gomorrah was hardly my scene; I pictured a MacMansion filled with bling, a triple garage stuffed with gas-guzzlers, and a swimming pool in which Angie and Calvin frolicked with their stoned guests before retiring indoors for a bout of wife-swapping. Extinction Rebellion didn't quite fit in with this, but never mind, it was none of my business.

'He was heartbroken when she died,' Lamonte said. 'He had to sell her horse last week. Lucky it couldn't talk.'

'Why?'

'Its stable overlooked the hot tub.'

Lamonte grinned at me; he was tall and rangy, the most

ravishing man. He pulled a giant spanner from the pouch slung at his hip. *Will I ever have sex again?* I remembered thinking this at the community hub a thousand years ago, Azra sniggering on her mobile. Was she sniggering with my husband? A wave of desolation swept over me. These brief hopes, so quickly snuffed out – were they worth the pain? Should I simply settle down to an embittered old age, like Pam, with her extensive collection of cacti? Was she to be my only companion?

I gazed into the rain-lashed garden. Testily I thought, can't it at least snow? It's February, for God's sake. Then I realised that it was Valentine's Day. Greg never took me out to dinner; he said it was too depressing, seeing all those silent couples. But we gave each other cards and he used to mix Negronis and cook us *boeuf en daube*. I did love him. Now he was gone, our moments of happiness seemed less muddy – more distilled, clearer. More intense than they probably were at the time. But still happiness.

I watched Lamonte packing up his tools, the muscles moving beneath his skin. The heating had come on full blast and his singlet was damp with sweat. He told me he had six children. The eldest was going to babysit while he took his missus out for a slap-up dinner in the West End. 'We met at school,' he said. 'And we've never had a night apart.'

'How much do I owe you?' I asked sharply.

'No worries. That's taken care of.'

I rang Calvin.

'You shouldn't have done it.'

'Why not?'

'You're too kind. It makes me feel uneasy. Guilty. Oh, I don't know . . .'

'Don't be daft.'

I flung myself on the sofa and put my feet on the coffee table. 'Anyway, thanks. It's so generous of you.' I watched a pile of newspapers slide onto the floor.

'A pleasure.' He paused. 'You said something about your car.'

'It's nothing. It just won't start.'

'Want me to have a look at it?'

'God, no.'

'Why not?'

'You've done enough, honestly.'

But the next day there he was on my doorstep, wearing blue overalls like a Pickfords removal man.

It was different this time. Calvin hardly spoke. He seemed distracted, even tetchy, bending under the bonnet in his foolish baseball hat. It was a heavy grey day, not like winter at all; even the weather seemed out of kilter. He poked and prodded, tut-tutting under his breath. When I brought him a mug of tea he merely grunted his thanks. If it was just a chore, why had he come? What had happened to our larky conversations about custard?

I'd been married to a moody man and couldn't face another. Besides, Calvin was obviously not interested in me and I wasn't in him. I watched him through the window, willing him to pack up and leave. How irritating that I'd tidied up the house for him and washed my hair. I was simply a foolish old woman with a thickening waist and her grey roots showing.

And yet there he was, straightening up when Mrs Feinstein appeared. The dentist's wife was pushing a double buggy containing her twins. Calvin bent down and said something to them; she laughed. As she walked off, her blond hair bouncing, he gazed at her, wiping his hands on his overalls.

'Hey, watch out!' I called through the open window. 'Traffic warden!'

While Calvin ran across to his Range Rover, I watched Mrs Feinstein disappear down the street in her black leather jacket. I thought: if her husband hadn't committed adultery I would never have met this man.

I gazed coldly at Calvin and thought: can I really take seriously a chap whose name is printed on a million men's underpants?

All except Evan's. Poor Evan, who wore his wife's knickers. Who chopped down the trees so she could have a last glimpse of the sky. Except by then it was too late.

That evening my phone rang. It was nine o'clock and I was already in bed. These winter evenings seemed to stretch for ever.

'You busy?' asked Calvin. 'Can I see you?'

'What, now?'

I kicked aside the duvet and heaved myself out of bed. It was a scramble to get myself ready, my face being smeared with rejuvenating serum and a sort of Tippex pasted around my eyes, allegedly to cure wrinkles. There was also a pungent smell rising from an ointment I'd put on my corns.

Reassembling myself for a stranger made me long for

marriage. How easy it was to be with a body that was as familiar as one's own, with no effort to be made! Surely any amount of boredom and resentment was preferable to this heart-pounding frenzy. When young, such preparations were thrilling. Nowadays it was a lengthy and humiliating operation and I wondered why I was doing it when I could be opening my door to an axe murderer. He'd sounded so strange and abrupt.

The doorbell rang as I was pulling on my leggings. Calvin must have driven at breakneck speed, or maybe he'd already been on his way and phoned from his car.

'What's happened?' I asked. 'Did you leave something behind?'

Calvin stepped into the hallway and kicked the door shut with his foot. He took me in his arms and kissed me.

Grabbing my hand, he led me upstairs, bumping against the wall as he kissed me again. We stumbled into the bedroom and onto my unmade bed.

'Let's get those panties off,' he muttered.

To be honest, that first time was disappointing – clumsy and hasty. I wished we'd stayed kissing, and had got to know each other's bodies before taking off our clothes. I'd felt so awkward that I'd switched off the light and couldn't see his face. In the blackness I pictured the beautiful Angie. Was I just a rebound shag, as Azra had warned? And Calvin had stayed silent throughout; what was he thinking?

As it turned out, the same thing as me. For he leaned over, switched on the light, and said: 'I'm glad we've got that over with. It'll be better from now on, I promise.'

I burst out laughing. The old familiarity flooded back. I adored him. *Adored* him.

He cupped my face in his hands and kissed me with great tenderness. 'You're totally gorgeous,' he said. 'Have I told you that?'

'No.'

'This bit here . . .' He lifted my arm and kissed my elbow. 'And this bit here . . .' He shifted himself down and kissed the dip behind my ankle bone. 'And then, of course, there's those eyebrows.' He stroked them with his finger.

'Are they that special?'

'No. I just thought nobody might have remarked on them. At our age most things have been remarked upon so there's not much choice left.'

'Your eyebrows are quite ordinary too.'

He laughed, and flung himself back on the pillow. 'I do like you,' he said.

'You didn't seem to, when you mended my car.'

'Yeah, but it seemed you couldn't wait to get rid of me.'

'And you couldn't wait to get away.'

He paused. 'It's Angie's birthday.'

'Oh.'

'She would have been seventy.'

We lay there side by side. I gazed at a stain on the ceiling, a tanned map from an ancient leak.

'She was dreading it,' said Calvin. 'She thought it was the beginning of the end. No, the *end* of the end.'

'I'm so sorry.'

He sat up and grabbed my hand. 'Let's get out of here.'

'What?'

'You eaten?'
'No,' I lied.

He drove me to a late-night place near Marble Arch, a Lebanese hangout where the proprietor hugged him like an old friend. I was to discover that this happened all over London.

It was midnight and the place still blazed with light. Shisha-smokers sat at pavement tables, zipped into flapping plastic rooms. I felt absurdly light-headed. I was young again, sticky from sex, eating baba ganoush with a man I hardly knew while law-abiding citizens were fast asleep.

Afterwards Calvin drove me through the deserted streets to the river and we stood on Waterloo Bridge. The clouds had cleared and a full moon hung in the sky. The city was ours, alone, as a distant church clock struck three.

Calvin was a man of impulse; I'd gathered that by now. As we leaned over the parapet, gazing into the water, he told me how, long ago, he'd met a woman in a bar. They'd struck up a conversation about Marilyn Monroe, and had a bet about whether she'd appeared in the movie *All About Eve*. He'd lost the bet and flown her to Le Touquet for lunch and a fleeting, afternoon fling, without ever learning her surname.

I was impressed. 'You're obviously not the sort of man who buys a copy of *Which?* before you invest in a tumble dryer.'

Calvin laughed. Of course I was jealous, but not stupid enough to let it show. Just for the moment he was mine. Besides, he'd said, 'It'll be better from now on,' which promised more than a lunch in Le Touquet. We drove home, climbed into bed and slept until the afternoon.

And so began our lost weekend. Calvin didn't go home that day, or the next. 'Don't you have any pets that need feeding?' I asked, thinking of Evan and his charming, vet's enquiry.

'Only a feral cat.' It was called Harrow, apparently, due to being found abandoned in a mailbag on the Harrow Road. 'Angie had a soft spot for waifs and strays, bless her.'

Angie's name had cropped up several times in our conversations but I couldn't yet make sense of her. A party girl who jetted around the world on fashion shoots seemed impossible to connect with a doughty campaigner against climate change. Had she undergone a Damascene conversion one day whilst immersed in the hot tub?

I didn't want to know, not yet. For Calvin and I were in a state of limbo. It was exhilarating to be locked away like this, outside time. We spent Saturday in bed, snoozing and talking, endlessly talking, and watching YouTube videos on my computer. Later we had a bath together. Later still we went to the twenty-four-hour shop at the local garage and bought food and rip-off wine. It was raining again and as we walked home arm-in-arm, the cars hissing past, my legs bendy from lovemaking, I thought: this is happiness, this moment. I shall always remember this.

It's hard to make Calvin sound attractive, particularly in the light of what happened. This beefy, freckly man with his sandy eyelashes and suspect political opinions was not the sort of person I'd usually meet, or indeed fancy. The clients he flew around the country sounded repulsive specimens of hubris and greed. His own morals were pretty dubious. One day he let slip that he'd bought his house from the classic little old lady who'd had no idea of its value. He wore loud shirts and made crude jokes.

I could go on, but what's the point? I just adored being with him. My loneliness had vanished; I knew I'd been acting strangely and Calvin restored my sanity. My feelings for him were a mixture of friendly intimacy and profound sexual gratitude. I had a man in my life – a man who made me laugh, and whose warm body protected me from the horrors of the night. *I don't want to die alone, buzzing with bluebottles.* Was that really so unusual a wish?

We were inseparable, those first weeks. I went to Calvin's place or he came to mine. His imaginary house lay like a hologram over the real building in Potters Bar. It took a while for this to fade away as my vision was not far from the truth. It was an ordinary 1950s building, much extended by Calvin and his wife – conservatory, pillared porch, plenty of garden statuary and, inside, wall-to-wall marble. Calvin was hugely proud of it and I found this touching. Who was I to sneer? His parents had been dirt-poor, back in Sydney, and he'd worked his way up in the world to build his own Shangri-la. Besides, he'd once saved lives. Admittedly he now ferried around corporate CEOs and reality TV stars, but hey ho. Compared to my *Guardian*-reading, Amazon-embargoing, fair-trade-coffee-drinking, electric-bike-riding, pious Muswell Hill friends he was a breath of fresh air.

Not that Calvin met any of my friends, in those early days. We kept ourselves to ourselves. Most of the time he was at my house. He managed to get a resident's permit for his Range Rover – God knows how, I didn't ask – and started to sort me out.

'This place gives me the heebie-jeebies,' he said. 'You're living in a slum, sweetie-pie.'

I thought: you should have seen it before I cleared it up.

He fixed things and glued things and replaced things, dashing around in his blue overalls. The energy of the man! When he couldn't sort something out, he got a guy in to do it. A lot of people seemed to owe him a favour.

I surrendered myself to this hurricane of activity. It blew away the cobwebs and the sadness. Calvin had brought me back to life. I looked back with wonder at the woman who'd gatecrashed funerals in her little black dress. What a surreal thing to do! For now I'd returned to the real world. I was a normal person at last, with a man who'd met in a normal way, who stroked my knee when he was driving and who reorganised my kitchen and fixed my computer. Who took me shopping and bought me underwear and, when he wasn't around, texted me six times a day.

'I miss our little chats,' said Pam one morning. She seemed to have materialised from behind her hedge. 'Still, I quite understand you're too busy for me, now you've got a boyfriend. I'm so pleased for you, because I'm the sort of person who likes to see people happy, even if it means they've got less time for others.' She buttoned up a toggle on her cardigan. 'And a very fancy car, I have to say. He's obviously wealthy. At least you can be sure he's not after your house.'

What was he after? My self-confidence had taken such a

battering that I asked myself this question. What did he see in a woman my age? Of course he was the same age himself, but I still felt insecure. I shrank from Calvin when he kissed my wrinkles but he told me I was beautiful.

'But you said my elbows were beautiful and they're even more wrinkled than the rest of me.'

'That's their tragedy,' he said. 'We'll leave them to deal with that one. At least they've got each other.' Suddenly serious, he pushed the hair back from my face. 'I can't believe a man would leave a woman as beautiful as you. He must have been a frigging moron.'

I'd told him that my husband had run off with my best friend, but Calvin hadn't asked me any more. That was fine. Calvin wasn't interested in other people; he lived instinctively, in the moment. It was part of his attraction. He had that in common with Azra, a woman he would have otherwise found incomprehensible. In fact they had more in common than he realised. They'd both had difficult childhoods, pulled up the roots and reinvented themselves. No wonder there was a certain recklessness about the two of them.

I'd realised this early on, with Calvin. We were lounging in his conservatory eating macaroons. It was April and unseasonably cold; outside, the swimming pool was still shrouded. We were talking about the most lawless thing we'd ever done. I confessed to shoplifting a bag of Maltesers.

Calvin said that he'd done a spot of joyriding when he was a teenager. Once, driving alone in an old jalopy somewhere in the Blue Mountains, he'd seen an empty car parked on the side of the road.

'A red Mercedes 190 SL convertible, what a beaut. She was parked on the edge, this big drop below.' He took a bite of macaroon. 'So I stopped my car, got out, walked across the road, released the handbrake and pushed her over the edge. Then I got back into my car and drove off.'

I stared at him. 'Why did you do that?'

'Cos I could.'

'That's a terrible thing to do.'

'You bet.' He dabbed his forefinger into the crumbs on his plate. I watched him suck his finger and lean back in his chair.

'Did you tell anybody?'

'You joking?' He saw my expression. 'Baby, I was totally out of control back then. I'm amazed I didn't go to jail.'

I was half horrified and half thrilled by this confession. 'Have you told anyone since?'

'Nope.'

'Not even Angie?'

He shook his head. 'She wasn't that sort of girl.'

I decided to take this as a compliment. The coke-snorting Angie, who'd mutated into a climate activist, now morphed into a pursed-lipped goody two-shoes. I couldn't get a grip on her at all.

'Well, it certainly puts my bag of Maltesers into perspective,' I said.

Needless to say, I was deeply curious about Angie. In fact, it was becoming something of an obsession, though I was wise enough to keep this to myself. They'd renovated their house together. What was Angie's taste and what was his? According to Calvin, the folksy, buttercup-yellow kitchen, with its gingham curtains and double Aga, was Angie's pride and joy. It was actually rather nice. Their bedroom, in which we slept, was also frilly and feminine. It overlooked her horse's stable and the notorious hot tub. The walk-in wardrobe was empty but Angie's spirit still lingered. In the bathroom, photographs of her in her modelling days hung on the wall. Of course she was beautiful – long blond hair, wide cheekbones, sexy cat's face. I spent a long time gazing at her while Calvin waited for me in bed.

'I was crazy about her.' That's what he'd said. However, he hadn't told me much more. It had only been a few months since her death and no doubt he was still grieving. The odd fact slipped out. When they'd met, she'd been something of a rock chick. She'd always loved animals, particularly horses. They hadn't had children because there was something wrong with her fallopian tubes. She'd been picky about her food, apparently, but it sounded to me as if she had a serious eating disorder. In fact, she seemed altogether fragile, both mentally and physically. She did Pilates and went to spas; she dabbled in interior design. Rich-wife stuff. Her conversion to the climate movement seemed to have happened overnight, but Calvin didn't talk about this. I think he found it threatening, in some obscure way. She'd died suddenly, of a suspected aneurism, and he'd been shattered.

Maybe he wasn't ready for another relationship, not yet. Angie's ghost still haunted him. Haunted me, too. Her presence was in the house. I sensed her just out of sight, wearing something loose and cottony, her tanned feet bare as she padded like a lioness across her marble floors. His boisterousness didn't fool me. Even when he was joking I'd catch a glazed look in his eye. Something a little forced, as if his mind were elsewhere. It was only natural; after all, they'd been married for thirty years. Needless to say, things were easier in my own house.

I wished I could confide in Azra. Her salty good sense would put it all into perspective. We'd have a laugh about my unlikely affair, which she would have found as bewildering as I did. *He must be dynamite in bed*, she'd say.

This wasn't entirely true. Calvin oxygenated my brain; that was our erogenous zone. Under the duvet we'd chat for hours, and if we had sex it was cosy rather than mind-blowing. Sometimes we started giggling and simply gave up. But I didn't mind. I'm sure I was no match for Angie, but I could make him laugh. From what I gathered, Angie wasn't the sharpest knife in the box.

As I said, during those first couple of months we lay low. I didn't even tell the children. Lucy would be instinctively hostile towards this new man in my life. *What do you know about him? Do you trust him?* In her gruff way she'd be worried about me. *I just don't want you to get hurt.* Max, on the other hand, would be pleased but incurious. *I'm just glad for you, Mum.* It would be easier to tell him, but if I did, Lucy would bristle at being left out. Despite their age, sibling rivalry lurked like a virus, ready to flare up at the slightest opportunity.

As time passed, however, I fancied coming out of hibernation. I was no longer a solitary, feral woman, and had rejoined the human race. Besides, I was curious about my friends' reactions. What would they make of Calvin? Would they like him? More to the point, how would *he* behave in their company? Like an internet date, I had no context for him, only his own word.

And I wanted to show him off. Look! I could still pull, even at my age. Tragic, I know.

In late May I got an email from Bethany Graham. We'd been friends for years, ever since our children's primary school days. I'd liked her the moment I saw her at the entrance. Her little daughter was burbling on about something or other and Bethany briskly pushed her through the gates – 'Just go in and get educated!' I'd liked her partner, too. Alex was a stay-at-home Dad so I'd meet him at the end of the day. My first sight of him was leaning against a lamppost reading *The Diary of Joe Orton*. Any man who read about anal gang-bangs outside his daughter's primary school was a man after my own heart.

They lived in the next street. Greg liked them too and for the next few years we were very close – children's sleepovers, supper parties, a lot of wine and some heavy flirtation. We were young and in love – with our children, with each other; there was an adulterous John Updike *frisson* to those golden days. We never used our front doors; the children ran through the alley into each other's gardens. We had our own secret world. We had fun.

Then Bethany trained as a psychotherapist and lost her sense of humour. They moved to Oxfordshire and we only saw them intermittently. But now she emailed to say that Alex had died. 'Brave to the last, after his long battle with motor neurone disease.' I hadn't even known he was ill. The funeral was in three days' time.

Calvin suggested we fly there in one of his helicopters.

He said it would be diabolical on the M40 and traffic jams were for wimps.

So I removed my little black dress from its polythene shroud. It smelled musty. Months had passed since I had worn it, in another life.

'Phoar,' said Calvin. 'You're a dead ringer for whats-hername, *Breakfast at Tiffany's*.'

'In the book she was a prostitute.'

'So, what's not to like?'

He drove me to Elstree in his glorious car. It no longer met with my disapproval. I wondered how Angie had come to terms with such a planet-polluter. I knew that Calvin had coarsened me, but what the hell. Safe in its creamy leather womb I gazed down at normal people, huddled at bus stops as we slid past. They looked at me the way I'd looked at people like me.

It was a beautiful day. Calvin wore a black suit, white shirt and bootlace tie. He looked spivvy, as if we were going to a mob funeral. I felt a lurch of lust. And, indeed, trepidation. I'd never flown in a helicopter. Ah, but it was thrilling, too.

'Who's been your favourite passenger?' I asked.

'A walnut cake. Every week I used to fly one from a bakery in Devon to Tesco head office in Welwyn Garden City.'

'Heavens, why?'

'For the Product Testing Panel. Not the most demanding passenger, a walnut sponge. No ego, know what I mean?'

He grinned at me and my heart jumped. I was alive, and the hedges frothy with hawthorn. We were having a jaunt, and I was very, very nearly in love with this brash, endearing cake-transporter. He'd brought silliness into my life, and I'd had precious little of that.

Let's never be grown-up, I thought.

His office was in a pre-fab building in a corner of the airfield. Monster dragonflies rested nearby, ready to clatter up into the clouds. Calvin was in high spirits. A guy came out of the office. This was apparently Doug, who nowadays did most of the work.

He patted Calvin's stomach. 'You're getting tubby, old bean.'

Calvin grinned. 'Yeah, because whenever I fuck your wife she gives me a biscuit.'

They roared with laughter. I'd never heard this joke and burst out laughing, too. Wherever Calvin went, it was a party.

And then we were off. A headset was clamped around Calvin's ears and he shouted into a mouthpiece. The noise was deafening. Strapped in my seat, I surrendered myself swooningly as he swung the helicopter around, round, the earth tilting beneath us, all those tiny houses, all those lives, the azure flash of a swimming pool. The glittering stream of cars on the motorway we hadn't taken because traffic jams were for wimps.

'We can't just land anywhere, can we?' I yelled.

'That's sorted!' he yelled back.

I didn't believe him, but who cared? This was a man who'd pushed a car off a cliff. We were daredevils, the two of us. And what a stir we'd make on our arrival!

The funeral was being held in a village next to the Thames. I could see the church and a cluster of cars as we circled, dizzyingly, our shadow scattering a herd of cows.

Calvin pulled a lever and the helicopter descended with a bump onto the grass. When he switched off the engine I heard the church bell tolling.

We got out and ran, bent double under the still-spinning blades. The field was spattered with cow-pats, smashed into the flattened grass. A few people paused to stare at the helicopter but most of the mourners were already in the church.

I won't bore you with Alex Graham's funeral. As always, my attention kept straying. Why does this happen in church, more than anywhere else?

1. Did I feed the cat?
2. Are the sachets better for the environment than tins?
3. Shit. I've forgotten my goddaughter's birthday.
4. Did I forget last year?
5. Shit.
6. What's the point of godmothers anyway? Now I'm close to you, Jesus, will you tell me?
7. Why are printer-ink cartridges so expensive?
8. What are they going to think of Calvin?

I tried to concentrate on Alex, whom I'd first glimpsed leaning against that lamppost in 1981. He'd become an avant-garde composer whose largely incomprehensible music was played late at night on Radio 3. Sitting in my pew I watched his daughter, Philomena, now a middle-aged matron, perform one of his tone poems on her oboe. In those golden days, that endless summer when we were young, she was my daughter's best friend. Her brother, Benji ('Bean'), had been Max's mate. Bean was now a consultant gastroenterologist at the John Radcliffe Hospital in Oxford. They certainly seemed more grown-up than I was.

'Who Knows Where the Time Goes?' We used to love that song. Craning my neck, I recognised various friends from that era, some of them still my neighbours in Muswell Hill. It seemed only yesterday that we were young and slim, having supper parties, flirting with each other and working on our allotments, our babies lying beside us in their Moses baskets, our most precious crop.

My eyes filled with tears. Various people were crying. I thought: it's not just for Alex.

Beside me, Calvin pushed back his cuff and looked at his watch.

We emerged into blazing sunshine. Sweat broke out under my black dress. Summer had arrived while we were inside listening to Alex's favourites – Emily Dickinson, Schubert, Nina Simone. The usuals.

The family lived in the old rectory next to the church. It had a large walled garden. Food and drink were laid out on tables under the trees, with artlessly arranged jugs of wild flowers. Tangle-haired granddaughters ran around, wearing the obligatory angel dresses that kept tripping them up. There was a great deal of hugging.

Bethany, the widow, held me tight. 'How are you, Pru? You've had an awful time, too.'

I told her I was fine and introduced her to Calvin.

She gazed at him with awe. 'It was you who drove the helicopter?'

'It's *flew*, love,' he said.

'We could hear it inside the church. So thrilling. Have a glass of fizz.'

'I can't,' he said. 'I'm driving.'

She laughed, and gave me a significant look.

I said: 'It's so funny coming by helicopter, missing all the normal stuff like traffic and whatnot, and just landing in the middle of a field. Like sex without the foreplay.'

Rosie approached, her face alight with curiosity. A stalwart of our gang, she'd grown very large and had recently retired from the Department of Work and Pensions.

'So you're Pru's new young man,' she said, shaking Calvin's hand. 'She's been keeping you very quiet and I can see why.' She gave him a roguish smile and swung round to me. 'After all you've been through, sweetheart, it's a tonic to see you so happy. You look ten years younger and I love the hair. Where did you meet, or shouldn't I ask?'

'In a dentist's waiting room.'

'No way!'

'In Potter's Bar.'

Rosie sighed. 'Such a shame it takes a death to bring us all together.' She turned to Calvin. 'You should have seen us, er . . .?'

'Calvin.'

'. . . Calvin, back in the day. Oh, the dinner parties! Rough red wine – Hirondelle, do you remember, Pru? Absolutely disgusting, but did we care?'

'Mackerel pâté—'

'Iceberg lettuce—'

'Boeuf bourguignon—'

'Duchess potatoes—'

'Black Forest gâteau!'

'Profiteroles!'

'Masses of dope.'

'Children asleep all over the place; sometimes we'd take the wrong one home. Remember, Pru?'

We drained our glasses of Champagne. Calvin was drinking elderflower cordial. I caught him looking at his watch again.

Rosie turned to him. 'Alex fancied Pru like mad, God rest his soul. She was absolutely stunning in those days. Greg got pretty arsey, didn't he, Pru? But they never came to blows, like Thingy and Thingy in *Women in Love*. On the floor, remember? In front of the fire? That wasn't Greg's style. He was more of an ideas man. Bit passive-aggressive, in fact, wasn't he, Pru?' She paused. 'And a very slow eater. It took him an hour to eat an artichoke. No wonder we all got so pissed.'

'Alan Bates and Oliver Reed,' I said. 'They weren't fighting, they were wrestling in a homo-erotic way.'

'Starkers,' she said. 'My God, it was sexy. You can still see it on YouTube.'

Calvin wandered off to inspect the cold meats. He'd removed his jacket and carried it under his arm. There was a damp patch of sweat on the back of his shirt.

I got drunk very quickly. So did the rest of our gang. By early evening most of the other guests had gone. It was still hot, though the shadows had lengthened across the lawn. The lilac branches bowed, heavy with blossoms; the scent made my head swim. Round our legs the little angels ran, their net skirts grubby and their wings askew. 'Shall

159

we take one of them home, like the old days?' said Rosie, who periodically loomed into view.

The garden was bathed in a golden, antique light. It was those old days we were mourning, of course. Our own golden, antique youth, all those possibilities ahead of us. Alex's death had simply triggered this group embrace. By now I was an old hand at funerals but this was different. It wasn't just Alex who was haunting our little band of stout women and balding men.

'Here's to us, the playground mafia,' said Rachel, swaying as she raised her glass. She'd had a brief affair with Rosie's husband and now ran a breast cancer survivors' group. 'And here's to the people who can't be with us today.'

We drank to them all.

'I'll always remember Greg on the allotments.' She turned to me. 'Not planting his potatoes. Standing there, a potato in each hand, giving me his latest theory about Cervantes.'

'Cervantes?' said Calvin. 'What team does he play for?'

Everybody laughed. Calvin wandered off, munching a slice of cake. I wondered if he was joking. I hadn't seen him for a while. He seemed to have spent most of the time in the gazebo, on his phone.

I can't remember who suggested skinny-dipping. I remember a hand grabbing mine and then we were running across the field, as fleet as deer. We were in our seventies, for God's sake! Somebody gave me a towel and now we were down at the riverbank, where the cows came to drink. The mud was pitted with hoof-prints and buzzing with flies.

I didn't feel self-conscious, unzipping my black dress and pulling off my underwear. These were my friends; we knew each other's bodies – from breastfeeding to holidays, to bacchanalian summer evenings like this one. So we were old? Who cared? We strode into the river, screaming as the icy water hit our legs and the mud slumped up between our toes.

Calvin stood on the bank. He'd taken off his tie but remained fully dressed.

'Come on in!' I called, but he shook his head.

As we swam, dragonflies darted above us, blurs of metallic blue and emerald. They hovered for a moment, then darted away. I watched Calvin trudge across the field to his helicopter. There was something pitiful about his hunched shoulders; the little boy who'd brought his prize toy to school only to find that nobody was interested.

Calvin was silent on the flight back. I couldn't have heard anything anyway. I combed my damp hair with my fingers and longed to be home.

It was dark when we landed. He was silent in the car, too, as he drove me back to Talbot Avenue. I looked at his grim profile. His lower lip stuck out.

'Sorry we were all so drunk,' I said. 'Shame you had to stay sober.'

He didn't reply. When he stopped outside my house he simply waited for me to get out.

'Calvin!' I said. 'Come in. Please.'

He shrugged, and followed me indoors. I led him into the kitchen and switched on the light. The glare made us shrink. I put on the kettle while Calvin stood at the window gazing into the blackness of the garden, or maybe his own reflection.

'It was a good party, though, wasn't it?' I said brightly.

'If you like that sort of thing.'

'Nobody *likes* a funeral. I just thought they laid on a good show.'

'What, old naked people making a fucking exhibition of themselves?'

I froze. 'Listen, Calvin, from what I've heard you did a lot of that yourself.'

'What?'

'Getting drunk and jumping into your pool, or your hot tub or whatever. Having a high old time.'

He swung round. 'Not since Angie died.'

'Look, I'm sorry.' I stepped over and laid my hand on his shoulder. 'I'm sorry.'

He stayed rigid. I turned away and dropped teabags into the mugs.

'I know you loved her and funerals must be painful,' I said, 'but I just thought it would be nice for you to meet my friends. You needn't have come if you'd known you were going to be upset.'

'I'm not upset.'

'Yes you are.'

He sighed. Finally he said: 'It would've been nice if somebody had taken a blind bit of notice of me.'

'Oh, Calvin.' I patted a chair. 'Come and sit down.'

He didn't move. 'And all that bollocks about sodding mackerel pâté, what the fuck was that all about?'

'We were just reminiscing, you know? I'm sorry you felt left out but I hadn't seen most of them for ages.' I passed him his mug. 'I can see you're upset but what was it really about? Was it all that talk about Greg, was that it?'

He didn't reply.

'Look, *I* feel weird about *Angie*,' I said. 'We all have baggage.'

'Angie wasn't baggage!' he snapped. 'She was my *life*.'

I flinched. There was a silence. The cat padded over and rubbed her face against his leg.

He put down his mug. 'Look, I can't handle this. I'm off.'

He shook Flossie off his foot and left the room. For a moment I couldn't move. Then I heard the front door slam. I jumped up and ran after him.

'Calvin!'

I ran out, but he was already driving away. I watched his brake lights disappear down the street.

The next morning the doorbell rang. Pam stood there, holding a Tupperware box.

'Comfort food,' she said. 'Coconut fingers with a chocolate base. It's a new recipe I got off the internet.'

She edged past me and went into the kitchen. I followed her. She sat down at the table.

'You poor love.' She sighed. 'Men, honestly.'

'You saw him leave?'

'Slamming the door, crashing the gears, what a performance! I sleep at the front, you see, and I couldn't help noticing. Honestly, sweetheart, you're too good for him. He's an idiot to treat you like that. I know I shouldn't say this but I believe in speaking my mind.' She picked some fluff from her cardigan and flicked it onto the floor. 'They're all the same. We girls have got to stick together.'

'I hope we didn't wake you up.'

I had a pounding headache and a raging thirst. Oh Lord, she'd be wanting a cup of coffee.

'Any chance of a cup of coffee?' she asked.

She already looked as if she'd been sitting there for ever. It was something to do with her size. As I boiled the kettle she said: 'It's no picnic being on your own, Pru, believe me, but there are worse things. Men having hissy fits being one of them.'

How did she know it was a hissy fit? Her words made me realise that's just what it was. A peevish, immature hissy fit.

She opened the box. The coconut fingers were packed on tissue paper, nestled side by side, a gift of love. Two rows of them, too. Tears sprang to my eyes.

'That's so kind,' I said, and sat down heavily.

'Enjoy them, you deserve it.' She pushed the box towards me. 'We've all been there, petal. Even me.'

I burst into tears. Wasn't that ridiculous? But once I'd started I couldn't stop.

Pam didn't hug me, for which I was grateful. She got up and made the coffee; I just pointed helplessly at the canister and the cafetiere. She picked up a little container.

'You shouldn't use sweetener, you know. It gives you a brain tumour.'

'I don't,' I sobbed. 'I got it for Calvin.'

'I told you he needed his head examined.'

I was so surprised by her joke that I stopped crying. Pam tore off a piece of kitchen towel and gave it to me. She sat down and slid a mug across the table.

'You don't have to talk about it if you don't want to.'

But suddenly the words poured out; once started, I

couldn't stop. 'He had this mega-sulk, you see. I've never seen him like that, I was so shocked, he's usually so, well, jolly, but I think he was a bit intimidated by my friends, he's not really their sort, more of an action man, and I think he wanted to make something of a stir when we arrived, we flew there by helicopter, you see, to this funeral, Alex Graham's funeral, but they'd all gone into the church by then so he couldn't make his grand entrance.' I paused for breath. 'And at the wake, well, we were all talking about the past, and Greg's name came up, maybe Calvin was jealous, and there were all these children running around and maybe he was jealous about them too, because he hasn't got any kids, his wife couldn't have them, in fact he hasn't got any family at all.'

I stopped, to catch my breath.

'Nobody told me Alex had died,' said Pam.

'You knew him?'

'Bethany and I sang in the same choir.' She sighed. 'Never mind. Silly old me. I'd probably have felt out of my depth too, like your boyfriend. That's why they didn't bother to ask me.'

I gazed at Pam, Pritt-Stick Pam, sitting there in her flowery blouse. My heart sank. Why had I so impulsively taken her into my confidence? I'd never get rid of her now.

Oh, for Azra to be there instead, eyebrows raised, smoke leaking out of her nostrils, talking contemptuously about men, and the impossibility of finding one. *Or else they've got a Japanese wife, slinky as a seal, hand sliding into his at a party. Maybe popping a canapé into his mouth. A Japanese wife, for God's sake! Might as well give up. Silky pubic hair, not like our old Brillo pads, probably got a high-powered job in the City but she's still a geisha at heart. Forget it, sweetheart.* The old Azra, my beloved keeper of secrets, who knew me better than I knew myself. Who made me laugh, and made me feel companioned in the world.

Seven

A week passed and I heard nothing from Calvin. When my mobile pinged it was British Gas telling me my payment was due. I relapsed into my old slovenly ways. *It's better to have loved and lost than never to have loved at all.* What rubbish. Better never to have met Calvin in the first place. I actually felt envious of my previous state of loneliness and despair. At least I could rely on being permanently depressed. Calvin, however, had given me an intoxicating vision of hope for the future. How foolish I'd been, to think I could replace his beautiful wife!

He'd gone for good. I suspected he was a bolter. He was certainly spontaneous – grabbing my hand in the dentist's surgery, *let's get out of here.* Pulling me out of bed at midnight to speed off to a Lebanese restaurant. Tipping a car off a cliff.

Well, now he'd spontaneously upped and gone. He'd left no trace. Even his sweetener was thrown away. My timid dreams of our living together had evaporated. And Pam had reclaimed me.

I didn't have the energy to resist. And there was a curdled sort of satisfaction in our mutual bitching about Calvin. My confession had loosened things between us. It had certainly encouraged Pam to speak her mind.

'I never liked the look of him,' she said. 'The way he

strutted around with his chest stuck out. And that little tuft of hair sticking out of the back of his baseball cap, didn't you find that annoying? And how did he get a resident's permit, perchance? There's regulations about that. Something dodgy going on, if you ask me.'

We were sitting in the tea-shop at the local garden centre. Pam had hinted that my front garden was letting down the street. Not in so many words, of course. 'You'd feel so much better if you tidied it up,' she'd said. 'I'll go with you. I need some pelargoniums for my patio.' I was too weak to resist. Besides, I had a car.

I was feeling particularly wretched that day. It was early June, the cruellest month. The young leaves on my neighbour's beech hedge made me want to cry – so soft and downy, like a child's skin. It had been a year since I'd last seen Greg, the harebells dancing around our feet. I missed him as much as I missed Calvin. I missed the *density* of living with somebody else. And is anywhere more depressing than the tea-room in a garden centre? Muzak tinkled as Pam passed me a cupcake. Around us were displays of pastel shirtwaisters, scented candles, trickling fountain features and ceramic blue tits. I wanted to die.

'You're right,' I said. 'It was hopeless from the start. I'm just terrified of being alone.'

Pam munched her cupcake. 'You've got me.' She flattened the paper wrapper onto her plate, smoothing it down with her finger. 'Men aren't the full shilling, are they, pet? I had a fiancé many moons ago – Teddy – but once he'd put the ring on my finger it all went pear-shaped. I think he was bi-polar.'

I looked at her wide, soft face, sheeny with perspiration. 'Oh, I'm so sorry.'

'It's all in the past. And Mother hated him, which should have been a warning. She had a sixth sense for such things.'

'You're right about Calvin,' I said. 'He's not the full shilling either.'

'He looked a bad 'un to me. And I saw him drop a wrapper in the street.'

'And such a silly name,' I said. 'I mean, men have it on their underpants.'

'Do they? I wouldn't know.' She took off her glasses and polished them with her napkin.

I was suddenly overwhelmed with pity. Maybe Pam sensed this, because she looked up sharply.

'If you think I'm a virgin you've got the wrong think coming. I had an active sex life before Teddy. I was a size eight then, believe it or not.' She put on her glasses. 'I'm fine, sweet pea. I just haven't defined my life in terms of men. And I know you thought Mum was a bad-tempered old cow, everybody did, but we were very happy together. Now she's gone it's like I've lost an arm. And it won't grow back.' She pushed back her chair. 'Now let's hit those pelargoniums.'

And then, midway through June, Calvin phoned. It was a Sunday afternoon and he said he was coming round. He said he'd been on the Isle of Mull.

'The Isle of Mull? What were you doing?'

'Clearing my head.'

I laughed. 'Mulling things over?'

He didn't respond. He said he'd be with me in an hour and rang off.

I rushed upstairs to change my clothes. So that's where he had been. I couldn't imagine Calvin mulling things over; he wasn't the type. But what did I know? In the last fortnight he'd become a stranger. Maybe he'd been a stranger all along – the most unlikely repository for my romantic dreams.

As I pulled off my tracksuit bottoms I thought: he's coming to tell me we're finished. He realised he wasn't ready for a new relationship. Who could possibly be ready, when their wife had just died? How cruel I'd been, to ambush men when they were broken with grief! What a tawdry little plan it had been!

Calvin looked wretched. It had been a hot day and he wore lime-green shorts and a shirt pattered with pineapples. This jaunty outfit mocked his grim expression. He was deeply tanned but looked wrinkled and diminished.

'Would you like some wine?' I asked. 'Shall we sit in the garden?'

He shook his head. 'Don't want the neighbours snooping.'

My heart sank. I poured drinks and we sat in the kitchen.

For a moment he didn't speak. The only sound was the plunk, plunk of the dripping tap. He'd promised to get a new washer; it had been on his list of things to do.

'So how've you been?' he asked.

'Fine.'

I was seized with panic. What on earth did we ever talk about? There seemed absolutely nothing to say.

'My mate's got this bothy,' he said. 'Great sailing. Gorgeous scenery. Place to clear your head and put things into perspective.'

'So?'

'Look, Prudence, I'll come clean with you.'

'Don't!' I laid my hand over his. 'Honestly, it's OK. The whole thing's been lovely but I quite understand.'

'I don't think you do.' He pushed his glass towards me. 'Got any more of this?'

I refilled his glass. He looked around the kitchen and gave a deep, shuddering sigh, like a beast of burden. I had no idea what was going on in his head. Who was this sun-dried man in his garish shirt? In fact, I longed for him to leave. I was too old to be dumped, yet again. Beginnings were easy but you needed stamina for endings, and I was nearly seventy-one.

'My wife was my world,' he said. 'You know that, don't you?'

'Of course,' I said testily. 'Of course she was.'

'But when I met you, something clicked. See, I'd never met a woman who could match me, word for word.' He stopped. 'Who could *more* than match me, to be honest. You see, my Ange, she wasn't blessed with a lot up top. To be perfectly honest.'

'I'm sure she—'

'No, hear me out. She'd never had an education, bless her. She'd had a dad who took the strap to her, too, like mine did. We had that in common, know what I mean? She was still that child, that damaged child. Men had abused her all her life – photographers, boyfriends – and I wanted to look after her and make her happy. Because nothing else

171

did, you know? All those fads she fell for, the mindfulness, the colonic irrigation, the diets and acupuncture, the quacks and charlatans, the Climate Extinction bollocks—'

'I wouldn't call it bollocks, actually. Extinction Rebellion.'

He raised his hands. 'Look, if it made her happy, fair play. But it didn't, none of it did, so I made it my job to save her.' He drained his glass. Oh Lord, he was going to be too drunk to drive. 'But in the end I couldn't. And I've got to live with that.'

'What do you mean?'

'She'd tried it before, to be frank. Twice. But I got there in time and they pumped out her stomach. But on this occasion she made sure I was away. Flying a customer to Antwerp. A diamond dealer. And I'll never forgive myself.'

I stared at him. 'I thought she had an aneurism.'

He shook his head.

'Oh God, I'm so sorry.'

'And I'd failed her.'

'I'm sure you didn't—'

'Look, sweetheart, what's past is past,' he said.

'Not really—'

'I'm dealing with it, trust me. I just wanted to fill you in.'

He refilled his glass. Dammit, he'd have to stay the night. My heart sank. He was a different man from the one who'd made me laugh and mopped up my dribble. I was filled with pity for him, and dread for what he was going to say. Just dump me and leave, I silently urged him. Get a cab and go.

'But then you came along,' he said. 'Know something? Once I couldn't have handled a woman like you.'

'Why not?'

'I would've felt threatened, know what I mean?'

'Bloody hell!' I snapped. 'Not that old chestnut. Why can't you men just get over it?'

He jerked back. 'Listen, babes. I came here to tell you I love you.'

For a moment I couldn't speak.

'I'm sorry I was such an arse that day,' he said. 'I just felt like a spare prick at a funeral. Will you forgive me?'

There was a silence. Finally I nodded.

'I think I fell for you when we were driving along the A1,' he said. 'That's probably a first.'

I laughed, shakily. 'It probably is.'

'So we're OK?'

'Yes,' I said.

He didn't touch me. It was nothing like that. We just sat there together, listening to the drip, drip.

'Remind me to fix that tap,' he said.

Calvin's mother was blind. This was one of the new things I discovered about his childhood. His father was a sadist and had enjoyed confusing her by moving objects around the house. He'd also enjoyed taunting his son.

'There was a pile of sand in front of our house,' said Calvin. 'From some building work the old man had never finished. He used to get me to load the wheelbarrow with it, wheel it round the back and empty it. Then load it up and wheel it round the front, empty it out, and so on, all bloody afternoon.'

'An early lesson in Nietzschean nihilism,' I laughed.

Calvin wasn't prone to self-pity; he just told me these things as a fact of life – which they were to him, of course.

'Maybe he was doing me a favour,' he shrugged. 'It's made me the man I am today.'

He didn't speak again about his wife's suicide. I didn't prod this tender spot; needless to say I was consumed with curiosity, but it wasn't my business. Maybe I should have asked him more – I realise it now. But at the time I was just revelling in his company, and our new openness together.

Calvin's declaration of love had taken me by surprise. It changed things between us. We were very close, that summer. I felt myself falling in and out of love with him, according to the chemistry and the weather. Sometimes he said something stupid and I thought: what the hell am I doing? Then the sun came out and I opened my heart. Sunshine is underestimated, in relationships. During those sultry days of August, the grass bleached and the trees heavy with exhaustion, only the *now* existed. The future had not yet closed in.

Did I tell you Calvin played stride piano? Fats Waller, whom I loved. Gershwin, whom I equally loved – how did Calvin know? I have no idea if he was any good but my insides melted and I was his. He played in his living room while I lay on his thick white rug, listening to him and thinking about his childhood. How strange, never to have been seen by his own mother! An invisible child, known only by the touch of her fingers. When I asked him he said, 'I bought this piano so I could play for her, even though she's long since dead.' See how he could surprise me?

Later we'd have a swim and I'd lie on my back, gazing at the last rays of the sun glinting on the weather vane above the stable. I even dreamed of getting a horse. I'd canter through the secret byways of the green belt – the fields behind Sainsbury's where cows still grazed; the bridle path, bordered with brambles, sunk beside the humming motorway. If you closed your eyes you could think it was bees.

I spent most of the summer at Calvin's place. I even brought along my cat, Flossie. London held nothing for me any more. My friends seemed permanently away visiting grandchildren and jetting off on their countless holidays. Maybe they just didn't get in touch, but I no longer minded. Max and Lucy seemed disinclined to visit, even though I'd now told them about this new man in my life. Plus there was Pam, another good reason to stay away. How could I face her, after we'd so enthusiastically slagged off my lover? It was too embarrassing for both of us. And I felt guilty for using her when I needed her, and dropping her now I was happy. So, like a coward, I avoided her. When I left the house I slipped out through the alley, the secret thoroughfare that had brought Calvin into my life.

One morning in September I emerged from Calvin's bed to find him downstairs, sitting at his laptop. His hair was damp from the shower and he wore his toweling dressing gown with St Regis Hotel stitched on the pocket. It turned out he was downloading the tide table for the Kentish coast.

'I'm taking you out of this world,' he said.

When I was a child I'd heard about the Goodwin Sands. They lay out to sea, a few miles from Deal, and were only visible at low tide. Once, on holiday, my father gave me a pair of binoculars and pointed out a vast expanse of what looked like sand in the middle of the North Sea. 'Those currents are deadly,' he'd said. 'More than two thousand vessels have been sunk in those treacherous waters.' He sighed his familiar sigh. 'If there's one thing I can teach you, my girl, it's never to trust appearances.' No wonder I was attracted to Calvin.

We flew there in Calvin's helicopter. It was our first jaunt since Alex's funeral. The weather was glorious; it was the end of summer and one of those Arcadian days that were suffused with nostalgia before they've even begun. Calvin was in high spirits as we flew over Deal, its toy houses and its toy pier where I'd eaten ice cream long ago, and then we left it behind and were flying over the water.

'I do love you!' I yelled, though Calvin couldn't hear.

Clamped in his headphones, he pointed down. Black dots were clustered around a vast expanse of sand in the middle of the ocean. As we grew closer, I realised they were seals.

Otherwise the Goodwins were empty. Rippled sand as far as the eye could see, pocked with lakes of water. The clatter was deafening as we landed. The seals slipped into the water and swam away. They soon reappeared, however, and gazed at us with their sleek puppies' faces as we stepped out onto the damp, ribbed sand. Seagulls cried, the wind blew. We were walking in the middle of the sea. We were walking on the moon. We were walking in the middle of nowhere.

There was no sign of the sunken wrecks. No sign of anything but our inquisitive companions who swam beside us as we jumped over the puddles. Far away, the white cliffs and the little town were irrelevant. Calvin wandered off and he was irrelevant too. I don't think I've ever been so happy. I thought of the sunken wrecks and, for some reason, I thought of my miscarried brother, also buried deep in silence, because my parents had never spoken about him. But I felt no grief, just a sense of peace. I was lost in space, in the middle of the sea, and time was irrelevant. Sunken ships and buried babies were just part of our history and one day we would join them. How could anywhere be so strange, yet so reassuring? *I'm taking you out of this world.*

The wind furred the sea and whipped my hair against my skin. I whooped for joy but only the gulls could hear. I felt lighter, wiped clean. My morbid resentments were blown away . . . my husband, my best friend . . . what were their names again? Who gave a toss?

Suddenly hands gripped my windpipe. I jumped.

'We're outside the territorial waters,' Calvin shouted into my ear. 'We could get away with murder and they couldn't touch us.'

I unpeeled his hands. 'That's reassuring.'

He said the place was constantly shifting and that the wrecks appeared and disappeared like ghosts. Nothing could be relied upon in this surreal non-world, even the sand beneath our feet.

Our exuberance lasted all the way home. I felt so light, freed from the burden of the past. Back at his house Calvin made a pot of tea and cooked us scrambled eggs. The homeliness of this meal moved me. For the first time, I felt that I could spend the rest of my life with this man.

During that day we'd stepped through space, between the past and the future, and I realised that Calvin had felt it too. For as we were eating he said: 'How about we get someplace together, babes? What do you say?'

My heart leaped. 'But you love your house.'

'Time for a new start. Too many memories.' He gazed at me, his blue eyes screwed up, his freckled face burnt from the sun. 'How do you feel about *your* gaff?'

'Too many memories.'

'It'll be worth a bob or two.'

'Even better.'

He said he'd pretty well retired from his business and it was time for Doug to take over.

'The man whose wife gives you a biscuit after you've fucked her?' I said.

'That was a joke, love.' He stroked my salt-sticky hair.

He said we could house-hunt in Deal, if that's where I wanted to live. Deal, where all this started, but I'd never told him about the charity shop and the little black dress. I'd just said I loved the sea and that I could never go back to Dorset.

So we Googled properties in Deal until we were gorged with possibilities and then we went to bed and made love. This time it was on another level, quite transcendent. He wasn't that sort of lover at all, not normally, but that night it was so intense it took away my breath.

Afterwards I couldn't sleep. Those sands had shaken up my inner kaleidoscope and resettled the pieces. My mind was racing with possibilities. A house in Deal, facing the sea. I was hanging up the washing in its back garden, seagulls standing sturdily in a row on its wall, watching me with their beady yellow eyes. Calvin was indoors, doing what? I had no idea . . .

Maybe we'd buy a vicarage in Suffolk, the church's shadow falling across the lawn. French windows, the curtains billowing in the breeze, a new Border collie dozing in a pool of sunshine, Calvin tinkering with something in his shed. Was he a shed man? I hadn't a clue . . .

How about a cottage in the Welsh Marches? We'd walk along Offa's Dyke, faces flayed by the wind, and come home to teacakes, our dog Beryl – a bitch this time! – lying panting on the hearthrug. My books on the shelves; Calvin didn't have many so all the more room for mine. A vegetable garden, of course. Maybe hens?

These scenarios flared into focus, stuttered and faded, like a dodgy connection. After all, I hardly knew this man. I'd seldom met his friends. He was unknown to me and yet, in some visceral sense, utterly familiar. It was thrilling that we would live together; I just had trouble picturing it. Would we marry? Maybe we'd elope to France in one of his helicopters and land in that village in Brittany where Azra bought her bedsheets. We'd live in a house with a cider orchard. We'd eat warm baguettes and spend the afternoons in bed.

I must have slept at some point, because it all became jumbled up and then dissolved into dreams. I seemed to hear Calvin in his shed, hammering at a piece of wood . . . I was in Suffolk . . . in France . . . Then I stirred awake and realised it was the rain, hammering on the roof . . . but loud, so loud . . . it must be hailstones.

Someone was hammering at the front door.

'Calvin!' I shook him awake and jumped out of bed. Grabbing a dressing gown, I ran downstairs. The clock said five thirty.

I opened the door. Two policemen stood there. I knew then that Max had died. Why not Lucy? A mother's instinct; I just knew. My son had no sense of direction. He'd got lost in the desert and died of thirst.

The policemen, however, were looking over my shoulder. I turned round. Calvin was approaching, his bare feet noiseless on the marble. As he walked, he knotted the belt of his bathrobe, the white towelling one from the St Regis Hotel. Maybe they'd found out he'd nicked it.

'Are you Mr Calvin Fox?'

He nodded.

The policeman cleared his throat and said: 'I am arresting you on suspicion of the murder of your wife, Mrs Angela Fox. You do not have to say anything, but it may harm your defence if you do not mention when questioned something you later rely on in court. Anything you say may be given in evidence.'

PART THREE

One

In her heyday Angie hardly unpacked her suitcase. She zigzagged the globe, crossing time zones, losing a day of her life here, gaining a day there, glimpsing the molten dawn through her window in Business Class, the curved horizon lit like a forest fire, tomorrow already, before she pulled down the blind. Props were flown across the world for photo-shoots in the Maldives, in Rajasthan and Bali. Once a sarong was flown to Tuscany by private jet because the assistant had ordered the wrong colour. In high summer false snow was blasted from massive nozzles across the Bavarian Alps, wintering the landscape for a shot that was eventually binned.

It was a profligate era, the late seventies. Angie was young, and so stunning that men, cycling past, crashed into lampposts. Tall and slender, honey skin, long blond hair, she was as lovely and fragile as a deer lost in the woods. For she was a vulnerable creature. All her life, predators had circled her, ready to pounce. She'd been molested as a child by an uncle with a damp moustache, an event that only emerged during a counselling session when she was a grown woman and suffering a breakdown. The effect she had on men had, in a sense, blighted her life, because great beauty can bring great loneliness. Women were jealous of her. Men just wanted to jump her.

They pretended interest in her opinions – not hugely fascinating, to be honest – but all they were doing was watching her lips.

Nor could she actually *be* alone, walking along with her own thoughts, because everywhere she went, heads swivelled. It was a peculiar irony, but who on earth would spare their tears for her?

Angie knew no different. She'd always been both blessed and cursed, and was swept along, an innocent really, her looks opening doors into other lives – celebrity lives, billionaire lives – until she was forty and met Calvin. He was flying her to the VIP suite at Glastonbury, where she was about to be dumped by her rock star boyfriend.

She was at a tricky age when she and Calvin fell in love. *Forty.* She felt walloped by a sledgehammer. She was middle-aged, her looks were fading, it was the beginning of the end! In fact, like many people with great bone-structure, she'd grown even more beautiful, but she'd always been insecure and she thought her life was over. Work had dried up, Calvin told me; a new generation was getting the jobs. The modelling world feeds off young flesh and there's always been an infinite supply of that. Besides, she was tired of living out of a suitcase. And even more tired of sleazeballs coming on to her.

But Calvin was a regular guy. He took her bowling and made her laugh. He might be a rough diamond – she knew people sneered at him – but that was fine. Who cared about their opinions? *He* certainly didn't give a toss. It thrilled her, hearing about his crazy adventures in the outback. She'd never met anyone like him. He'd no interest in flaunting her in restaurants, the paparazzi nonsense, nothing like that.

And Calvin didn't jump her, not at first. He played the long game. This intrigued her. Finally he said, *Come to bed. Honest, it's so small you'll hardly notice.* This sent her into such paroxysms of laughter that she had a choking fit. Calvin the paramedic came to her aid. And when they finally collapsed, giggling, into bed she totally surrendered herself. She trusted him, and until then she'd never trusted anyone in her life.

Silly woman.

Another thing about Angela, almost the most important thing: she was rich. Her father was the Marquis of Something and had a baronial pile in Wiltshire. Like much of the aristocracy they were a pretty dysfunctional lot, drink and drugs running through them like a fault line, various siblings in and out of The Priory's revolving door. Calvin called them alco-toffs and despised the lot of them. Indeed, he found the entire British class system baffling.

When Angela was thirty her trust fund matured. Though she was considered something of an airhead she invested wisely, due to having a banker boyfriend at the time, a dull German who had enough money for them both. She'd also hoped to secure her children's future, a hope that was dashed when she found she was infertile. She was still mourning this when she met Calvin.

'I didn't marry her for her money,' said Calvin. 'Straight up, that's the honest truth.'

What difference did it make? Did he really think I cared? People can have a strange set of priorities.

These conversations took place when Calvin was on remand in Belmarsh Prison. His friends had faded away; I seemed to be one of his few visitors. After my initial horror I had a compulsion to see him, during those weeks before his sentencing. I had so many questions; I needed answers and he opened up. In fact, he was eager to talk; I had the feeling that it was something of a relief. He'd already pleaded guilty, which meant a shorter sentence, and maybe he felt he had nothing to lose.

Each visit he looked greyer and more shrunken. More unshaven too, because why would he bother to smarten himself up, just for me? He had no desire to please me or entertain me any more. That Calvin had gone, that man who'd joked about chutney and kissed my elbows. My easy-going, chatty friend had been replaced by a stranger. A prisoner. A *murderer*. The disconnect was so dizzying that I couldn't link them up. Instead, I just listened to his story, delivered in a monotone with sometimes a cocky tilt of the head as he looked at me, challenging me, like those seagulls in Deal. Sort of pitying me, too. Why would he do that? Because I believed him? He was right. Why *did* I believe him, after he'd spun me so many lies?

Why, for instance, did he tell me his wife had died from an aneurism and then changed it to suicide? What was the point of that? Was he just a congenital liar? A sociopath? A psychopath? If any of this had taught me anything, it was that you never know anybody.

So there I was, driving into the hinterland of south-east London, week after week. Heaven knows how I found the place; each time I got lost and came to a halt under some godforsaken flyover. I was propelled by a need for some sort of explanation.

Which came out eventually as I sat in the visitors' hall, facing the man upon whom I'd once pinned my hopes. He didn't try to justify himself or make excuses. In fact he seemed strangely detached from his own actions. Not a flicker of interest in my reaction, either, which was chilling. But then I thought: he'd never been that curious about me, or indeed found out anything about me at all.

A sociopath. Psychopath. Whatever. Why hadn't I realised?

And more to the point: had he been planning on murdering *me*? Once or twice this flashed through my mind but I dismissed it. I wasn't rich enough. We'd have to be married for him to get his hands on my house, and marriage had not been mentioned by either of us. He'd only suggested living together. Of course, he could have been playing a long game, as he did with Angie, but I'd never been as attractive as her and, quite honestly, I felt too upset to speculate about the future. I had enough horror to deal with, in re-examining the past.

For it had all been poisoned, a chemical spill seeping into the landscape of our months together. Had it all been a lie? I felt nauseous, but with a dogged compulsion I went back over every contaminated moment – the silliness and chattiness, the lovemaking, the impulsive jaunts to late-night restaurants where Calvin's entrance had turned the place festive. I hadn't felt this sense of betrayal since Greg and Azra. This time it was even more sickening.

But I needed the facts. Sitting in the visitors' hall, we were cut off from the outside world. Far off, the faint roar of the inmates was like the roar of the ocean. We were marooned together. I remembered that day on the Goodwin Sands,

Calvin's hands clamped around my throat. *We could get away with murder and nobody could touch us.*

'Tell me more about Angie,' I said. 'What changed between you?'

'You really want to know?'

'Of course.'

He gazed at me with his small, piggy eyes. Yes! I could admit it now. I'd romanticised this man, so strong was my longing for companionship. He sat there in his plastic chair – sandy eyelashes, lizard skin, all the life drained out of him. A pathetic little murderer who had almost got away with it.

'I don't know why you come here, week after week,' he whined. '*Why* do you come here? Why don't you just get on with your life?'

'Tell me what happened. Don't you owe me that?'

He tore the wrapper from his KitKat. 'All right then.'

For years they were happy. Angie loved animals. Animals wanted nothing from her and gave her unconditional love; many abused women find solace in pets. She loved her horse, Conker, and won prizes for eventing. She dabbled in interior design. She and Calvin held their legendary parties, where she binged on drugs and on several occasions passed out. For sure, Angie had her problems but Calvin looked after her; that was his role. He was a traditional sort of chap and it suited him fine. His business couldn't support their lifestyle but in the early years that wasn't a problem. It was Angie's money that bought the house and paid for the renovations, but she understood men and their need to be in control – she'd had plenty of experience – and passed the financial matters over to him. The fact that she paid the bills was never mentioned.

Calvin didn't tell me the details. I filled them in for myself – the men colliding with lampposts, the uncle's damp moustache. I've always had a strong imagination. As she became fleshed out, my reconstructed Angie was no doubt an altered creature from the Angie he'd known, but I was getting a picture of their marriage and the trouble that started brewing towards the end.

Angie was a gullible woman. That's how he put it, anyway. I think she was a troubled soul who was looking for answers, seeking some sort of guidance through life. Calvin wouldn't understand this; it wasn't his sort of thing. I was finding myself getting more and more defensive on Angie's behalf. In fact, I was getting rather fond of her. Maybe because I knew what lay ahead.

Calvin took a sip of the disgusting prison coffee. 'But then she got into the climate lark. Big time.'

It was triggered by something she read online. Whatever it was, it had a profound effect. First, she stopped eating meat. In fact, she wouldn't have it in the house.

'Bloody lentils,' said Calvin. 'Bloody rabbit food. I was farting from here to Christmas.'

Calvin wasn't this unreconstructed; we'd eaten Lebanese *mezes* often enough. Prison seemed to be bringing out the Neanderthal in him. Maybe it was the company he was keeping.

At first he thought it was just another fad. He soon realised, however, that this was something different. Within weeks Angie's character changed. She'd never been a bossy woman but now she started haranguing him about the pollution levels of his beloved Range Rover; she turned off the heating in the swimming pool and cancelled their holiday to the Maldives. She became increasingly militant, lecturing their friends, going on marches and mounting petitions outside the Potters Bar Tesco. Calvin suspected she was donating large sums of money to Extinction Rebellion but he had no way of knowing this, not yet.

'She swallowed the whole thing, hook, line and sinker,' he said. 'You'd think she was on a one-woman mission to save the world. And – get this – she started nagging me about my job. She said it was immoral and poisoning the planet. She'd spout these statistics about flying and carbon emissions. It was my *work*, for fuck's sake! I'd built up that business from scratch, it was my baby and I was proud of it. She started showing me up in front of my friends, humiliating me, know what I mean?'

'Maybe there was a touch of *mea culpa* about it, that she'd been so guilty herself, whizzing around the place burning up fossil fuels.'

He shrugged. He wasn't interested in my opinion; that wasn't the point.

His fragile, dim wife became a battleaxe. Worse still, a depressive.

'Where'd she gone, my Ange? Into some black hole, and I couldn't pull her out. One day I came into the bathroom and there she was sitting on the floor, crying her little eyes out, banging on about plastics in the ocean and turtles tangled up in fishing lines and whatnot. She was spending half her time on her computer, scaring herself witless.'

Angie was simply filled with grief. I could understand

that. I felt it too, of course – the helplessness and despair. I, too, wept for the world as I uselessly recycled my newspapers and switched off the lights. Thank God I didn't have grandchildren.

'I tried to be reasonable,' he said. 'Hand on heart. At first I tried to talk to her, but suddenly I'm the enemy. Men the oppressors, all that shit. It was men who were destroying the planet. She'd had some bad experiences with them, of course, but she didn't have to take it out on *me*.'

He was sounding more and more aggrieved, as if the whole thing was Angie's fault. He didn't quite say *she brought it on herself*, but near enough. His new Angie was almost unrecognisable; he felt he was living with a stranger. But then, how many of us really know the person with whom we share our life?

'And a fuck was certainly out of the question,' said Calvin. It was the only time I saw a glimmer of humour.

But something else was happening too.

'See, I'd got into a spot of bother,' he said. 'Finance-wise. Things were going down the tubes, big time.'

I won't bore you with the details. Basically, his business was haemorrhaging money and he was borrowing heavily to bail it out. Angie knew nothing about this – Calvin had his pride. Finally, without her knowledge, he'd taken out a large mortgage on the house – maybe its deeds were in his name; maybe he forged her signature. I suspect there was something even dodgier going on, but only Doug, his partner, was in on the secret.

And then, a week before she died, Calvin learned that Angie was going to change her will and leave everything to Extinction Rebellion. He learned this from Angie's closest friend, Johanna, who happened to be Doug's wife. Johanna told him this in confidence.

'We were in bed at the time,' Calvin said.

'You were *what?*'

It transpired that they'd been having an affair for years, he and Johanna. Nobody knew – not Doug, the husband; not Angie, his own wife.

I was astonished. 'So did she give you a biscuit afterwards?'

Calvin didn't laugh. He was past laughter. The biscuit joke was another double-bluff, I realised. A dangerous one, but this was a man who liked to push things to the edge. That's how he got his kicks. It was part of his attraction. And to think I had my doubts about him simply because he called women 'girls' and voted Tory.

Sitting there amongst the prisoners I suddenly longed for Greg. Dear, gentle Greg, the Greg I once knew. Who cooked Ottolenghi recipes with plenty of lentils and read me *Middlemarch* when I had glandular fever. Who was the father of my children. I was utterly adrift, half in and half out of a world of criminality at which I'd been a helpless bystander but yet . . . but yet, it had been my *life*, my hopes of a future in a Suffolk rectory or a Welsh farmhouse with a dog, and hens, and a man whistling in the kitchen.

So how did he do it, and why did he escape detection for so long?

Escape detection. It's laughable, isn't it, that I was using that sort of vocabulary. That this had become my new normal.

Although, of course, it didn't have to be. I could have walked away and had nothing to do with Calvin. In fact he urged me to do this – the nearest thing he ever managed to an apology.

And he was right. We weren't officially together. I'd never known Angie; all that was in the past. The police had briefly questioned me but realised I had nothing useful to tell them. I was irrelevant in all this.

'So how did it happen?' I asked. 'And how come nobody found out?'

I suddenly felt as light as air. Calvin was in deep trouble. So were the other men in the visiting hall, leaning across the tables, talking to their wives while their children ran riot. It was so bleak and touching, those efforts at connecting, under the eye of the officers stationed around the room. Soon we'd be free, but these men would be swallowed back into their underworld, banged up again, doors clanging shut. Soon Calvin would be swallowed up for good. He'd already gone from my life, that day the police arrived.

I knew, then, that this was my last visit. Whether he'd loved me or not was irrelevant. I sloughed off his jokes and his companionship and no longer felt betrayed. It wasn't his fault, it was mine. I'd built this unlikely man into the repository of all my hopes and dreams, and now it was time to say goodbye. But first I would sit back and listen to his story.

Calvin, remember, had been a paramedic. He'd saved people's lives, but he also knew how lives could be ended. Once, when he and Doug were drunk, he'd bragged to him about ways of killing someone and leaving no trace. You could press two fingers into a person's temples, in a certain tiny spot. You could inject them with insulin, which didn't show in the bloodstream. Or you could inject air into a vein. Inject it through a mole and it wouldn't even leave a puncture mark.

And this is what he did. Maybe he gave Angie some sort of sedation first – at that time she was heavily reliant on sleeping pills – I'm not sure. He didn't go into details and I felt too awkward to cross-question him like a detective; he'd had enough of that.

I *did* ask him why he'd changed his story about the cause of her death, from an aneurism to suicide.

'Did I?' Calvin's eyes were dull. He didn't remember – or, indeed, care. By now he'd been in prison for three weeks and had drifted even further away from me. His new surroundings were claiming him. When the children were small, and stirring awake from some nightmare, there was the same absence in their eyes as they returned from somewhere I couldn't reach them.

I suspect he was just a congenital liar and liked playing with people's reactions. He'd certainly lied about his finances. I'd had no idea how deeply he was in debt. 'Your house must be worth a bob or two,' he'd told me. He'd also found out that Greg and I had paid off the mortgage. No doubt it was me who was going to pay for the house in Deal or Suffolk or wherever. An ageing, desperate woman who couldn't recognise a con man. It wasn't part of my education.

And he'd certainly omitted to tell me about Johanna. I finally plucked up courage and asked him if the affair had still been going on during the past year, when he and I were together.

'What's that got to do with anything?' he snapped.

I stared at him, open-mouthed.

I'd had my answer. I got up and left.

When I got home I found a Tupperware box of pastries on the doorstep. Pam must have seen my car arrive because soon the doorbell rang.

Pam pushed ahead of me into the kitchen as if she owned the place. Though it was a chilly day, she was damp with sweat.

'I'm bushed,' she said, plonking herself down. 'Been clearing up the garden.' She pointed to the Tupperware box. 'Only shop-bought this time, I'm afraid. I've been up to my ears in bindweed. It's been throttling the life out of my climbers.'

I thought of Calvin's hands around my throat. She inspected me over her spectacles. *Don't crow,* I urged her, silently. *Don't say I told you so.* Since Calvin's arrest we'd had a few brief conversations but now her curiosity had got the better of her. I suspect she was relishing it all.

'You been visiting him again?' she asked. 'Isn't that a bit masochistic?'

Like a dog returning to its vomit, I thought, too exhausted to reply.

'It must be difficult, it being in all the papers,' Pam said. 'Any reporters been snuffling around?'

I shook my head.

'I must say, I haven't seen any,' she said. 'If I had, I'd have sent them packing.'

'There's no connection to me. Anyway, it's yesterday's news by now.'

Deborah Moggach

'I'd have offered my house as a refuge – you could have
had Mother's room – but I knew you had closer friends
who'd be offering the same thing.' She gazed at me pity-
ingly. There was a smudge of earth on her nose. 'You'll
just have to put it behind you and move on.'

I felt overwhelmed with weariness. It took a superhuman effort to lift the kettle. How did she know I'd been
visiting Calvin in prison? Actually, I didn't care.

I was still reeling from the discovery about Johanna.
The affair had obviously been carrying on all this time;
he'd said as much. Just now I pushed it to the back of my
mind; I couldn't bear to think about it yet.

'There hasn't been such excitement in the street since the
Forsters' chimney caught fire,' Pam said. 'Even Elaine – you
know, the brothel-keeper, who must have seen a thing or
two – even she was chatting to me about it in Waitrose.
Thank goodness you're safe, anyway. I mean, he could've
been planning to murder *you*.'

This had, of course, crossed my mind. As I made the
tea I felt grateful to Pam for putting it into words.

She patted my knee. 'You've had a lucky escape, and
thank goodness for that.'

For the first time, I smiled at her with genuine warmth.

My friends had rallied round, of course. Bethany had
asked me to dinner, with Rosie and her husband. To my
surprise, their various grown-up children had joined us,
taking time out from their busy, high-powered lives. I
realised I'd become something of a celebrity. Feeble
attempts to stay off the subject had soon foundered. 'Did
you ever feel threatened?' asked Bean, the gastroenterologist son. 'He seemed perfectly pleasant at the wake,'

196

Bethany said. 'A bit quiet, bit of a dark horse, but then that's often the case, isn't it?' As if she'd known murderers all her life.

Tish and Benji also had me round. They'd invited some friends of theirs, people I didn't know; it was quite a party. No doubt they wanted to show me off. Again, any attempts at general conversation were soon abandoned. Gentle hints turned into an eager barrage of questions. I felt too raw to pull it together into any sort of coherent story, especially in front of strangers, and resented the pressure to entertain them, even though I'd have behaved exactly as they did. Ah, but it was so exposing, so humiliating. For a mad moment I thought: wait till I get home and tell Calvin. He'll have a laugh.

At this point I burst into tears. Benji jumped up and said: 'Pru, I'm so sorry. Let me drive you home.'

'But I've got my car.'

'You've had a few drinks, though, haven't you?'

I'd always been fond of Tish and Benji, though with a bitter-sweet edge, as theirs was one of the marriages I envied. They had a thriving landscaping business and danced the tango together. I've told you how they joshed around as they'd dished up dinner all those years ago, and how I'd felt a stab of jealousy. That's what they were like – larky, companionable, and according to Tish still enjoying a vigorous sex life. So what happened next totally threw me.

As Benji parked his car outside my door he turned to me. 'Poor Pru, you've really been through the wringer, haven't you? First Greg and now this.' He switched off the engine. Then he lunged forward and kissed me, just missing my mouth. His beard pressed into my cheek.

I froze. He drew back and gazed at me wonderingly. 'Prudence . . . Prudence.' He brushed the hair from my face. 'I've been wanting to do this for years,' he said. 'You've sensed it, haven't you? Have you? Has it been that obvious?'

I shook my head and grabbed the door handle.

'I always remember when I first saw you.' His voice throbbed. 'When we'd moved into number seven and you knocked on our door with little Max on your hip. You were wearing a long blue dress and your hair was loose around your shoulders, a Botticelli painting, a Madonna. You'd brought us a quiche. A *quiche*. We'd never seen one of those, we came from Dudley.'

'I really should be going—'

'No!' he gripped my arm. 'Hear me out, please.'

He took my hand and kneaded my fingers, one by one, his head bent over them as if they were holy. His bald patch gleamed in the streetlight.

'Me and Tish . . . our marriage has been dead for years.'

'I don't want to know—'

'We don't talk to each other, we have no pleasure in each other's company any more, we haven't had sex for three years. Three *years*. If it wasn't for the anti-depressants we'd probably have killed each other by now.' He stopped. 'Sorry, that was tactless. I just mean, it's not what it seems. Basically we're leading separate lives. It's just the grandchildren and the business that keeps us together.' He cupped my head in his hand and drew me to him. Stroking my hair, he murmured: 'I'll have to get back to my guests but can I call you tomorrow? Tish'll be at the hospital all afternoon. Colonoscopy, the poor duck.'

I pulled away. 'I don't think that's a good idea.'

I managed to get out of the car and hurried to my front door. It was late and the street was empty. I fumbled for my key and tried to put it into the lock but my hand didn't work. He was right, I was drunk.

I heard him start the car and drive away. Finally I wrestled the door open. I glanced up and down the road. The houses were dark – all but Pam's. There was a light glowing in her upstairs window; no doubt she'd seen the whole thing.

I went into the kitchen and drank a glass of water. My hands were trembling and some of it spilled into my lap. I thought: I've lost two more friends. Things will never be the same between us after this.

I suddenly had an urge to hear my children's voices. I'd told them by now, of course, but I'd kept my tone light, even jokey, as if I were describing a cop show on the television. I didn't want them to feel obliged to fly over. Trouble was, it had worked rather better than I had imagined. They'd both been sympathetic enough – Lucy in particular had been eager to hear what she called 'the gory details' – not the most sensitive way of putting it, but my daughter had always been something of a blunt instrument. 'You were just sitting in a dentist's waiting room,' she said. 'How did Calvin know you were single, and had a nice big house in Muswell Hill?' I'd replied tartly: 'He just found me attractive. Is that so difficult to believe?' A long silence had followed this.

Neither of them had offered to come and support me. As I said, I'd played it down, but I couldn't help feeling abandoned. It was too late to phone Reykjavik but in

199

Pasadena it would be early evening, so I rang Max. However, I only got his answerphone.

So I took two sleeping pills and went to bed. In the morning I had a crippling hangover; nothing unusual about that.

I couldn't see Calvin again, not after the Johanna revelation. Though 'revelation' sounds too awe-inspiring – even biblical – to describe something so grubby. However, I needed to find out more about what happened, so I decided to visit Doug, Calvin's business partner. This required some courage. After all, I hardly knew the man and suspected he'd colluded in Calvin's financial dealings. Commercial aviation was not my speciality – nor, indeed, was murder – but Doug and I did have betrayal in common and he'd seemed amiable enough when I met him.

So I drove to Elstree Aerodrome and made my way past the helicopters to the office.

It was empty but I heard a lavatory flushing. An inner door opened and an enormously fat man emerged, zipping up his flies.

'Whoops,' he said. 'Sorry about that. Can I help you?'

'I'm looking for Doug.'

'He doesn't work here any more.' He eased himself into his seat. 'You come about the booking to Birmingham?'

I explained that I needed to talk to Doug. At first he wouldn't give me Doug's address but when I explained the situation he looked at me with a mild flicker of interest. I suspected his curiosity was seldom roused.

'No skin off my nose,' he shrugged, and wrote the

address down on a piece of paper. 'But don't tell him or he'll have my guts for garters.'

I sat in the car, suddenly drained of energy. Across the airfield a private jet shot into the sky. The rich can always escape; they have the lawyers and the private islands. They can be out of this world, sealed off in their own Goodwin Sands somewhere in the Caribbean. And even if they look like toads, which they often did, they have the beautiful women. For thirty years Calvin had flown them to their corporate shindigs and gated mansions. I wondered whether the greed that finally undid him sprang from envy, from his proximity to these people, or from the cruelty of his childhood. He had the beautiful wife, however. He had the pool and all the trappings.

I'd never truly understood him. One day I might be able to look back on it and laugh at my stupidity. But not now, not yet.

Doug's house was only a mile away. At least I wouldn't have to meet Johanna; their marriage had broken down when Calvin was arrested, and Doug had kicked her out.

Still, my heart pounded as I parked outside his house. Doug was there in his front garden, bent over a motorbike. He straightened up, frowning, when he saw me. Then his face cleared.

'Well, well, it's Patience,' he said.

He flashed me a smile. I guessed he wasn't too pleased to see me but he was a smooth operator – deeply tanned, white teeth, a man who'd spent a lifetime charming the rich. He wore a boiler suit with 'Texaco' emblazoned over his heart.

'So what can I do for you?' he asked, wiping his hands on a rag.

'I just wanted to, you know, have a chat.'

He glanced up and down the street. 'You'd better come in.'

He opened the front door. A huge dog leaped at me, growling. It put its paws on my shoulders and I staggered back.

'Don't worry about Bella, she's a pussycat.' Doug pulled the dog off me and playfully hit its nose. 'Just a big baby, aren't you, sweetie?'

The room was a mess. On the floor, dismembered engine parts lay spread out on newspapers.

'Take a pew.' Doug gestured to a sofa. I sat down and he leaned against the wall, watching me. He was still smiling. 'I have to say, this is a surprise.'

'The whole thing's been a bit of a surprise.'

'You could say that, for all concerned.' He pushed himself away from the wall and opened the back door. 'Garden!' He pointed outside. The dog lumbered out and barked at nothing in particular. Doug sat down on the arm of a chair and inspected me. 'Well, well, Patience, I didn't expect to see you again.'

'Prudence.'

'We've both been royally shafted, have we not?'

I nodded.

'But I've put it behind me,' he said. 'I've had some hard knocks, Patience, but believe me, I've never let it drag me down. Tomorrow's another day, that's my mantra. Let bygones be bygones. You pick yourself up, dust yourself down, and just get on with it.'

'I just wanted to know, well, what exactly happened. I've been visiting him in prison, you see—'

'What, Calvin?'

I nodded.

'Blimey, I wouldn't touch that cunt with a bargepole, excuse the language.' He looked at me, eyes narrowed. 'Listen, love, I'm sorry I can't help you. If you've come here for answers you've come to the wrong place.'

Just then the front door slammed. Before Doug could get up a woman strode into the room. She wore motorbike leathers and carried a helmet.

'What are you doing here?' Doug snapped.

'I've come for my CDs.' The woman squatted down and opened a cupboard; she started throwing CDs into a carrier bag.

'Hey, some of those are mine!' said Doug.

'I'll sort them out later.' She looked at me. 'Who are you?'

'Prudence.'

'Wow, what are you doing here?'

She was so different from my imaginary Johanna that for a moment I couldn't reply. A strapping, beefy woman, something no-nonsense about her. Plain face, mousy hair cropped short, a jutting, determined chin.

'I came to talk to Doug,' I said.

'Huh. If you think you'll get anything out of this knobhead you've got another think coming.' She shoved the last CDs into the bag. 'I'm Jo, by the way. Calvin's friend.'

'*Friend!*' snorted Doug.

'I'm outta here.' She stood up, breathing heavily.

'See you in the divorce court,' said Doug.

'Don't be an arse, we're not on the telly. I'll be back to-morrow for the garden tools. *You* won't be needing them. You wouldn't know a yucca if it came up and slapped you in the face.'

Johanna strode to the door. I got up and followed her. I'd lost confidence in Doug. Besides, I was intrigued by this leather-clad Valkyrie who'd whirlwinded in and out of her marital home and seemed unfazed by meeting me.

Her motorbike was parked in the street. 'Want a lift?' she said.

'I haven't got a helmet, and anyway my car's here.'

'Don't be a wimp.' She playfully punched me in the ribs. 'Come to the park; it's just round the corner. I've been wanting to meet you.'

So I got on the back of Johanna's bike and we sped off, my arms around her sturdy midriff. A moment later we dismounted at a small playground. It was deserted, as playgrounds always are unless they're in a TV drama. Nitrous oxide capsules were littered around the swings. Johanna pulled off her helmet and flung herself down on the grass.

'Look at that sky!' she said. 'The freedom, oh, the freedom! The swallows have gone, bless them.' She clicked her fingers. 'Just like that, just like me. We're all off to better climes. Wow, the relief!'

I removed some KFC boxes and lay down beside her. She turned towards me, her leathers creaking.

'So you're Calvin's woman.'

'Well, sort of . . .'

'Did he tell you about shovelling the sand, and pushing the car off the cliff?'

I nodded.

'Lies, all lies,' Johanna said. 'His family was quite wealthy. His father was a civil servant and it was a perfectly happy childhood.'

'And his mother wasn't blind?'

'Of course not.'

'How do you know?'

'His sister came to England for a visit. She and I smoked some weed together.'

'Did he work as a paramedic?'

'Christ, no. He got into some financial scandal and fled to England. It's only then that he learned to fly.'

I realised that none of this surprised me. In fact it was something of a relief. My feelings for Calvin had been numbed; one day they might come tingling back to life, like my gums after the dentist's jab, but I doubted it.

'Did he know?' I asked. 'That you knew he lied?'

Johanna shook her head. 'I played along with it.' She shrugged. 'In fact, it gave me a sense of power.'

'It didn't stop you loving him?' *Loving.* The word jolted me to my senses. This woman had betrayed me, month after month. Why was I being so friendly?

'I'm sorry.' Johanna laid her hand on my arm. 'I know what you're thinking and I apologise. To Doug and to Angie. And to you, of course. I didn't feel too great about it either, to be honest.'

'I should think not.'

'Did it stop me loving him?' She rolled over onto her back and gazed at the sky. 'He and I were like peas in a pod. It's hard to describe. People talk about soulmates but it was deeper than that. Back in Utrecht I did some work with twins, and that's the nearest I can describe it. My lost twin. As if we'd shared a womb, as if we knew what each other was thinking before they'd spoken. In fact, we'd forget who said it. Oh, it's hard to describe.'

Her voice was dreamy. It reminded me of Greg talking about Azra, that day in Dorset with the harebells dancing.

'It wasn't even hugely sexual, if that's what you're thinking,' Johanna said. 'Oh, we had sex – sorry about that – but that was just an added delight. Part of the mix. And we never felt guilty because it was all so inevitable.' She laughed. 'Basically, we're both fantasists.'

It turned out she was a child psychologist and had trained in Holland. Though she was Dutch I could hardly detect an accent. At one point she'd worked with young offenders in a high-security unit. She'd met Calvin through Doug, when they started up the business together.

'Have you been visiting him in prison?' I couldn't call Calvin by his name. 'Are you going to forgive him for what he did? Will you be there for him when he comes out?'

She shook her head. 'I'm as shocked as you are. I could take the cheating, I could match him at that, lie for lie, but I do draw the line at premeditated murder.'

'So how did he get found out?'

'Because the business went bankrupt, back in June, and Doug discovered that Cal had been swindling him. He'd been taking money out and forging Doug's signature. And when Doug started ferreting around he discovered some emails between me and Cal and realised we'd been having an affair, so the whole thing blew up, big time. They'd been best friends, for Christ's sake! Our marriage was pretty well dead by then but this was the last straw and we had one hell of a row and I moved out.' She sat up and pulled a cigarette case from her pocket. 'Want a puff?' She pointed to the silver case. 'This was my grand-father's. It saved his life in the trenches. That dent was where a bullet would have hit him.'

The joints lay neatly in a row. There was something touching about them – the care with which they'd been rolled and assembled; their cosy nestling together like confidantes. They reminded me of Pam's coconut fingers. For some reason my eyes filled with tears. For those young men in the trenches, the ones unable to be saved from a bullet; for the children and grandchildren they never had; for the children disappeared from the playground, leaving just the nitrous oxide bullets scattered on the grass. Where had they all gone?

What had happened to all of us? Lucy and Max, my darling bat-babies, hanging upside down on their climb-ing frame. The joy of it all. Our swimsuits hanging side by side on the washing line in Dorset. Greg's and mine; the children's. We'd eat supper with the windows open and the moths blundered against the lamps. The next day we'd be swimming again and we'd wring out our cos-tumes and peg them on the line and have supper and nobody would grow up.

Yet we did, because here was I at seventy-one, lying on the grass with my lover's lover in a litter-strewn play-ground in Elstree, sharing a spliff.

Johanna said: 'So I might be lacking in empathy but I'm still a human being and I thought: poor old Doug. Shafted by his best mate, business down the toilet. Cal had been such a shit.' She paused. 'And you come into this, too.' She inhaled deeply, and held it in for a long time. I waited tensely. Finally she blew out a plume of smoke. 'I might as well tell you, now you're here. How I hated you, too.'

'Me?'

She didn't pass me the joint. Carefully she raised it to her lips again. Her hand was trembling. 'When Angie died I thought he and I would finally get it together. Me and Cal. I thought, give him a few months to mourn her. Remember, there was no hint of anything dodgy; it was apparently an aneurism. Angie had high cholesterol but she kept forgetting to take her pills. So it was presumed to be a clot. There wasn't even a postmortem.' Johanna took another drag. 'So when she died I expected him to be devastated and I kept my distance. Just sympathetic, you know, a shoulder to cry on. But then, blow me down, *you* came along. Pipped me to the post, didn't you? For a while I didn't see him – he was with you I guess – but soon he came sneaking back, presuming things were going to carry on as before. Of course I was hurt, but know what? I welcomed him back with open arms. What a wuss! Who'd believe I'm a Black Belt? What's that song? "I'm Just a Woman".'

'Look, *I* was pretty hurt too. When I found out about you.'

Johanna ignored me. 'I was dead sorry for myself, and even a bit sorry for my husband, so to spite Calvin I told Douggie everything. Including Angie's decision to change her will and leave it all to Extinction Rebellion. How she'd made an appointment to see her solicitor, the week before she died. I'd no idea how significant this was, but Doug was spitting furious with Calvin, of course – the man had ruined him – and he started digging around. I don't know what he found but it was enough to go to the police.'

At last Johanna passed me the spliff. I took a drag, deep into my lungs. For a moment I thought I was going to die. Industrial-strength skunk had arrived since the last time I'd smoked what we quaintly called 'pot'. It blocked my breath and made my brain dissolve. I realised Johanna was still talking, her voice echoing from Derbyshire.

'The police interviewed Angie's solicitor, who confirmed he was drawing up a new draft of her will, cutting out her husband. Doug told them that Calvin had bragged about ways of killing people without leaving a trace. I told them he'd once pressed his thumbs on my temples and said I'd be dead within a minute.'

I remembered Calvin speaking about Greg: 'Shall I go and sort him out?' He'd said it in a matter-of-fact way that had startled me. I remembered the day a magpie fell down my chimney, flapping its wings in a cloud of soot, and how he'd casually wrung its neck.

'And there was all the fraud and forging of signatures, the lies and cheating,' said Johanna. 'I still can't see how that would be enough to charge him so long after the event, and Angie cremated, but maybe those policemen found out more. Enough, anyway, to convince the CPS they could go ahead and arrest him. Maybe they hinted to Calvin that they had more evidence than they actually had, and gambled on him simply throwing up his hands and confessing, to reduce his sentence. He was a cornered rat. Maybe he was just weary of the whole thing and found it a relief to tell the truth, for the first time in his life. Maybe – you know how arrogant he was – maybe he wanted to brag about how he'd so cleverly pulled it off.' She shrugged. 'You tell me. Your guess is as good as mine.'

It was only then that I noticed the children. They'd arrived while we were talking – an Indian couple with two little girls. They were twins and wore identical pink dresses. They rose and fell on the swings, their plaits floating up and down. Their parents pushed them in silence.

'I'll give you a lift back,' said Johanna. She put out her hand. 'Help me up, will you? These leathers weigh a ton.'

I hauled her up.

'We're none of us getting any younger.' She brushed grass clippings off her arms. 'Doug's mate Terry has taken over the business now.'

'I know. I met him this morning. God, it seems like a week ago.'

Walking to Johanna's motorbike, we waved to the little girls but they didn't wave back.

'Terry's a big bloke, isn't he?' I said. 'With him at the controls, I'm amazed a helicopter could even get off the ground.'

Johanna burst out laughing. Her square, sallow face was transformed; suddenly she was beautiful. This woman was made for merriment. No doubt she'd had plenty of that, with Calvin.

At my car she shook my hand and said, gruffly: 'I'm

glad we met.' She cocked her head, one eyebrow raised, and gave me one last look. Then she clicked down her visor and became a spaceman.

She roared off, and I never saw her again.

Two

Calvin was sentenced to sixteen years. I read about it in the papers, though they seemed more interested in Angie. Posh totty always pulls in the punters, especially when they've dated rock royalty and had a history of mental illness. Angie's beautiful face gazed at me from beyond the grave. There was even a photo of her horse, Conker, in the online *Daily Mail,* a website to which I'd become briefly and shamefully addicted. No photos of me, of course. I was a bystander in this soap opera, and felt more and more detached as the weeks passed. Briefly, on waking, I forgot that I'd had anything to do with it at all.

In November I put my house on the market. It was a sudden decision. I'd been walking to my car, which I'd had to park three streets away. This irritating situation had been happening more often. I realised, then, how my neighbourhood had changed. Many of my old friends had gone and the bankers had moved in. My familiar streets were now jammed with SUVs and Porsches. Half the parking spaces were blocked by skips and the houses sheathed in flapping plastic behind which thunderous renovations were being carried out – basements dug out for gyms and cinemas, roofs removed for penthouse extensions. Nobody knew anyone any more. And my old-established neighbours had given way to transients. Nights were punctuated by the trundle of luggage wheels as strangers sought out their Airbnbs. New people had bought the house next door and suffocated their garden with decking, silencing the birdsong. I'd seen no signs of life; like many of the houses theirs remained dark, its only illumination the security lights around the garden and the winking entry-phone set in the prison wall they'd erected at the front.

I hadn't registered this. For the past fourteen months I hadn't really noticed anything. Now I'd emerged like Rip Van Winkle from my long hibernation and found the world had changed. Pam had been bemoaning it, of course, but I'd been too distracted to listen. Besides, whenever she waylaid me I was itching to escape.

By the time I arrived at my car I'd decided to sell my house. As Calvin had observed, it was worth a bob or two. The property was mine, Greg was out of my life, I could do what I wanted with it. I could sell up and start a new life in Deal. I'd been thinking about it since that conversation with Calvin. Deal was a charming town, familiar from my childhood. Greg and Azra had never set foot in it. I'd be free.

And rich. Homes were a lot cheaper in Deal. What would I do with all that extra cash? Give it to Max and Lucy?

I sat in the car, thinking long and hard about this. I had to admit that over the past months my children had been something of a disappointment. They hadn't even flown over for Christmas; at the time they'd had no idea that cousin Dorothy would come to my rescue. The trouble was, as I've said, I'd kept assuring them I was fine. Who could blame them for taking me at my word?

Maybe I'd give the money to Extinction Rebellion.

I burst out laughing. A passer-by looked at me. I realised an hour had passed and I was still sitting in my car. A Pimlico Plumbers van had come and gone, and it had started to rain.

Still I didn't move. I felt a surge of euphoria. I hadn't expected this; I loved my house and had lived in it for nearly forty years. Life, however, is full of surprises; we can all agree about that.

'Look at that sky!' Johanna had said, flinging herself on the grass. 'The freedom, oh, the freedom!'

I got out of the car, walked home, and rang the local estate agent.

To my surprise I had three offers within the week. 'Unrenovated homes like yours are becoming increasingly scarce,' said Barry, from Murray and Brookes. Like many estate agents he was barely out of his teens, with gelled hair and smooth beige skin, as if he'd been polished with a chamois leather. 'Our overseas buyers like to put their own stamp on a property and of course it's a very safe neighbourhood with good schools. Five bedrooms and a larger-than-average garden are another plus, and of course there's Waitrose on the doorstep.'

Needless to say I bridled at the *unrenovated*. Had Barry no tact? He'd certainly no idea of the years of toil it had taken Greg and me to rip out the Formica kitchen units and sand the floors and raid skips for shutters and fireplaces; of the thrill and exhaustion of creating a home. Barry hadn't been born then, of course, nor had my children. This long-lost age was now bathed in a golden glow; it was a time of newly married love, and neighbours who would soon become our dearest friends and who were also hammering and painting and throwing impromptu dinner parties. And soon the babies came thick and fast and we carted them around in slings and thought: nothing's going to change us, it'll always be like this. Those days seemed so innocent now, those days of laughter and flirtation, my jeans spattered with paint and my breasts leaking milk.

I accepted an offer from a Chinese family who were relocating to London. I think the husband was a physicist. I chose them because they offered the asking price and could pay cash. They wanted to exchange as soon as possible and complete in March.

'I can't blame you,' said Pam. 'I'm sure it's hard to resist that sort of money. And I'm not a racist but I can't help noticing that the neighbourhood's changed. You hardly hear English being spoken any more. Still, that won't be your problem.'

The house was in my name; it was mine to sell. I'd told the children my plans and for once they both agreed – *Great idea, Mum, you need a change.*

My euphoria didn't last. The moment I signed the papers I was hit by the enormity of it all. Was I mad, to step into the unknown? I'd be alone in a strange town. 'You're so brave,' said Bethany, giving me one of her penetrating stares. I'd never been to Deal in the winter, with the arcades closed and the dark streets lashed with gales. Maybe I'd even miss Pam. And how on earth was I going to pack up my life? Even the understairs cupboard would take me a week. I glanced inside and slammed the door with a shudder.

Maybe I *was* mad. I'd been behaving oddly, I knew that. I flung myself on the sofa. My heart pounded and I was suddenly overwhelmed with grief. For my life; for the past, jammed into every corner of this house; for the disappearance of all the people I loved most dearly. I thought of Greg and Azra leaning towards each other in that Turkish restaurant, how they cracked my world open. And all I was left with was Greg's exercise bike and old school reports and his cupboard full of clothes and . . . and *so much stuff*. What had he said? *People bust their guts doing jobs they don't like to buy stuff they don't need, just to help corporate criminals ruin the planet.* Thanks, Greg, so what the hell do I do with it?

I climbed the stairs and crawled into bed, fully clothed. I thought I'd got over my depression but it came roaring back, I heard the creak of its greasy black wings as I pulled the duvet over my head.

The old torpor descended on me. I wandered like a sleep-walker around the house. Limply, I stuffed stuff into bin-liners and then collapsed on the sofa, overwhelmed by the scale of the task. I remember gazing at a heap of clothes hangers, the wire ones you get from the dry cleaners, locked in their communal, clattering embrace. Would I ever, ever manage to untangle them?

For days I did nothing. There was a finality to packing that I couldn't quite face. Throwing away things seemed so brutal but what was the point of keeping them when nobody had wanted them for years? And the memories came flooding back. Max on his bicycle seat, clinging to his father, his arms around Greg's corduroyed midriff. Lucy leaning against her father's legs as he fixed a picture to the wall. Tiny moments from long ago. Was Greg adulterous even then? He'd once admitted to finding Rosie Hargreaves sexy, with her avid mouth and bony Egon Schiele body. When she and her husband were going through a bad patch Greg had walked her home and hadn't returned for two hours.

Then there were my own long-ago snapshots – always the holidays, always in Deal. The photos were black-and-white, of course; the Sellotape had dried, decades earlier, and when I opened the album my childhood dropped off the page. I picked up the photos and remembered the arcade, to which I was addicted. How I trembled with hope as I slotted in one more penny. That tottering cliff of pennies, surely one more coin would dislodge them in a clatter of riches beyond imagining? Then there was the grabber, roving over the stuffed toys and never quite grabbing, being just too feeble. Ah, the rush to the blood, the beating heart, the inevitable, gutting disappointment!

I refused to see this as a metaphor for life. I gathered up the photos, shoved them back into the album, opened my laptop and Googled properties in Deal.

That winter of 2019 would turn out to be the warmest and wettest on record. There was no sign of snow, or even a frost; my nasturtiums hadn't yet dissolved into slime. I thought of Angie, and her fears about climate change. Her campaigning for Extinction Rebellion now struck me as both courageous and intelligent. She'd done her best, little knowing that she herself would soon become extinct. I thought of Calvin, standing on tiptoe to look through his prison bars and only seeing the driving rain. Their story played over and over in my mind. I dreamed it at night.

And around me, my house closed down. Once I'd decided to leave, the rooms withdrew, as a person does when they know a relationship is over. It was no longer my home.

I didn't do much clearing out, partly from inertia and partly because I had plenty of time. That's what I thought, anyway. Once we'd exchanged in January, the sale would be secure and I'd get a removal firm to put everything into storage while I rented somewhere in Deal and started seriously looking for a house to buy. Maybe something would crop up sooner and I'd make an offer, who knew? I was becoming addicted to property websites and became as intimate with people's rooms as they were themselves. Many in Deal had a nautical theme – watercolours of sailing boats, and the obligatory wooden seagull in the window. My spirits skittered between terror, excitement and dread at the monumental task ahead of me. I lost weight and couldn't sleep.

'It's not too late to change your mind,' said Rachel. It was the first week in December and we were having lunch. Rachel was one of my few remaining friends who still lived nearby; we'd bumped into each other at the post office and she'd invited me home. 'I'm not sure that now's the best time for you to make decisions.' She passed me a bowl of soup. 'I mean, what with all you've been through, you poor love, first Greg and then Calvin.'

I willed her not to say, *You're so brave.*

She put her hand on mine. 'Actually, Pru, to tell the truth, I envy you. Being utterly free, able to do anything and go anywhere. Not listening to someone blathering away and asking when's suppertime. Jim's in Scotland till Friday and, honestly, I'm loving every moment.'

'It's not the same!' I snapped. 'You know it's not. It's utterly different when you know it's only temporary and the person's coming back. It's like working in a chicken-gutting factory but only for the summer holidays.'

Rachel withdrew her hand. 'Sorry, you're right. Stupid of me.' She shrugged. 'Anyway, I just think you're being so brave.'

I walked home in a foul mood. It was still raining, and so murky that you couldn't sense when day ended and night began. Rachel's words had irritated me. Why couldn't she just have said: *Good luck! Can we come and stay? We'll miss you!* This was compounded by my abortive visit to the post office. I'd gone there to tax my car, only to be told I'd brought along the wrong insurance document. Boring things like this had been Greg's job. In some ways I was shamefully unreconstructed. Poor Greg, lumbered with insurance documents, and boiler instructions, and rip-off plumbers, and anything to do with my computer. He used to spend half the day trying to get through to call centres while I sat in the kitchen, feet on the table, swigging wine and complaining to Azra about male oppression.

I suddenly missed him so sharply it took away my breath. This was happening more and more often nowadays; the Calvin episode had cast a new perspective on my marriage. And saying farewell to the house reminded me so painfully of those early days, when Greg and I were newly married and moving in with such high hopes. There were sitting tenants on the top floor – an elderly couple who soon conveniently died. Heavens, I hadn't thought about them for years. As I trudged home, my hair dripping, I suddenly longed for Greg. Not for the first time, I thought how very much nicer he was than Calvin. And more honest. And better read. And more left wing. And not a murderer.

I arrived home. I had a shower. I looked at my watch and saw it was nearly six o'clock, not that this made much difference. I opened a bottle of wine and poured myself a glass. I took a Serves One moussaka from the freezer and put it in the oven. I went into the living room, sat on the sofa and opened my laptop. Flossie jumped onto my lap and kneaded me with her needle claws. I lifted her off. She jumped back again. I drank some wine and started looking at my emails.

The front doorbell rang. I flung away the cat, walked down the hallway and opened the door.

A woman stood there, haloed by the light of the porch. For a moment I didn't recognise who it was; her hair was grey and shingled short.

It was Azra. She held out a carrier bag for my inspection, as if I knew what it contained.

And I did.

'Can I come in?' she asked, and stepped into the hall. She took a pot out of the bag. It was a small ceramic urn, grey-green and painted with lotus blossoms. Its lid was firmly sealed with black duct tape.

'I've been feeling so guilty,' Azra said. 'Having him all this time.' She gave it to me. 'Fair do's. It's your turn now.' She tapped the pot with her finger – an odd gesture, as if she were admonishing it. 'Bye-bye, Greg.'

PART FOUR

One

I didn't tell you about Greg. I know, I know. No doubt you think this strange but, to be frank, I just found it too upsetting. And I didn't know quite where to fit it in. Too casually, and you'd think me heartless. Too detailed, and I wouldn't know where to stop. Besides, at the time I'd been mentally somewhat rocky and I'm not sure I'd get the facts straight. Anyway, I apologise now.

He'd been diagnosed with Parkinson's. I didn't know this, but it explained his shakiness on our walk, that day in June. I'd noticed his hands trembling during our stilted and meagre lunch, but presumed he was just discombobulated by my sudden appearance.

I didn't tell you about his funeral, either. It was held in Weymouth Crematorium, ten miles from the cottage. Wicker coffin strewn with wild flowers, beautiful weather, a full house. This time, not surprisingly, most of the faces were familiar. Max and Lucy had flown over; Lucy was accompanied by her new partner, Helga, an elfin child who held my daughter's hand throughout the service. They both wore pillbox hats with little veils – a startling look, as if they were about to break into a song-and-dance routine. Max wore a black suit, which made him doubly a stranger. He'd also put on a great deal of weight; for years I'd only seen his head and shoulders on Skype.

225

Of course my friends greeted me warmly – why wouldn't they? But I detected a certain constraint. It was an awkward situation, of course, and their loyalties were divided. This hadn't been the case in the past. Many of my old gang hadn't taken to Azra – she was too abrasive, too challenging. She was *my* friend rather than theirs and seldom socialised with them; she lived her own singular lifestyle and hunted alone. Now she'd stolen my husband she'd been further ostracised, and their sympathies were mainly with me, as far as I knew.

Now, however, all that was forgotten. Her lover had died and she was quite undone. Gaunt, ashen-faced, her hair scraped back from her face, Azra was scarcely recognisable from the woman I'd last seen, a few weeks earlier, in the window of Yassar Halim. She wore baggy black trousers and her old velvet jacket buttoned up to the throat. When she hugged me I could feel her ribs.

'I'm so glad you came,' she murmured into my hair. 'I thought, for a moment, you might stay away.'

Why would I do that? He was my husband, for God's sake! I said nothing, however, and Bethany gripped my arm and led me into the chapel. My children followed me to the front pew, reserved for family.

Max and Lucy had arrived the previous day and were staying with me in London. It had been hugely comforting, eating dinner together for the first time in years. Helga went to bed early, leaving us alone. I drank too much – no change there – and grew maudlin as I blathered on about their childhood and the happy times we'd spent together. From time to time Max patted me awkwardly on the shoulder but Lucy briskly interrupted.

'Come on, Mum, you and Dad were at each other's throats.'

I stared at her, astonished.

'I used to climb into Max's bed,' Lucy said, 'and we'd put pillows on our heads to block out the rows. Sometimes we added *Encyclopaedia Britannica*s for extra weight. Why did we have them in the house when we never read them?'

'Granddad left them to me in his will,' I said.

'She's right, Ma,' said Max. 'We used to dread the holidays. You and Dad, quarrelling in the car about what you'd forgotten to pack—'

'—and having to play Scrabble,' Lucy said, 'which we all hated, and Dad endlessly nagging us to go outside and seize the day, and you muttering about spending your whole time in the car going to the shops and cooking and clearing up, and why did men only do barbecues and make the most awful fuss about it.'

Max chimed in: 'And it was always raining.'

'It didn't rain!' I said. 'It was sunny, all the time.'

They both snorted with laughter. It was nice to see them united, even in mockery, but I was bewildered. Whose version was the truth? If, indeed, such a thing existed. But Greg and Azra had stepped into another life and had seen nobody, unless my friends had been lying about it, to save my feelings.

There were many versions of Greg, too, in the eulogies at the funeral. Azra had organised it. This had been something of a relief. I was in no state to do anything. Grieving is hard work at the best of times, but even more so when muddied with rage and unresolved bitterness. Azra's grief was no doubt a purer emotion. She'd simply loved Greg and was simply mourning his loss. It was yet another reason to hate her.

We both behaved impeccably, however. We hugged; we said a few words. In the chapel she sat across the aisle from me, bolt upright, her sister's arm gripping her shoulder. I gazed at Azra's grim profile, that face I'd once loved. Behind us I could almost *hear* people's curiosity, like corn rustling in the breeze. It wasn't an unusual situation, of course: the dumped wife and the mistress united briefly in mourning. A hush fell as she stepped up to the lectern. What was Azra going to say?

Nothing. She just read a poem. The Auden one, 'Stop all the clocks' from *Four Weddings and a Funeral*. I was dumbfounded. Greg had hated that film! 'So indulgent and middle-class,' he'd said. 'Didn't any of them have a job? And that awful simpering American woman, Andie Thingy, simper simper, just put in cynically to appeal to the Yanks, God, she stuck in my craw.' I'd loved it, and we'd quarrelled all the way home. 'Didn't you at least think it was funny?' I asked. 'Didn't you at least like the poem?' He'd replied, 'Huh! Another cynical Curtis ploy to inject some gravitas and leach off a superior writer. I can't believe you were taken in.' I'd snapped, 'I was actually crying. Not that you'd notice. Or care.' We'd arrived home in stony silence, to find that the teenage Max had had some schoolfriends round and left the house a cesspit.

I glared at Azra. She stood, clutching the lectern with both hands, her head bowed over her piece of paper. She read the poem in a flat, formal voice, swaying slightly from side to side. How could she have chosen something so perverse? Not content with stealing my happiness, she'd now stolen one of my rows. That evening rushed back, in all its misery. Surely she couldn't have done it on purpose?

Azra had emailed asking if I wanted to speak and I'd said no. Max, however, got to his feet and said a few words. He was perspiring heavily, and read from his iPad.

'Dad was always there for me,' he said shakily. 'When I had problems at school, Dad always had time to listen and offer some wise words.' He paused to wipe his nose. I remembered Greg scuttling out of the room whenever the children entered: *Just got to finish my marking . . .* 'Of course he supported Arsenal but nobody's perfect!' said Max. 'Seriously, though, our happiest times were spent down here in Dorset. Summer holidays were always magic when Dad was around. He taught me to swim, he was very patient with my initial efforts! He taught me how to play Scrabble. We had some epic games, the four of us, and a lot of laughs. He was the best dad in the world and I miss him to the bottom of my heart.'

I listened to this with some surprise. Then Lucy got up and stood behind the lectern. She tossed her head like a filly, but her veil floated down again and she irritably pulled off her hat and became more recognisable. As she spoke about her dad's kindness and generosity I felt the Greg I knew evaporating. By the time she finished he'd disappeared completely. Of course my heart bled for my children, and I admired their courage in speaking to us all, but I felt curiously betrayed. Couldn't they find the right words? These clichés weren't Greg at all – certainly not the Greg they'd slagged off so enthusiastically the previous night. Or maybe I was the one with the warped memory.

Music played: Gloria Gaynor's 'I Will Survive'. I looked at Azra but her face was buried in her sister's shoulder. Would this anthem to female resilience really have been Greg's choice? Then I wondered: did Greg and Azra dance to it around her kitchen, as he and I had once, grabbing each other when it came on the radio and we were doing the washing up? That lightning bolt of joy. Had Greg done the same thing with her? Had they done it often?

'Here, Mum,' Lucy whispered, and passed me a Kleenex.

Lionel, Greg's brother, took the stand. He was a quantity surveyor from Godalming and always finished his sentences.

'It's been a shock to us all that Gregory was taken from us so suddenly,' he said. 'And so soon after his diagnosis. As you probably are aware, those suffering from Parkinson's can carry on relatively normal, active lives for many years but in my brother's case it was not to be.' He cleared his throat. 'However, Gregory lived each day as if it were his last. He never lost that childhood joy, as we can all attest. He was a life-enhancer, with a bottomless fund of rude jokes.'

Good Lord, in forty years had I missed something? However, it got worse.

'What is a particular tragedy is the cruel timing of his passing,' said Lionel. 'For, as you all know – you, his friends, as well as ourselves, his family – Gregory was just embarking on a new chapter in his life, a new beginning, and as his brother I have to say I'd never seen him so happy.'

I must have passed out. When I opened my eyes my head was bowed, as if in prayer. Maybe it was just a blip – nobody seemed to have noticed. But, just for a moment, I knew I'd lost consciousness because, horror of horrors, my knickers were wet.

Maybe I wasn't there. That's why I didn't mention it earlier. Sometimes I had the feeling it had all been in my imagination. The person they were mourning was a stranger. Azra was wearing any old clothes and hadn't even brushed her hair. My tomboy daughter wore a pill-box hat and veil – a *veil*. My son was fat. I can't remember a single detail about the crematorium. Nor can I remember who was there, or if I talked to them. An air of unreality hung over the whole experience. Wetting one's knickers was the stuff of nightmares – perhaps that was what it had been. Memory plays tricks on us all, doesn't it? Doesn't it?

It must have happened, surely, and there must have been a wake back at the cottage. I wasn't there, however, because what I do remember is driving fast along a country lane, past a cornfield scattered with poppies like carelessly strewn drops of blood. The sun was sinking.

What I do remember is waking up in a single bed, my phone dead and my knickers dry. The twin bed next to mine lay shrouded in an unlovely mauve nylon quilt. Mauve was the theme throughout; on the wall hung a framed print of a lady in a crinoline. It all spoke B&B, which indeed it was.

My gorge rose and I knew I was going to be sick. I stumbled into the bathroom. The toilet was concealed by layers of what looked like petticoats – creamy rayon, creamy lace. I fought through them like a man rifling under a woman's skirts, lifted the lid and vomited. Was this still a bad dream? For when I fumbled for the toilet roll it too was hidden beneath the skirt of a shepherdess, complete with bonnet and crook.

I tried to find the B&B a few days later, when I drove back to Dorset, but gave up. My children were certainly with me this time. My brain had cleared after what we called my mini breakdown and they'd forgiven me for disappearing so abruptly.

'You were there and then you weren't,' said Lucy. 'We just thought you couldn't face the wake. But you could have told us. We were so worried, we were going to call the police!'

We were driving to Mortimer's Creek to sort out the cottage. Greg had left it to Max and Lucy in his will. We'd long ago agreed that we would bypass each other as the world was tough and our children had more need of support than we did. Max and Lucy were in no state to decide anything just yet and planned to rent it out until they came to a decision.

Azra wasn't mentioned in the will; it pre-dated the break-up of our marriage. She disappeared from sight and I had no idea where she'd gone, nor did I want to know. I heard nothing from her until that rainy December night, eighteen months later, when she turned up unannounced on my doorstep.

Two

'Can I come in?' she asked. 'I'm soaking. Even my knick-ers are wet.'

'Your knickers?' My head reeled. Suddenly time tele-scoped. I was back at the funeral; she was back as she used to be, strong and healthy, with a full head of hair.

Azra pushed past me into the kitchen, like Pam used to do, and flung herself down in a chair. Her fake-fur jacket, being sopping wet, looked strangely lifelike.

She gave a huge, shuddering sigh. The shorn hair didn't suit her somewhat monumental features but she had the confidence to carry it off. I placed the urn on the table and we both looked at it.

'Do you think we ought to give him a memorial?' Azra asked. 'Or is it too late? Everybody's probably forgotten him by now, except us. And some day we ought to scatter his ashes somewhere. Where do you think it should be? He didn't say anything in his will.'

'Where have you been?'

'On the bus.'

'I mean, all this time?'

'New Mexico. Then I got cancer.' She stood up. 'I'm freezing. Can I have a shower?'

I nodded. 'There's a dressing gown behind the door. A

posh towelling one.' I'd stolen it from Calvin's house, just as he'd stolen it from the St Regis Hotel.

Azra sloughed off her sodden leopard-skin and went upstairs. I sat there in a daze, gazing at the pot. Why had my husband been brought back to me? There had been no arrangement. I'd presumed Azra would have scattered him by now, probably at Mortimer's Creek, their love-nest and future home.

I couldn't take my eyes off Greg. Azra must have transferred him from the crem urn to this more tasteful storage container. It had previously held her herbal teabags. Now, sitting on the table, it radiated a powerful magnetism, as if lit from within. The surrounding clutter faded into meaninglessness. This was my husband, and I was alone with him at last.

I didn't speak to Greg out loud. Upstairs, Azra's footsteps creaked across the floorboards and then stopped. Maybe she was listening. Silently, I urged my words onto the urn. My mother used to take me to church and I made the same effort when I was praying. I remembered pressing my forehead against the pew in front, my body straining to concentrate on the unanswering void.

I tried the same thing with the tea-caddy, urging it with my questions. *Were we happy, Greg? It's so hard to tell, after all that happened. It's all become so muddy and confused, how can I make sense of it? We were happy, and we were unhappy. You were controlling, and you were amenable. You were irritable, yet patient. You liked playing Scrabble, yet you didn't. You were gloomy, but apparently had a fund of rude jokes. Who can I trust, to tell the truth? I trusted you, and see what happened. But then I can't even trust myself.*

I gazed at the flowers, painted on the pot. Were lotus blossoms a symbol of rebirth and renewal? Azra could tell me; she knew about things like that.

I looked at the duct tape, thick black bands of it, brutally sealing the lid. Next to the delicate flowers it was shocking in its finality. I thought: it's what rapists use, to truss up their victims.

This time I spoke aloud: 'I'm so sorry, darling.'

A few minutes later I heard footsteps on the stairs. Azra came into the kitchen. She was wearing my little black dress.

She saw my face and stopped.

'Do you mind?' she said. 'My clothes were soaking. I'll give it back tomorrow.'

I didn't reply.

'Where on earth did you get it?' she asked. 'It's so not you.'

'*I* was so not me,' I said.

'The sort of thing you'd wear to a cocktail party in Esher.'

'It was an aberration.'

She held out one of my cardigans. 'And can I borrow this?'

'Take them both. I don't want them any more.'

'Are you sure?' She smoothed the dress over her hips. 'I could probably do something with it. Take it in, here. Wear it with my Ghost jacket.'

'Or give it to your Syrians.'

She sat down. 'Have you been sorting out your wardrobe? Half of it was empty.'

I nodded. 'I've been having a clear-out. I'm selling the house.'

Azra stared at me. 'You're kidding.'

The atmosphere shifted. Until now it had been curiously relaxed, almost like the old days. This was surprising, to say the least, but this was Azra all over.

Now the blood had drained from her face. She murmured something but I couldn't hear.

'What?'

'You can't do that,' she whispered.

'I've already got a buyer. I'm going to live in Deal.'

'You can't go,' she muttered. 'Don't go.'

'Why not? There's nothing for me here.' I suddenly snapped. 'You put paid to that. And don't tell me what to do. It's none of your business!'

She jerked back.

'You cheated on me for five years,' I said. 'You stole my husband, you ruined my life and then, just because you feel like it, you waltz back here months and months later and bang on my door without even bothering to phone, and now you're telling me what I should be doing with my life. For fuck's sake, Azra, why don't you just fuck off and leave me alone?'

A moment passed. She cupped the back of her head and stroked it – a new gesture, this, as if ruminating on her skull.

'You didn't realise, my love, did you?' she said.

'Realise what?'

The air thickened. 'What this was all about.'

I pushed back my chair and got up. 'Want a drink?'

She grabbed my arm. 'Look at me, Pru.'

236

She pulled me down. The rain had stopped drilling on the roof. A snap, and Flossie escaped through the cat flap.

She said: 'It wasn't really about him at all.'

My throat dried. 'What do you mean?'

She leaned across the table and took my hand. 'It was you I wanted.'

'Me?'

Her voice was husky. 'All the time, all those years.' She turned my hand over and stroked my palm. 'When I was fucking him, I was fucking you.'

She raised her head and looked at me. The blood rushed to my face.

She stood up, came round to me and took my hand. 'Come upstairs.'

In the bedroom she turned her back to me. We didn't say a word. I stood behind her. Slowly I unzipped the little black dress and it fell to the floor.

Afterwards, as we lay in bed, she murmured: 'I told you, didn't I?'

'Told me what?'

'That it would be better with a woman.'

Three

It was always about you and me, she said. I'd had no idea how right she was. It was the most natural thing in the world to explore each other, skin to skin, tongue to tongue. Over the next few days the past was forgotten. All the recriminations dissolved away. All that was irrelevant. At night we slept soundly, Azra's long dry legs around mine, her breasts pressed against my back.

I know this sounds strange but I started thinking of her as Linda; this was a lot less exotic, but it somehow felt more truthful. This was her birth name, her real self. In fact we talked a great deal about our childhoods. She'd never been the greatest listener but now she avidly asked me questions. And she'd become more vulnerable, more uncertain. 'Do you mind my hair like this?' she'd asked, stroking her shorn head. My fearless friend had changed. Maybe it was our love affair; maybe it was her brush with death. During her long disappearance she'd developed cervical cancer. Though she'd now been given the all-clear, it had – not surprisingly – had a profound effect on her. Even her new growth of hair was softer.

What we didn't talk about was her relationship with Greg. I wasn't ready for that, not yet. She must have sensed this because she kept quiet. This was unusual behaviour, for her, but then these were unusual circumstances.

What a lot of time we'd lost! Both of us were greedy for some sort of new life together. We decided to move out of London and live in Deal. We'd get a dog. We'd swim all year round, even in the depths of winter, wearing bobble hats to keep our heads warm. We'd be two merry widows. We'd have a laugh. The whole thing seemed possible, exhilaratingly possible, compared to those pitiful day-dreams I'd had with Calvin.

We looked at seaside properties on my computer, jos-tling each other for a better view. We were seized with energy and started clearing out my house. *Dump, dump, dump!* Azra shouted, piling up the bin bags. Every day we drove to the recycling centre and flung stuff into skips; we knew all the staff and gave them doughnuts. We were open and profligate in our exuberance; we smiled at babies and joked with traffic wardens. All December it poured with rain but we didn't care as we sorted out my past, Azra shouting, *Keep, chuck, keep, chuck* ... only pausing at Christmas to tear apart a turkey. So she was a vegetarian? So what?

It was a sort of madness, I can see it now. But a mad-ness born out of joy and the surprising sense that I was coming home. With Azra's arms around me I felt safe at last. I didn't tell her about my funeral-hopping; it creeped me out, just to think about it. That *was* a derangement, of another kind entirely. So, in a way, was my affair with Calvin. *Tell me more about your murderer,* urged Azra. Put into words, he sounded even more unlikely.

I preferred to hear about her time in New Mexico, after Greg's death. She'd lived in Taos, decades earlier, with a charming but violent sculptor. She said she'd longed to be

239

back in the desert, breathing the pure, dry air and burning away the past. She'd worked at a pottery, and showed me the hideous jugs she'd made. And then, on her return, she'd fallen ill.

'Why didn't you tell me?'

'You've never had cancer,' she said. 'If you had, you wouldn't ask that question.'

'But I could've looked after you.'

'You don't understand.' She sighed. 'I needed all my strength, just to get through it. I couldn't face *you*, of all people. *You*, sweetheart. My sister was there – she cared for me. I had to wait till I was strong, to come here.'

'With Greg.'

'With Greg.'

We gazed at the urn. It had been sitting on the mantelpiece for three weeks.

'I think we should do something about him, don't you?'

On New Year's Day we scattered his ashes. We chose the beach at Deal.

By now I'd told the children about my new love affair. Max had reacted with his usual laconic: *Great news, Mum, I hope you'll be happy.* Lucy had been astonished. *But I thought you hated her!* I'd tried to explain, but gave up. Skype is too inadequate for complex conversations, especially with a dodgy connection. I longed for them to be with me on the trip to Deal. We'd sit on the train, chatting and reading our books, just being normal, despite the significance of the occasion. I'd ruffle Max's hair, even though it annoyed him, and hear Lucy's corncrake laugh. We'd crunch across the beach together, gather up handfuls of their dad, and scatter him to the wind. We should have been together. Needless to say I'd offered to pay their airfare but they both said they were working over the New Year and that we'd make a plan to have a ceremony in the summer.

So it was just me and Azra, standing on the shoreline. It was raining, and suspiciously warm for January. What was happening to our climate? Angie was right – dear airhead Angie, murdered for her money. She'd done no harm in the world except to be beautiful and increase carbon emissions. And she'd understood what was happening – all of us with any sense understood that. Holding Greg's urn, I was glad he'd been spared this ever-lengthening list of destruction that was now spiralling out of control. God knew how our children were coping with it. They'd been conceived in love and now were let loose in a world my husband and I had never envisaged when we'd lain together, sated with sex and surrounded by objects that were now in landfill.

'Are you crying or is it the rain?' Azra's words were whipped out of her mouth.

'Just saying goodbye to Greg.' Together we shook the urn.

'Goodbye, darling!' shouted Azra.

The ash blew back into our faces.

'Ha ha!' I shouted. 'He always got up my nose.'

Afterwards we lay in bed in a seafront hotel, the rain rattling the window. Like many momentous events, it hadn't been as significant as we'd hoped. Bit of a damp squib, to be honest. We lay side by side, deep in our own thoughts. Drunken voices boomed in the corridor and a door slammed.

'Where did you disappear, after the funeral?' Azra asked.

'Some B&B, God knows where.'

'I knew you wouldn't stay for the wake.'

'No.'

Lights from a passing car chased over the ceiling. She was waiting for me to speak.

'I had the nearest I'd got to a lesbian experience there,' I said, 'in the B&B.'

'What happened?'

'I rummaged under a shepherdess's skirt, trying to find the bog roll.'

She didn't laugh. She hadn't a clue what I was talking about. Nor had I, actually.

'You should have come. You were missed.' She spoke into the darkness. 'If you'd come to the cottage it might have helped you, to see that nothing had been changed.'

I froze. No way was I going to tell her that I'd been there, to the cottage, that day in June.

There was a constrained silence. We lay there side by side, not touching.

'Well, too bad,' I said. 'Night-night.'

I kissed her cheek and turned away, pulling my half of the duvet with me.

The next day, back in London, I had a phone call. It was Barry, the estate agent.

'I have some news for you,' he said. 'You'd better speak to your solicitor.'

'What's happened?'

'You know about this virus thing, this flu thing, in China?'

'Of course.' I'd seen it on the news, everyone had.

'Your buyers want to move the completion date forward, to a week after exchange. January the twenty-second. You OK with that?'

'Sure, but why?'

'There's rumours of a lockdown where they live, a place called Wuhan, and they want to finalise the sale before it happens.'

It didn't give us much time.

'Us.' Lovely word. Azra seemed to have put her life on hold and was devoting herself to me. 'Devoting' seemed another unusual word, certainly when applied to my scratchy friend, but as I said, she'd changed. Sometimes I caught a thoughtful look in her eye that I'd never seen before; sometimes she seemed positively needy. She'd given up smoking; gone were the eccentric outfits and painted fingernails. Day after day she wore the same jeans and sweatshirts, like a wife who no longer made an effort. The sort of clothes a Linda would wear. I didn't mind; during those weeks I didn't mind anything. I was still intoxicated with her and the vision of our life together.

Besides, most days we were busy sorting out the house. In mid-January contracts were exchanged and we had a week to pack up the furniture and put it into storage. When the house was sold I'd move in with Azra until we found somewhere to live in Deal. I felt, then, that our adventure was just beginning.

Such was our self-absorption, and physical exhaustion, that we hardly turned on the radio. We were too busy heaving boxes of books and hauling wardrobes through doorways.

As the house emptied, the past flooded back. The joy when Greg and I moved in; the ghostly laughter of the children when they were little, their footsteps pattering on the stairs. With the carpets gone the rooms echoed with lost voices, I was living in a haunted house. And look – the old stains on the walls, the children's scribbles, and the hole in the corner where Lucy's gerbil disappeared for ever. No doubt every house in Muswell Hill has a mummified gerbil under the floorboards.

So we had no idea what was happening in the world. January 21 was our last night in the house. Only the bed remained – I was giving it to Azra's niece, who would be collecting it the next day.

We spent our last night in it, the room empty around us. Moonlight shone through the uncurtained window. Azra snored but I lay awake. In this bed I had dreamed a thousand dreams and made love a thousand times. I'd conceived two children and now it was all over in the blink of an eye. The house no longer belonged to me. Another family was moving in and our occupancy that had so briefly fluttered into life was now extinguished. As for me and Azra – we were flimsy creatures at the end of an era; our presence had barely registered.

My heart pounded as I lay there in the dark. The minutes ticked by and I was seized with panic. What had I done? It was too late now to turn back. This woman lying beside me suddenly felt like a stranger. This happens when people are asleep: they return to their unfathomable, private selves. I told myself this but I was still filled with foreboding as I lay drenched with sweat, waiting for morning.

The next day the house was sold. When it happened I

felt a throb in my bloodstream. I'd heard a twin feels this when their fellow twin has died.

And the following day we heard that Wuhan had been put into lockdown. My buyers were now trapped in China, in the midst of what was now called a pandemic.

'Don't worry, darling,' said Azra, patting my knee. 'It's just a local thing. They caught it from their food markets. I didn't know they existed, did you? With wild animals in them, horrible. Still, it won't happen here.'

Four

Azra's flat was small. There was a bedroom, overlooking the side street and a rowan tree, and an L-shaped living room-cum-kitchenette, overlooking the busy high road at the front and rooftops at the back. Its window opened onto the flat roof of Karim's takeaway, where, in summer, Azra grew tomatoes.

They fitted her perfectly, those two sunny rooms where she lived freely, unencumbered by the weight of possessions. A few plants, a few pictures and a wardrobe of clothes; that was it.

My own possessions filled up half the bedroom. Suit-cases and carrier bags, we were always tripping over them. In those early days this wasn't an irritation. We were in love. The novelty was thrilling – shopping for two, cooking chickpea curries together in a haze of frying spices, swaying in unison like the couples I'd once envied, Bessie Smith belting out on the CD player. I didn't feel an intruder, not then; both Azra and her home enfolded me in their arms. And how cosy it was in mid-winter, the wind rattling the windowpanes and bed waiting for us at the end of the day!

The loneliness was gone. My house was sold, the phone never rang, neither of us seemed to have any work; despite the filthy weather there was a honeymoon feeling to those weeks. I felt untethered from my former self; I was as liberated as Azra had always been, I had joined her world and she seemed to welcome me into it.

Well, yes. Up to a point.

To be honest, there were tensions from the start. Looking back, I can see some early signs, but I chose to ignore them. My cat, for instance. Azra had always disliked Flossie. She said she gave her the evil eye. And the litter tray stank. Azra was fussier about such things than I had expected. She was forever wiping down surfaces, brushing crumbs into her cupped palm with a sigh. We'd never lived together, of course, and I realised now how much tidier she was than me and how she needed to keep things under control. Maybe the cancer had changed her; she said she was nervous about picking up an infection, that's why she hadn't returned to her Syrians. *Sorry I snapped,* she'd say, *I'm just so used to living alone. This is your place as much as mine, you know that, don't you?*

I also realised that she had few friends. Those long phone calls, I guessed, had been to my husband, a subject we never discussed. Now her mobile was silent for days on end. But then so was mine. Few people knew that I'd gone to ground in Tottenham. Autumn had been a time of such upheaval – emotional as well as physical – that I'd lost touch with people, and had no desire to go back to Muswell Hill, least of all to see my empty house.

Besides, there was a strange feeling in the air, a sense that people were retreating from public spaces back into their own lives. Azra didn't listen to the news so I didn't either, but by the first week of March it was becoming clear, even to us, that this flu thing was more serious than we'd imagined. Now we had a stronger desire than ever to move out of London. We were visiting Deal every week, looking at properties, but hadn't found anything yet. Too small, too dark, not enough garden. Our hunt united us. *We'll know it when we see it,* we said.

No, we didn't talk about Greg. I didn't want to hear about their time together, God, no. But I thought about him, obsessively. I thought about him with Azra. It was uncomfortably prurient. I remembered her lounging on the sofa in a fug of cigarette smoke, cradling a cushion against her belly as if it were her baby. She was telling me what a tosser Greg had been and how I was well rid of him. *He'd become such a pompous old git. Didn't it annoy you, the way he cleared his throat before giving his opinion on anything?* Was my husband's semen still inside her as she elaborated on his shortcomings? Was her bush still moist? By now I was as intimate with it as with my own.

As with my own.

Bush. Pussy. How strange and wonderful it was, that we were the same! It was Greg's penis that was the interloper. Yet he had been inside her many, many times, like a former picnicker in a much-loved wood. A long-dead picnicker, with an unsettling connection to me.

Another wonderful thing – why had I never realised this? – she and I had no *rigmarole*. No diaphragms (in the early years of my marriage), no Viagra (latterly), no cumbersome preparations, sometimes no undressings. None of that kerfuffle. Our lovemaking flowed in and out of our days, with no beginning and no ending, clothed and unclothed . . . our lips, our fingers, our breasts, our electric skin. Sometimes our lovely moist pussies that answered

each other, and sometimes just our mouths and our stroking hands. It was the most natural thing in the world. It
seemed bemusing that a big cock barging into one's body
was considered natural when women had been there all
along, in plain sight. Why had I been so dense?

This ardour sailed us through the squally moments,
and there were bound to be some of those. Azra was not
the easiest person to live with, as she herself admitted.
Like all of us, she was a mass of contradictions. Whilst
berating me for leaving on the lights – *what about the
planet?* – she habitually washed up under the running tap.
That sort of thing. It seemed petty to even notice this and
I kept quiet – it was her flat, after all. Besides, it was only
temporary. Soon we'd have a proper house together with
our own space. It was only a matter of time.

And by mid-March we'd found somewhere to rent,
near the seafront in Deal, and arranged to move there at
the end of the month. We'd then look around for somewhere to buy.

How blind we were! Blind to the gathering storm as we
sat there talking and laughing, entwined together on
Azra's shabby green sofa. We talked a lot about the past,
as if we'd only just met and needed to catch up with each
other. She described her early memories of her father:
how, aged four, she clung to his back when they went
swimming; how one day he vanished and another man
walked out of her mother's bedroom, zipping up his trousers. We talked far into the night while down in the street
police sirens wailed. Often we forgot to cook, and went
out to eat – never at Yassar Halim, where I'd seen her with
Greg; we avoided that.

I remember sensing a tremor in the air but presumed it was just me, feeling jittery about the future. Such is the solipsism of lovers. Why people romanticise them I'll never know.

So the news took us by surprise. Events moved fast, and on 23 March 2020, the country went into lockdown.

Five

It's hard to remember those early days. We were all in a state of shock. The enormity of it didn't sink in for a while. In fact it still hasn't sunk in. I remember feeling safe in our love-nest – we had each other, after all – and then I'd become overwhelmed with grief: for the world, for those people who were lonely and frightened and dying. For what might lie ahead.

Down in the street life carried on, eerily normal. The Turkish and Bangladeshi shops seemed as busy as usual, though a lot of customers seemed to be bulk-buying toilet rolls. Nobody seemed too concerned, not then. But when I borrowed Azra's bike and cycled into the centre of London I found a deserted city – echoing canyons of emptiness, post-apocalyptic. Shuttered shops, dark restaurants and dead theatres. Now there were none of the usual distractions, no traffic or people, the buildings had stepped forward and taken over ownership of the streets. It was strangely moving and utterly desolating. I don't need to tell you all this.

At first I was thankful to be with Azra. After all, we were already in a sort of lockdown together. Our plans were on hold but we were in no hurry. Our phones were silent and we had no work. No financial worries either, as I'd just sold my house for an eye-watering amount of money.

I could save my sorrow for other people, and my fury for the government's ineptitude and lack of compassion.

As the days passed, however, I was aware of growing tensions between us. I blamed it on the virus. Everything was out of kilter and we were in the vulnerable age group. Azra was mercurial at the best of times and now she had every reason to be jittery. Still, I was surprised by her growing obsession with infection rates, and vitamin supplements, and sanitising everything we touched or bought or practically breathed upon. 'Of course you should wash the bag of rice!' she told me irritably. I'd never taken her for a hypochondriac, but then the longest we'd previously been together were weekends in Dorset, when she'd come to stay. I remembered once, when Greg had friends round, how she dropped a dish of ratatouille and scraped it off the kitchen floor and back into the pot. 'None of them'll notice,' she'd whispered. That was my Azra, I thought. Blithe and careless, afraid of nothing – certainly not a bit of dirt.

But these were strange times, as everybody kept repeating. Nobody felt quite themselves. Under our feet the tectonic plates had shifted and we were living in a parallel universe, with new rules and, far off, the jungle-beat of fear. No wonder our behaviour had altered.

That's what I told myself. That must be the reason.

It was the most beautiful spring. Everybody noticed this. The grass was greener, the sky bluer. With little traffic, we could hear the birdsong ringing out. For our daily exercise Azra and I jogged around her local park. It wasn't much to look at, just some taped-off swings, some grass and bushes.

But even here, now the world had closed down, nature exploded into life with glorious abundance, as if in compensation. Flowers burst out of the cracks between the paving stones. And next to Azra's flat, seemingly overnight, the rowan tree erupted into blossom. Nature was taking over, even in Tottenham. *Look! I've been here all this time. You've ignored me at your peril.* With no exhaust fumes, we could smell the fragrance in the air.

There's a before and an after. In hindsight, you can see the moment when everything changed. At the time, it was all confused by the pandemic. Azra's edginess with me, I presumed, was due to the general stress. As I said, she seemed more doomy about the whole situation than I was. And there was no denying that, now we were locked down together, the flat was increasingly claustrophobic. Nor did it help that my elderly cat was suffering from incontinence, and the vet's was closed. But I presumed that in a few weeks this strange period would be over.

It was now mid-April and Azra was looking more like a Linda. Her hair had grown back not just softer, but in prim curls, like a perm. 'It looks so suburban!' she wailed. The hairdressers were shut, of course, so I suggested I cut it back into what we called 'the Annie Lennox elfin look', and she'd dye it blond.

It was a beautiful day and we climbed out onto the roof terrace, carrying a couple of chairs.

Azra sat down. She paused, then swung round to look at me. 'Do I trust you?' she asked, squinting against the sun.

'Of course.'

There was a silence. She was about to say something, and stopped. She shrugged and turned back.

I was puzzled. She wasn't just talking about my hair-dressing skills. There was something odd about her tone, something laboured. I'd heard that an actor who was playing a child abuser was told by his director to keep a large stone in his pocket throughout the weeks of filming. *So you never forget,* he was told. I realised, then, that I'd had this sensation for some time now, some secret freight Azra was carrying around. That day, however, I simply presumed she was nervous about having an amateur cut her hair.

She kept up a stream of disconnected chatter. 'Now we're in the firing line we really should update our wills, don't you think?' she said. 'I'll leave everything to you, of course, not that there's much to leave. That reminds me, we need more teabags. By the way, have you noticed that Ali's disappeared? In the corner shop? I hope he's not ill. It's his brother who's working there now.' She swung round, jerking my scissors. 'You're not cutting off too much are you?' She glared at the hair scattered on the ground.

By this time I'd lost my nerve. 'Hardly any. I'll just neaten up this bit . . .'

'That's enough.'

She pushed back her chair and climbed back into the kitchen. I followed her. She was inspecting herself in the mirror. 'Hmm,' she said. 'Give me the scissors.'

She trimmed a bit here and there, and then shook her head like a dog.

'That'll do.' She walked across the room and flung herself onto the sofa. 'It's not as if anybody's going to see us. God, it's depressing; can't even go out for a *coffee.* Hope Max and Valeria are getting on all right, stuck in lockdown together.'

'Who's Valeria?'

'His fiancée.'

I sat down. '*What?*'

'She sounds a real control freak. And he's so passive.'

I tried to swallow. 'Max is engaged?'

'Didn't he tell you?'

'I didn't even know he had a girlfriend.'

'That's Max for you.'

'No it's not.' I glared at her. 'Why did he tell you and not me?'

Azra shrugged. 'You've never really got on, have you?'

'Of course we have.'

'Why do you think he lives halfway across the planet?' She looked at me. 'Whoops, have I put my foot in it?'

'I don't understand what you're talking about.'

'Same with Lucy. They couldn't wait to get away.' Azra laid her hand on my knee. 'Look, darling, I've never had children so I'm hardly one to judge, but I would've thought it was pretty blindingly obvious.'

'What was?'

She sighed. 'It doesn't matter. We're all weird. I'm sure *I'm* weird. Forget it.'

Her hand slid under my skirt, up my bare leg.

'I'm sorry, sweetheart,' she murmured. Her fingers fiddled with the edge of my knickers. 'It's probably easier to teach them than to have them. Don't be upset.'

I snatched her hand away. 'Of course I'm upset!'

'Come here.' She turned my head towards her.

I pushed her off and went into the bedroom, slamming the door shut. There was nowhere else to go.

I sat on the bed, trembling. How could she attack me

like that? If anyone was weird, it was Azra, with her pho-ney voice and dressing-up-box clothes. My friends had always found her peculiar, hadn't they? A bit of a fraud.

Basically, she wasn't well-liked. Some of the time *I* didn't like her. What business did she have, to criticise me so brutally? Especially about my children. She'd changed, no doubt about it. Now I was locked down with her, unable to escape, she was becoming something of a bully. I'd noticed this recently. More proprietorial. That hand up my leg – she didn't *own* me. I wasn't her *sex slave*. Once I'd found it thrilling, the way she'd suddenly ravish me, but now she kept misreading my mood.

Nor was I her skivvy. For I was starting to resent the way she bossed me around. Of course it was her flat and she wasn't used to having somebody else there, especially somebody with an incontinent cat. Lockdown seemed to be bringing out another side to her, a fearful, fretful side I'd never seen before.

So I blamed it on the virus, and comforted myself with thoughts of the future. When we emerged into normal life and found somewhere to live, our new home would belong to me and the balance of power would shift. And thank God we'd have more space. For it was fast becoming apparent that we each needed a room of our own, to sulk in. Doesn't everybody?

I had no idea what was coming. No idea at all, of the secret Azra had been harbouring, or the bombshell that was about to explode. I was too busy brooding about my chil-dren. Azra refused to explain herself and it became a sullen black weight between us. By now it was late April and she insisted that we wore face coverings when we went out. The masks wiped the smiles off our faces, if indeed there were any smiles beneath them. All they exposed were our gimlet eyes.

This was happening all over the country, of course. We were all in it together. Yet we were alienated: masked strangers in fear for our lives. It both pushed us apart and drew us together. Friends disappeared and old, unexpected connections were rekindled, like messages through wartime static. I had an email from Evan: 'Are you all right? Stay safe.' What a darling man! Life with him would surely have been less volatile, and he would have sorted out Flossie's bowels.

Women were so tricky, especially women like Azra. Passive-aggressive, laying traps, festering. I was guilty of this myself. Men were such simple creatures. The bitterness I felt towards Greg had long since faded and I started to feel nostalgic for the old days of our marriage. At the same time, my long-suppressed resentment of Azra was working its way to the surface, like shrapnel from an ancient wound. Our flare-ups became more and more frequent.

'Do you think you should?' she said one day.

'Should what?'

'Open that second bottle.'

'*Everyone's* drinking too much,' I snapped. 'Next week we might be on ventilators.'

'It's just that – oh, never mind.'

'What do you mean, *never mind*?'

'It's nothing.'

'Look, it's *my* liver.'

She paused. 'It's not that.'

'What is it then?'

She stood up. 'Forget it.'

'For God's sake, Azra, spit it out.'

She walked towards the bedroom, our only refuge.

'Azra!'

She turned, her hand on the doorknob. 'All right.' She sighed. 'Don't take this the wrong way, Pru, but you know we always go half-and-half, at the shops?'

I nodded.

'Well, you might be able to buy stuff without a second thought,' she said, 'but I can't. I haven't got your sort of money. And, to be perfectly frank, I can't afford to sub your wine habit.'

I reddened. 'I'm so stupid. Sorry.' I jumped up and hugged her. 'Everything's so surreal nowadays, I've completely forgotten about, you know . . .'

'You know what?'

'That I've just sold a house. It's like another world. And money's become strangely meaningless.'

She loosened herself from my arms. 'Only people who've got it can say that.'

I said that from now on I should pay for the shopping. She promptly agreed.

I remember being surprised but told myself that I had the funds and Azra didn't. However, it marked a subtle shift in our relationship. I don't think Azra noticed this, but I found myself growing more and more resentful about the past. As I said, we hadn't discussed her affair with Greg – it remained unspoken between us – but I'd find myself watching her with hostility as she sat at her sewing machine stitching yet more masks. *YOU were that silent retreat in Rutland, weren't you? Did you concoct that story together? Maybe had a laugh? 'Let's think of the most unlikely county in England!' Wasn't I an idiot, to think he was working on his spiritual enlightenment!*

I'd always felt protective of Azra. Once, in her actress days, I overheard another actor murmur, 'I can't work with that woman, she's a total nightmare.' I remember bristling on Azra's behalf. Now I was living with her, I could see his point.

Maybe I was just as difficult. I certainly had a difficult cat.

'She gives me this superior look *at the same time* as she's crapping on the floor,' said Azra. 'She could at least look guilty.'

'She doesn't mean to crap there. She just misjudges the litter tray.'

'By about a mile.'

'She usually gets there in time.' I scooped it up. 'I think she's going blind.'

'It's her attitude I hate.'

'She's getting old, like us.'

'Yeah, but we're not shitting on the carpet.'

Azra gave a martyred sigh. Once we would have been able to laugh, but those days seemed to have gone.

Then there was the episode with the antlers. By mid-April, rubbish was piling up in the street. Stuck in their homes, people were busy decluttering and flinging their old stuff out. One day I spotted a pair of antlers lying on an old mattress – stag's antlers, mounted on a plinth, an unlikely sight in Tottenham. I carried them back to the flat and dumped them on my pile of belongings.

Azra was out for her run. When she returned home she went into the bedroom. I heard a crash, and a scream.

'What the fuck is this?' Azra emerged, carrying the antlers.

'Aren't they amazing?'

'I nearly broke my fucking leg.'

'I thought we could use them as a hat-stand. When we get a house.'

Holding them at arm's length, as if they were contaminated, she lowered the antlers onto the floor. She glared at them, wiping her hands on her legs.

'They're repulsive,' she said. 'Some fat twat's *killed* an animal for *fun*.' She looked at me. 'I can't believe you'd be so insensitive, Pru. I'm not only a vegetarian, I'm a *pacifist*. I don't want this disgusting object in my flat.'

'I'm sorry. I'll put it into the storage place with my other stuff.'

'Don't be daft. It's closed. Everything's closed – haven't you noticed?'

Suddenly she burst into tears. I stared at her.

'I'm sorry I'm sorry I'm sorry.' She grabbed me and crushed me against her breasts. 'I'm just so frightened,' she muttered into my hair. 'Come into the shower with me. I need to have an orgasm.'

She led me into the bathroom, her hand gripping mine so tightly it hurt. We pulled off our clothes and a moment later we were squashed together in the shower cubicle. Water poured on us as she pressed me against the wall, grabbed my hand and pushed it between her legs. For a moment I resisted, but then she was rubbing me with her expert fingers and soon I was weakened by waves of such pleasure that my legs buckled and she had to hold me up. The water was scalding but neither of us could reach the controls and then I brought her to orgasm and she shuddered against me, moaning.

Afterwards we laughed. I felt restored to her, but only briefly. She'd become more aggressive, no doubt about that. In some obscure way she was punishing me, but I had no idea why.

Trouble was, there was no escape. *Be careful what you wish for.* Don't get me wrong; we still had good times together, of course we did. They'd just become rarer. I'd been married; I'd been through this. With us, however, the whole thing speeded up. Do you remember how lockdown had this effect on us all, stripping away love, restoring love, cutting it short, igniting it, deepening it, challenging it? Making us violent? Or causing us to simply hunker down and sit it out in a sort of paralysis? Long-term prisoners say the same thing, that time is out of kilter – simultaneously both speeded up and slowed to a standstill.

The day of reckoning was stoppered up, like a dam, and we were all waiting for the end of lockdown when we would be released, for better or worse.

With the two of us, it happened sooner than that. In fact, the very next week.

We'd woken up to bad news. The virus was spreading and lockdown was being extended. Azra was plunged into gloom and paced up and down the bathroom with a thermometer stuck in her mouth. Every day she took her temperature and swallowed handfuls of supplements; she was becoming more and more paranoid. I was surprised she didn't wear a mask in the flat. Recently I'd catch her looking at me warily, as if *I* might be a cause of infection. I presumed this was the reason for her bad temper.

She went into the living room and put on the kettle.

'Shit!'

I joined her at the window. Our roof terrace was littered with beer cans. This had been happening more and more often nowadays. The flat above Azra's was occupied by a quiet Korean family but the flat above that, the top flat, was rented by a group of students. They'd obviously had another of their lockdown parties. Our trays of tomato seedlings looked pitifully frail amidst the rubbish.

Azra clambered out and yelled up at their window, but it was Sunday morning and their curtains were closed. Then it started to rain.

All in all, we were both feeling wretched. I emailed Max and Lucy but I literally had nothing to say. Nothing had happened. By now I'd spoken to Max about his engagement and how thrilling it was. He'd told me about Valeria, who worked in his office and was a keen cyclist. But I was still brooding about Azra muscling in on his news – why had he told her first? More to the point, how dared she criticise me and my parenting? Where did that spring from? Jealousy?

We still hadn't had a showdown about this. I couldn't risk a full-blown row in such a tiny flat with no possibility of escape. But it curdled the atmosphere between us.

There was something else, too, that was making me feel uncomfortable. It was to do with money. I could hardly bear to put it into words, even to myself. Azra was my beloved friend – surely she wasn't using me? But why did she drop that hint about rewriting our wills? And should she really let me buy all the groceries? Wasn't it enough that I was buying us a house?

Just occasionally this thought shouldered its way to the surface. I'd push it back down. Nothing in the past had led me to believe that Azra was money-minded. She lived like a gypsy, free as air, sometimes skint, sometimes solvent. She didn't seem to give a toss, either way.

A few hours later, however, all that became irrelevant.

I remember every detail of that Sunday morning. It was too rainy to go outside and clear up the rubbish. The wind blew and we could hear the cans rolling around the terrace. Azra and I didn't speak. I was leafing through the Sunday papers, preoccupied, and she was sitting at her computer. I sensed she was only pretending to look at the screen. Sometimes she took a breath, as if she were about to say something, and then fell silent. She wore her old Rolling Stones T-shirt, the one with the big red tongue, which she'd worn in those heady days when we were clearing out my house. When she raised her arm to scratch her face I noticed how papery her skin had become. Mine, too. I was thinking about ageing, and the wrinkled bodies of my friends when we'd run naked into the Thames, all those months ago. I remembered those little angel girls with their gauzy wings, flitting around like fireflies in the long shadows. How we'd had no idea, when we were young, that the years would be over before we knew it, and our children would be gone. Then I remembered Calvin sulking that day, and wondered whether he'd found comfort later in Johanna's arms. I'd long ago ceased caring. I pictured him in prison and thought: we're all in lockdown now.

'Want some coffee?' I asked.

Azra nodded. She sat back in her chair, her hands laced behind her head, and gazed at the screen.

I unscrewed the canister of coffee beans. 'Sundays are still different, aren't they?' I said. 'Even when every day is exactly the same.'

She nodded again.

'I'm still going online to look at houses, aren't you?' I said.

'What?'

'I'm still Zoopla-ing, even though they're always the same ones. By now I know every inch of them, don't you? The one with the greyhound cages in the garden, re-member? The one with the glimpse of the sea from the upstairs loo. We were well out of that one. Do you re-member, we flirted with it for a bit?'

Did I know what was coming? Was that why I was babbling?

I poured the beans into the grinder. 'I wonder what's happened to Calvin's house,' I said. 'Whether they've impounded it or something. The fridge had one of those icemakers in the door. I've always fancied one of those.' I screwed the lid on the grinder. 'It was one of those houses that has dodgy money written all over it. *So* not our sort of place. Marble everywhere, like a morgue. And eerily tidy – he was quite obsessive – not a speck of dust. In fact, now one knows the truth, it looks exactly like the house of a murderer.'

I pressed down the lid. The motor sprang to life and the

beans ground, noisily. Azra's mouth opened and closed. She was saying something but I couldn't hear.

I finished grinding and unscrewed the lid. 'Sorry. What was that?'

Azra looked at me steadily. 'I said, it takes one to know one.'

'Takes one what?'

'A murderer.'

Six

There was a silence.

Azra said: 'You pushed him off that cliff, didn't you?'

I filled the kettle. 'I don't know what you're talking about.'

'I've always known,' she said. 'Greg wasn't that unsteady. He was still in the early stages – Parkinson's takes years – he was keeping himself fit, jogging every day.' Her voice was calm, almost conversational. 'There's no way he just fell off a cliff. Were you having a quarrel or something, was that it?'

'Azra, darling, I wasn't even there.'

'Oh yes you were.'

'Look, I know it was horribly upsetting for you – for all of us – but there's no need to take it out on me.'

'You were there that day.'

'I wasn't.'

'You were.'

'I wasn't—'

'The farmer saw you.'

'What?'

'Your neighbour, the farmer.'

'He couldn't have. There was nobody around, just the dogs—' I stopped dead.

Azra snapped shut the lid of her laptop. 'Exactly.'

*

Do you know? Just for a moment, it was a relief. Just for a moment, I felt weightless. Only then did I realise the burden I'd been carrying around, all this time.

In fact, it's the most enormous relief, telling you.

Azra sat back in her chair, her head cocked, considering me. She laced her fingers together.

'You're one crazy woman,' she said. 'Bat-shit crazy.'

I didn't speak.

'Did you plan it?' she asked. 'Did you go there, knowing you were going to do it?'

'*You're* the crazy person, thinking I'd do that.'

'Did you think: if I can't have him, she can't either?'

'Do you want this coffee?'

'I haven't told anyone, if that's what you're thinking.'

I poured the coffee into the cafetiere. Look! My hands were steady.

'I knew it, the moment they found the body,' said Azra. 'On the beach. You see, I know you through and through. You're not well. I knew it the moment I met you. That's why we were drawn to each other.' She smiled. 'Takes one to know one. We're both damaged, sweetheart, but in my case I'd draw the line at murder. At least I hope I would. Who knows?'

I pushed down the plunger. The coffee wasn't brewed but this seemed a minor thing, in the circumstances.

I poured the coffee and passed her a mug. As she raised it to her lips I noticed, with gratification, that *her* hands were trembling.

'Since we're being frank,' she said. 'I have to admit that I used to envy you.'

'Why?'

'Because you had a beautiful house and garden, dummy, and two lovely children, and you took them totally for granted.'

This startled me. 'But you didn't want any of that. You always said you liked being free.'

'And you had Greg.' She put the mug down and gazed at it. 'The love of my life.'

Outside, the street was silent. Nowadays, the whole of London was silent.

'I knew it the first moment we met,' Azra said. 'At the wholefood café, remember? It was so crowded that I joined you at your table.'

'Of course I remember.'

'And little Lucy was refusing to eat anything and you snapped at her and Gregory lifted her onto his knee and was so sweet and patient with her, and I thought, what a lovely man, and even then I thought you didn't deserve him.' Her voice quickened. 'All those years I watched you sniping at him, undermining him. No wonder the children were so unhappy and were dying to get away. No wonder he was so depressed.'

'That's not true! Any of it—'

'All that time I watched you playing happy families, with your dinner parties and your allotment and *we did this* and *we did that*, and it was all a lie.'

'It wasn't a lie!'

'And I'd come back to my miserable flat—'

'I thought you loved your flat—'

'I hate my flat! Who'd want to live here? Would you? And I was so fucking lonely. He resisted me, of course; he was an honourable man, and so sodding dense, bless him. But I knew that if I stayed close to you I wouldn't lose contact with him. Oh, there were other people, remember them? But I always ended up chucking them. I guess I was punishing them because they weren't Greg. I knew that I'd have to bide my time and he would come to me in the end.' Her voice softened. 'And he did. After all those years, he did. That night at the Odeon . . .'

She sank into her memories. For a moment she'd forgotten I existed. It reminded me of that moment on the cliff with Greg, how his voice became as dreamy as hers. How I realised I was utterly irrelevant.

Azra said: 'You'd had him all that time. It was my turn now.' She said this in a matter-of-fact way, with a shrug of her bony shoulders.

Then she jumped up and joined me on the sofa. She put her arm around me and gave me a squeeze.

'Look, darling, I still love you. This isn't going to make any difference to anything, is it?'

I was too astonished to speak.

'We're peas in a pod,' she said. 'Crazy peas in a crazy pod. Your secret's safe with me, sweetheart, you can trust me on that. Honest injun.' She gazed at my breasts with a speculative look, as if she'd never seen them before, and started stroking one of them with her finger. 'We'll find a nice house and live together at the seaside and nobody will ever know.' She grabbed my chin and turned my face to hers. 'Give us a kiss,' she crooned. 'Say you forgive me. After all, *I've* forgiven *you*.'

And then she kissed me deeply, her thick tongue exploring my mouth, pressing against my teeth.

I sat, rigid in her arms. I was literally frozen with fear. What was she playing at?

I was wearing my old blue cotton dress. Azra pushed it up, yanked down my knickers and flung them onto the floor. And then her hand was busy between my legs, and she'd unzipped her jeans and thrust my hand into her own wiry bush.

It wasn't rape, not really. But all sorts of thoughts swirled around my head as she got to work on me. I remembered her laughing about Japanese women with their silky pubic hair, *not like our Brillo pads*. Where had that woman gone?

What had happened to us?

I squeezed my eyes shut and pictured the trees in Burnham Beeches, that picnic with Greg and the children, Max reading his *Beano*. I tried to concentrate on dappled sunlight and butterflies, anything to block out what was happening as I lay squashed on the sofa under Azra. But I knew my survival lay in pleasuring her, so like a whore I detached my mind from my body. And amidst it all was my horror at the loss of my friend, my beloved merry-maker and soulmate.

My mind was working fast. Azra had finished with me and fallen asleep. I eased myself from under her, picked up my knickers and shut myself away in the bedroom. I needed to think.

For I'd realised something else. I'd worked out the dates, you see. That evening in December, when Azra came downstairs in my little black dress – that was the moment I told her I was selling my house. And the next moment she was busy seducing me.

Because she knew I was going to be rich.

*

I know I should have told you about Greg. To be honest, I thought you would have guessed by now. Perhaps you have. You knew the state I was in, and the provocation. It was more than any human being could bear. Think of it as a moment of madness, like Calvin's when he pushed that car off the cliff. Except, of course, he lied. In my case I didn't exactly lie; I just didn't finish telling you. Call it a crime of omission.

I could hear Azra snoring in the next room. She'd told me she started snoring when she was sixty. *Snoring, spectacles, whiskers on our chins. Oh God, Pru, what's to become of us?* We'd been lounging on that very sofa, drinking tea, sunlight streaming through the window. We'd laughed, slumped against each other, partners in our voyage into old age.

Now her snores sounded ominous, like an approaching thunderstorm. My nipples were sore. She'd gnawed at them – no other word for it. Gnawed as if she were attacking a piece of gristle. I felt like an abuse victim, groomed and then assaulted.

I paused, listening for the snores to stop. Azra was now my enemy and I had to make a plan. 'Your secret's safe with me,' she'd said, but I couldn't trust her. I was totally in her power. At any moment she could call the police – tomorrow . . . next year. From now on I would never, ever be safe.

I sat on the bed gazing at my pile of belongings. I'd covered them with a blanket to make them less obtrusive. The antlers were propped on top. This lumpy, sinister creature looked strangely alive, as if it were about to shake off its shroud and rise up to confront me.

My heart thumped against my ribs. Azra had a plan, I realised that now. Whether she was conscious of this or not was irrelevant. I would buy a house and look after her, for the foreseeable future. Sexually she could do what she liked with me. In return, she'd keep her mouth shut. Never again, however, would I be able to sleep easy. She knew, and I knew, that she could break our Faustian bargain at any time. I could never escape.

Half an hour had passed. Azra was still snoring but soon she'd wake up. I didn't have much time.

I removed the antlers and pulled off the blanket. Quietly, very quietly, I slid out my suitcase.

It took ten minutes to pack it with essentials. What *were* essentials? I was too flustered to gather my wits. The bathroom cabinet creaked as I opened it and grabbed my toiletries. In the wardrobe the hangers rattled as I pulled out some random clothes. Ah, my laptop! I'd nearly forgotten it. I shoved it, with its charger, on top of my clothes. The zip screeched as I pulled it round my bulging suitcase. I'd have to walk past Azra but the sofa faced away from my escape route to the front door.

I couldn't risk the noise of the wheels so I carried the suitcase, as cumbersome as a human body, across the living room. I glimpsed the top of Azra's hair, jutting above the back of the sofa.

I paused, to listen. She'd stopped snoring. Was she faking it? Nothing would surprise me any more.

The grey hair didn't move. For a mad moment I thought it was a wig. Azra had laid it on top of the sofa and was actually standing behind me. *Where do you think you're going?*

But by now I was by the front door, fumbling with my suitcase and shoulder bag while rifling amongst the layers of garments hanging on the hooks. It wouldn't be warm forever; I'd need my winter coat.

Finally I got everything down the stairs. I had to make two trips. A few moments later I was outside in the street, loading my stuff into the car. I was breaking lockdown, of course, but that was the last thing on my mind.

Seven

'I hope you don't mind sleeping in Mother's room,' said Pam. 'The others need a good old clear-out. I'll get round to it one day. And the boxroom's absolutely chocka, shall I show you? Look! There's enough in here to last us months – pasta, tinned tomatoes, toilet rolls, flour, sugar, tins galore. We could feed an army! And, of course, now I can put my baking skills to good use. It's so lovely you're here, Pru, because it's no fun baking on my ownsome and I know how you love my cakes.

'And if you need any more clothes – just look in here! For my sins, I never throw anything away and these date from when I was a size eight, some of them as good as new. You'd look lovely in this dress, it's just your colour, you've always had such marvellous taste and it's got an elasticated waist because we've all put on a little bit around the tummy, let's be honest, even someone like you, who's always had a lovely figure! So do rummage around and help yourself. Consider this *your* home now.

'Oh, I know I'm a silly sausage to bang on about it but, seriously, I'm so thrilled you're here. It's been no fun on my own. I mean, I'm used to it normally but this is different, isn't it? The new normal. And don't worry, your secret's safe with me—' Pam stopped. 'Whoops, sorry. Don't look at me like that. I won't say a dicky-bird. I know you've

274

broken the rules coming here, but it's not as if you've *murdered* anybody, and from now on you can lie low, I can do the shopping and nobody will know you're in residence. It can be our little secret. We're a bubble now! I mean, it's not like number twelve: they've had people going in and out of their house. Of course, in their culture it's different but that's no excuse. And it's not just them. Look, here's my little book – it's got all the violations so far. The Wilmots had eight people there last night, *eight*, and he's a deputy headmaster. What sort of example is that? I'll report them, of course, but just now I'm biding my time and noting down the evidence.

'Come downstairs and we'll have a nice cup of tea. I'll keep the curtains closed; no one will see you. Besides, it's not as if anyone knows you're here – all your friends, all those leftie types, they never knew *we* were friends, did they? To be perfectly honest I used to find it just a little bit hurtful – even that woman who was always in and out of your house, the one with the funny clothes, I once waved to her and she looked straight through me but never mind, I've got you to myself now.'

Pam chuckled.

'We're like my cacti – see, over there? Prickly on the outside, so nobody comes near. And on the inside – well, we've got everything we need, haven't we, petal? It's all stored up inside us. We can live off it for months without even watering.' She raised an imaginary glass. 'So here's to succulents!'

She smiled, her spectacles glinting in the electric light. Then she put her arm around me and gave me a squeeze.

'They say it's an ill wind . . . but to be perfectly frank,

my love, and I know I shouldn't say this – naughty me! – if it's taken Covid to bring us together, then it's been a blessing in disguise.'

In the kitchen the kettle boiled but Pam didn't move. She squeezed my shoulder tighter.

Pritt-Stick Pam and me, stuck together for the duration. However long the duration might be.

Epilogue

The next time I wore the dress was at Azra's funeral. The next, and the very last time. It had been hanging in her wardrobe; I found it when I went back to her flat for the rest of my belongings.

Our little black dress.

Two months had passed. It was July and lockdown had been lifted. The country had emerged from its long hibernation, blinking in the light. My God, wasn't that summer beautiful? The sun beat down on our little group as we stood around the grave. We watched Azra being lowered into the earth, taking her secrets with her.

I was dripping with sweat. The lining of the dress stuck to my skin. Janey, Azra's sister – *Linda's* sister – passed me a tissue to mop my face. She dropped a bunch of peonies onto the coffin. As they hit it, the petals scattered; a peony's life is over almost as soon as it's begun.

It was Janey who had emailed me with the news. 'It happened so fast,' she wrote. 'The cancer had spread to her spine. It was all over in a matter of weeks.'

The funeral was held in Sunderland. The next day I returned to London and took the train to Deal. The dress was packed in my overnight bag. I'd presumed that at some point I'd take it out and dump it in a rubbish bin but

I couldn't quite bring myself to do something so insignificant. So dingy.

The beach was crowded with families released from their imprisonment. En masse they'd rushed to the seaside. There was a carnival atmosphere as they frolicked by the waves; who knew how long this would last?

I found a space, took out the dress and spread it on the shingle. I lay down on it, closed my eyes and surrendered myself to the sun. The voices echoed far away. I heard Azra's husky laughter. I heard the scrunch of the pebbles as she ran towards the sea, lithe and lovely in her lime-green swimsuit.

I lay there for a while, feeling the weight lift off me. I was free at last. My secret was safe, buried for ever. Soon I could begin to mourn the Azra I'd once known, before all this happened – if, indeed, I had known her at all, or she had known me. What mysteries we are to each other! Me and Greg; me and Calvin. All those strangers whose funerals were simply a hall of mirrors, reflecting back a multitude of truths, and half-truths, and lies. For they were simply mirroring back our own selves. If I'd learned one thing over the past months, it was this.

Dizzy from the sun, I got to my feet, picked up my bag and walked towards the road.

I left the dress behind. It was late in the afternoon, but the beach was still crowded. Amongst the bodies it lay unnoticed, a small dark shadow, woman-shaped.